THE WHISPERING DEAD

Also by David Mark

Novels

THE ZEALOT'S BONES *(as D.M. Mark)*
THE MAUSOLEUM (aka THE BURYING GROUND) *
A RUSH OF BLOOD *
BORROWED TIME *
BLOOD MONEY
INTO THE WOODS
SUSPICIOUS MINDS *
CAGES *
GRAVE OF THE GOBLINS
ANATOMY OF A HERETIC
THE WHISPERING DEAD *

The DS Aector McAvoy series

DARK WINTER
ORIGINAL SKIN
SORROW BOUND
TAKING PITY
DEAD PRETTY
CRUEL MERCY
SCORCHED EARTH
COLD BONES
PAST LIFE *
BLIND JUSTICE *

* *available from Severn House*

THE WHISPERING DEAD

David Mark

SEVERN HOUSE

First world edition published in Great Britain and the USA in 2022
by Severn House, an imprint of Canongate Books Ltd,
14 High Street, Edinburgh EH1 1TE.

Trade paperback edition first published in Great Britain and the USA in 2023
by Severn House, an imprint of Canongate Books Ltd.

severnhouse.com

British Library Cataloguing-in-Publication Data
A CIP catalogue record for this title is available from the British Library.

ISBN-13: 978-0-7278-5055-3 (cased)
ISBN-13: 978-1-4483-0817-0 (trade paper)
ISBN-13: 978-1-4483-0816-3 (e-book)

All Severn House titles are printed on acid-free paper.

MIX
Paper from
responsible sources
FSC
www.fsc.org   FSC® C013056

Typeset by Palimpsest Book Production Ltd.,
Falkirk, Stirlingshire, Scotland.
Printed and bound in Great Britain by
TJ Books, Padstow, Cornwall.

For Phyllis and Milly

AUTHOR'S NOTE

Some of the events outlined in this novel actually happened. Most of them didn't. I'll trust you to work out which is which. I rather hope you're wrong.

Spies cannot be usefully employed without a certain intuitive sagacity.

They cannot be properly managed without benevolence and straightforwardness.

Without subtle ingenuity of mind, one cannot make certain of the truth of their reports.

Be subtle! be subtle! and use your spies for every kind of business.

If a secret piece of news is divulged by a spy before the time is ripe, he must be put to death together with the man to whom the secret was told.

Sun Tzu, 544–496 BC

PROLOGUE

Browndown Beach, Gosport, Hampshire
March 11, 1968

The sea's a joyless grey, cloudy as milk. There's no line where water meets sky, just a smudge as the slow-moving sea merges softly into low, cloud-coiled sky. Drizzle greases the stones on this shingly, isolated beach; a near-invisible rain suspended in the chill air, misting a horizon the colour of unbaked clay.

A young woman is sitting on the sea wall, gazing at nothing. She's as colourless and unremarkable as the emptiness into which she stares. Such appearance marks a change in philosophy and deportment; a transformation of sorts – a butterfly worming back into its muted cocoon. She is capable of extravaganza, of genuine visual spectacle; adept at clothing herself in gaudy hues and luxurious modes, splendid in short skirts, vivid nails; big earrings, big hair. She favours plum-coloured berets and large sunglasses, calf-hugging platform boots and bangles that clank as she swigs her brandy and lemonade. But here, now, she is equally comfortable in her monochrome anonymity. Were she to sit still long enough, she fancies she could pass for a stone.

She shifts position, ignoring the throbbing pain in her ribs. She's getting good at disregarding pain. She didn't even wince when she applied the blusher to her bruised cheek; her knuckles prodding her tender flesh as she worked her kohl around the contours of her strikingly blue eyes.

She's an attractive woman. Knows it too. She's in her mid-twenties. Mouse-brown hair recently chopped into an unremarkable bob. The salt air and the sea spray has undone her ministrations with the brush and wet strands cling to her pale face. She wears wellington boots beneath her long corduroy skirt. Wears a man's shirt and a tatty leather jacket, three sizes too big. There's a paperback book on the damp stone beside her. It's dog-eared and well-thumbed. She would say the same about herself, if prompted. She has a wicked tongue, does Cordelia Hemlock. The nuns used to tell her that as they did God's work on her buttocks and back. So did the silly boys she dallied with at university, though it was said in a spirit of grateful esteem rather than chastisement.

She's smoking. She doesn't really enjoy cigarettes but she's gotten into the habit and has convinced herself that it calms her nerves and that she's entitled to do what she wants. Her son hated the smell of cigarettes and used to forcibly try and pull them from her mouth. She stopped for him. Stopped most of the things she did for pleasure. And then he died and the icy fires of grief consumed her from within and without and it had seemed absurd to deny herself something that might, if she were lucky, hasten her own descent towards the grave.

She has been sitting here for almost an hour. She has a thermos of hot coffee in the satchel at her feet but has yet to open it. Her wrist is badly sprained and she cannot work up the enthusiasm to further aggravate it by untwisting the lid. She's been through a lot these past weeks. She's learning her trade. They're showing her the ropes. They're putting her through her paces. Retired sergeant majors are teaching her how to shoot a pistol and whereabouts to thrust her blade if called upon to put an enemy beyond return. She has been thrown around as if she were a scarecrow. Big, broad-shouldered, ruby-playing types have kicked her legs out from under her and struck her beneath the jaw with the heel of their hands. She has had her head yanked back with a fistful of hair and dirty water poured into her gaping mouth and nose, hands pinioned at her back, eyes round and blind and popping as questions were whispered in her ear by a man who smelled of American cigarettes and bourbon. She hasn't yielded yet. Her group has already lost three members, dismissed for giving in, giving up, giving themselves away. Cordelia is now the only woman left in the intake. Even if she wanted to she knows she can't give up now. Can't quit. She feels a responsibility to her sex. People have spent a lot of time telling her what she can and can't do and she's never taken any notice of their opinions. She's not going to start now. She has serious doubts about her own suitability for the role but she has the sense to keep them to herself. She's started this and she'll finish it – even if doing so means a career to which she is hideously ill-suited. She fancies that she'll make a rather good spy. She just isn't sure whether, in so doing, she will be making the world better or worse. Her moral and political philosophies lean more towards the subversive than the state-sanctioned. She dabbled with Communism at university. She's marched for women's rights and wrote letters to foreign governments urging them to alter foreign policy or at the very least, remove themselves from Vietnam. She's not remotely patriotic. How can a person be proud of being born in a particular country? It's not as if they have any choice. She doesn't mourn the death of the Empire and cannot understand those who wish to once again paint the maps of the world in glorious pink. In truth, she finds the whole business of international espionage faintly ridiculous. It all seems to come down to stealing secrets, and she can't help feeling that a secret isn't even interesting until somebody else knows about it. Nevertheless, she'll see it through. She's clever and tough and dogged and can't think what the hell else to do with herself for the next fifty years. She's been given an opportunity, a reward for her small part in unmasking a killer, and the idea of returning home to the big empty house in the Borders fills her with the kind of dismay that the grey sky and opaque seas seem to be trying to mirror. The only thing she misses about home is her best friend, Felicity. She writes to her often though she rarely posts the letters. She can only be truly honest with herself when writing to Flick, and true honesty is something that is going to be denied her if she continues down this path. So she writes what she thinks and what she feels and then she burns them in the grate and watches the ghosts of spilled words climb blackly, greasily, into the haze of cigarette smoke that swirls in the low roof of the barrack room where she is quartered.

Cordelia doesn't turn her head when she becomes aware of the man to her left. She uses her peripheral vision as she has been taught. She's surprised at how close to her he has managed to get without her noticing. This is a shingle beach. The sea wall is to her back. He must have made barely a sound as he approached. She examines him from the feet up. He's shoeless. He's got socks on and they're thick with damp sand. He must have approached her through the sand dunes. He wears baggy blue suit trousers, shiny at the knees and with three different crease lines poorly ironed into the shins, giving the seam the appearance of an abandoned pleat. He wears an unfashionable raincoat, fastened to the very top. A woollen hat, the sort that might appear in a comic as a gift from a half-blind aunt, is pulled down over his ears. It's a garish clash of blue-and-white zigzags, entirely without any discernible pattern or form. He wears thick glasses, their lenses speckled with rain. He's not even close to being handsome, but there's an absurdly confident smile on his face as he stands there, shoes in his hand, and waits for her to give him her attention.

'Can I help you?' she asks, turning her head and glaring at him with hard eyes.

He makes a face, pretending to look distressed. 'Good Lord, Hinny, is that where the nickname came from? The Basilisk. Well played. If we could weaponize that quality we'd have won the war by next Tuesday.'

Cordelia licks her lips. Takes her time. Lets the moment stretch out like a cat in front of the fire. She has to fight the urge to smile. She doesn't know whether she's passed or failed but she feels as though she's achieved something simply by spotting him before he was close enough to hit her with his shoe. She finds herself curiously beguiled by the odd little man, though she'd be hard pressed to explain why. He has a Rumpelstiltskin look about him – a sense that he could play the happy imp up until the moment he tore himself in two out of anger. She's certainly not alarmed at having her nickname relayed to her by a stranger. She knows that such encounters are part of her training. She's been followed by active agents and tasked with losing them on hectic London streets. She's had to make spur-of-the-moment decisions about whether or not to proceed with simulated dead-letter drops based on her own instincts as to whether she is being observed.

'Hinny?' she asks, at last.

'The Geordie twang,' he says, rummaging in his coat and

producing his cigarettes. He lights up and observes her through a cloud of blue-grey smoke. He doesn't seem compelled to say anything else.

'Will you be joining me?' she asks, making room on the sea wall. 'Room for one more.'

'I won't, if it's all the same,' he says, with a look of genuine apology. 'Takes an age for me to get myself properly situated and once I start walking I prefer to remain upright. I don't so much walk as fall down over a considerable distance. It's a controlled totter.'

Cordelia permits herself a smile. 'I didn't hear you approaching,' she confides. 'Is that a mark against me?'

'You spotted me before I got close enough to do anything outlandish.' He shrugs. 'I'd call that a win. All a bit silly, isn't it? All this simulation and dissembling, this learning how to lie. Good God, the whole organization is made up of public schoolboys and they learn how to dissemble at the teat. One must never show emotional honesty, you realize that, yes? Not a whiff of humanity. Otherwise, how the devil can you be expected to lead? How can one make decisions about what is good for people if you are beset by those God-awful feelings every moment.'

Cordelia isn't sure how to reply. He seems genuine in his contempt for the upper classes and yet his own accent is pure old Etonian.

'You're reading Orwell,' he says, with a genuine grin of approval. 'My *my*, what a splendid find you are. True subversive literature within a spit of Fort Monckton. I can't decide whether you don't give a damn or just want to be *seen* as somebody who doesn't give a damn. Or perhaps you're too guileless to realize it might not be the wisest choice of reading material when your every spit and cough is being pored over by men who want you to fail. Either way, with the Geordie accent and the steel blue eyes, you really are a discovery. I feel like Sir Joseph Banks poking around Botany Bay.'

Cordelia lights herself a cigarette while she considers her response. 'That's a very odd way to compliment somebody.'

'And a compliment it is, my dear,' he says, nodding vigorously. 'I'm one of the troublemakers, if you were wondering.

You might hear my name from time to time. A face-card. Jack of Clubs, let's call it that. Have you got to the hierarchies yet? Basic structures? Oh, I shan't spoil it for you. They do like to do things in the correct order and in their own good time. Suffice to say, I always have a little poke around in the heads of the new recruits. It's incredible what one might find. I had such a good feeling about you when I saw the file. Bastard child, born to an unstable mother in '42, father unknown, convent educated and bloody clever. Scholarship student. Grammar school. Up to Nuffield, Oxford, in '62. Abandoned your studies when you fell in love. Wife of one Cranham Hemlock, civil servant. Your son, Stefan – meningitis, wasn't it? I'm truly sorry for your loss.'

Cordelia doesn't let her change of mood show in her face. Inside, she feels as though all the blood in her body has turned to smoke. She feels as though her face is a sponge full of tears, just waiting to spill down her bruised cheeks. But she doesn't let it show. She's very good at not letting it show.

'Seems odd that a woman as beguiling as yourself should marry a gentleman of such astoundingly homosexual persuasion,' he says, with a little shake of the head. 'I'm not a romantic, I'll leave that to the French, but I should imagine that it causes one or two problems from time to time. Still, least said, soonest mended, as they say. And you have done rather well out of the arrangement. That's the establishment, for you – everybody knows, but nobody lets on.'

'He's not part of this,' says Cordelia, coolly. 'Cranham doesn't even know. If you think I got special treatment because of who I'm married to . . .'

'Whom, my dear,' he corrects her, with a smile. 'Gosh, you become even more of a coal miner's daughter when you're cross, don't you? And please, do accept my apologies if I implied that you were being given special treatment. I very much doubt that Cranham would spot a trainee spy if it sat on his face and started reading Tolstoy. No, have no fear on that score, my dear. I'm more than aware of what you've done. Mind sharp as a razor, that's what your instructors say. They fear your political affiliations, of course. You're not, shall we say, one of us. The whiff of the socialist about you, and they'll never understand that a whiff of socialism falls well short of a love of communism. I'm a firm believer that we need a few more like you.'

'And what am I?' asks Cordelia, grinding out her cigarette. She feels combative, irritated, unsure whether she's being tested or teased.

'I believe the popular phrase used by your apparent betters is *"lebbage"*. Latin, of a sort. Think *hoi-polloi*. The great unwashed. The masses.' He clicks his fingers as if searching for the right word. 'The poor.'

'I heard "Plebian" a lot at university,' she says, with a slight smile. 'I heard "slattern" a lot too.'

'I don't doubt it. Terrifying to them, I shouldn't wonder. They wouldn't know what to make of a girl like you.'

'A woman, you mean,' she replies, with a twitch of her lips.

'Touché,' he replies, and stoops, holding his side, to pick up a rock that has caught his attention. He turns it over and over as if checking it for something and then wrinkles his nose, throwing it away. He winces a little, as if the action has pained him.

'Not what you were hoping?' asks Cordelia. She feels an inexplicable warmth towards this man. There's something oddly genuine about him; as if he can play any role required of him without ever really changing his fundamentals. She envies him. Wonders if, should everything go the way she'd like it to, she will be able to maintain who she truly is.

'It will be hard for you, Cordelia,' he says, the smile fading as he looks into her eyes; a sudden intensity about him. 'They won't want you to do well. They won't ever trust you. They don't trust me and I'm one of them. I have feelings, you see. I actually believe we have certain moral imperatives. I have this bizarre notion that in a world where we are no longer a true power, we can at least be influential. We could, for example, fight the good fight. We could help people regardless of political affiliation. It's a fanciful notion but in you, in people who care about decency first and queen and country second, I see something that breathes on the dying embers of my optimism.'

'The dying embers of your optimism?' repeats Cordelia,

with a grin. 'Jesus, Hinny, you've got quite the turn of phrase. You're a poet and *ya divvent* know it.'

He laughs properly, head back, delighted with her sudden thrust of Geordie. She does her best to hide the accent but he's right – it creeps back when she's angry or drunk or in love, and she's one or all three most of the time. She can't help thinking that she'll make a rather ridiculous spy. She likes people. Feels awful if she hurts somebody's feelings. Thinks the government is both too big and too small and sees nothing about capitalism to suggest that it's any better than the alternative. She's doing this because she's been given the chance and because she doesn't like to waste an opportunity.

'I'm Walt,' he says, with a twirl of his hand and an exaggerated bow. 'You can dig around and ask the questions and see if I'm somebody you'd like to get to know. I have no romantic interests in you, before you worry – quite the eunuch below the waist. Never had much interest in any of that silly sticky business. Incidentally, I have to fill in a rather inane report stating when and where you saw me following you and how you responded to my knowledge of your record, so if there's anything you'd like it to say, just tell me and I'll fit it in to my conclusions.'

'How long have you been watching me?' she asks, and behind him she sees the thick block of clouds reassemble themselves like shifting tectonic plates.

'Don't trouble yourself,' he shrugs. 'I think you're rather marvellous. My opinion counts for quite a lot, as it happens, and this little chat has only served to reassure me that you are exactly what I'm looking for. I have a few ideas, you see. Here and there, bits and bobs – put your hand in the bran tub and pull out the cliché of your choice. Suffice to say, there may come a time when I need to know who's on the side of the angels, and who . . . well, let's just say, those who aren't.'

'I'm a bit confused,' says Cordelia. 'I don't even know if this is right for me. I don't agree with half of what we seem to do. It's not exactly glamorous, is it? And look at the mistakes we've made. Nobody ever seems to answer a question properly. I mean, is there any point to any of it? Intelligence, counter-intelligence, stealing secrets, selling secrets, finding out who's selling to who and whether what they're selling is worth the price. It's just, I don't know, I suppose that I had it in my mind that the people who knew these things, who made the big decisions – I thought they'd be a bit more . . .'

'Impressive?' asks Walt, sucking his lips back over his teeth and pulling a face. 'Yes, we are something of a disappointment, aren't we? Not really one of them, that's my problem. But not really anything else either. I'm damnably good at what I do, you see. And I'm an excellent judge of character. So, well . . . there's paperwork and oaths and a little more back and forth to worry about, but supposing I extended my hand and welcomed you as a Friend – you'd be pleased, yes?'

'A Friend?'

'What we call ourselves, my dear. The Service.' He shrugs, keenly aware of their absolute solitude. 'I'm sure we will do our damnedest to turn you into something you're not, but I do really rather hope you continue to be the young lady who reads Orwell in the gathering storm.'

Cordelia holds his gaze. Gives the slightest nod. He returns it, then turns away. She glances down to gather up her cigarettes and her book. When she looks up again, she's alone on a deserted beach.

Cordelia sits for a while trying to work out how she feels. She smokes. She reads. When she gets back to the barracks she will write to Felicity. She won't post it, but she'll enjoy writing it. She's joining MI6. She's going to be a bloody spy. She'll go mad if she doesn't share the news with somebody.

On balance, she decides she should probably keep that particular gush of excited honesty to herself.

ONE

**BRAVE SPY 'SENT TO HIS DEATH' BY
BRITISH TROOPS**
By Paolo Fergus, *Aletheia.com
Investigations Team*
14.08.2016

BRITISH troops manning a border post
in Belize betrayed one of MI6's top
informers to a ruthless death squad,
according to top secret documents
unearthed by Aletheia.com

Documents found in the National
Archives indicate that the British
government cooperated with a succession of genocidal presidents and leant
support and expertise to the Guatemalan
military during their decades in
command of the war-torn Central
American country.

Our exclusive investigation suggests
repeated collusion between British
politicians and the most notorious of
Presidents Rios Montt, who stood trial
for genocide and has died without ever
facing true justice for the atrocities
carried out at his command. The role
of the CIA in arming, training and
funding Rios Montt has already been
ruthlessly exposed by United Nations
investigators who suggest that President
Reagan's administration deliberately

turned a blind eye to the wholesale
massacre of Guatemalan peasants. It
was seen as a price worth paying to
halt the spread of communism on
America's doorstep.

Now, 35 years after the murder of a
British intelligence source, Britain
faces calls for a public inquiry for
its role in the capture, detainment
and later execution of a Guatemalan
soldier who escaped a massacre and
fled to neighbouring Belize. Our
sources suggest that the man was actually an agent, loyal to the British
intelligence services, and that he
was given over to the notorious
Kaibiles special forces unit to avoid
causing embarrassment to President
Reagan, who spoke of Rios Montt as
'a man of integrity'.

In 1983, Britain had a garrison of
1,500 soldiers stationed along the
Guatemalan border, which had been a
UK colony until a recent independence
vote. Politicians in Westminster and
the public believed that the British
Army was there to prevent Guatemala
invading Belize, which it has long
claimed as its own.

We can now reveal that Prime Minister
Margaret Thatcher regularly allowed
her troops to help the brutal Guatemalan
military dictatorship eliminate its
internal opponents. Senior officers
within the British forces routinely
dined with figures from the Guatemalan

military, including the officers from
the infamous Kaibiles special forces
unit.

A source in Belize has now come forward
with astonishing claims about the
execution of a man named Alejandro
Ruano, whose mutilated body was delivered to his family's door a week after
the British authorities handed him to
the Kaibiles — along with a taped
recording of his claims about the
massacres occurring among the indigenous Mayan population.

Alejandro's younger brother, Diego,
said: 'He was the bravest of all of
us. We knew he was working for the
British intelligence service. He risked
life and limb to feed information to
his handler about what the Kaibiles
were doing. He was part of a network
that nobody has ever admitted to — a
unit run by a few half-decent people
who wanted to undo the damage caused
by their governments.

'Alejandro trained as a Kaibile. He
went through the absolute hell of their
training regime. He almost lost his
humanity to bury himself in the heart
of the enemy but he stayed true to
his belief in a democratic Guatemala
and managed to help get the truth to
his British handlers about the worst
of the atrocities. The military claimed
that it was the guerrillas, the Left-
wingers, who were annihilating all the
villages and wiping whole communities

off the map. He provided the proof that it was the Kaibiles in plain clothes, following counter-insurgency plans drawn up and drilled home by American special forces. When he made it to the military base he thought he would be safe. He was a hero, after all. But when the commanders contacted Westminster they were told a different story. He risked causing embarrassment and difficulty for the Americans. He was to be treated as a potential enemy agent. He was to be quizzed about guerrilla encampments that may or may not have been concealed in the jungle in Belize. And when he couldn't provide that he was handed back to the Kaibiles and they took such delight in his death that there was almost nothing left of him to parade in front of his family as a warning to those who threatened to betray the Kaibiles.'

A file found at the UK National Archives supports this allegation, and shows that a Belizean major visited the Kaibiles' notorious training academy, even drawing a crude map of the camp.

A former British paratrooper stationed in Belize has confirmed reports that the British troops were regularly sent on missions into the Guatemalan jungle looking for enemy combatants. They were told that these men were drug runners but many former combatants claim they were insurgents fighting for the right to hold democratic elections

and bring an end to the decades of
bloodshed.

The Ministry of Defence did not reply
to our approach for comment.

***

National Archives, Kew, London
November 10, 2016
9.56 a.m.

Paolo Fergus.
   Journalist. Proprietor, editor, senior reporter, photographer
and pot-washer and eighteen times Employee of the Month
for the award-winning, if little-read news and features agency
Aletheia.com.
   Last of a dying breed.
   He's an affable, big-boned chap. Isn't given to the doldrums.
Optimist, moderated by experience. Believes that there's still
an important place in society for newspapers and that the
internet will eventually burn itself out.
   Paolo's in his early forties and is one of the few half-decent
journalists still making a living from secrets. His business
cards describe him as an 'investigative reporter' though he
has to resort to a bit of court reporting and showbiz piffle
to really keep the wolves from the door. He's dabbled with
podcasts and briefly had his own attempt at a true-crime
show on YouTube but it was amateurish and time-consuming
and didn't really play to his strengths. He's not got the slick-
ness that a good presenter needs. He's a bit scruffy for all
that. Even when he's trying to impress people he manages
to look like he's been mugged, stripped and forcibly inserted
into his attacker's clothes. He's got big hands that look silly
as they hammer away at a keyboard. He's forever scratching
his grey beard and sending flakes of dead skin spinning away
to blizzard down onto the collar of his checked shirt, his
zip-neck jumper; his photographer's waistcoat with a pocket
for every conceivable lens – none of which currently contain

lenses and which hang open, limp and pointless, like slack mouths.

He looks up and around him. Gives a sigh through his thick lips and badger whiskers. He usually finds the church-like silence of the National Archives a restful environment; a place where a fellow might get away from other people's inanity and be left to focus on things that matter, such as his own opinions, a gentle doze, or how to make more money from the dead.

Paolo scratches his beard again. He's read that he needs to moisturize more: needs to really lather it into the flaky epidermis beneath his bristles. He found some skin lotion in the medicine cabinet of a lady-friend and in the spirit of a chap high on the promise of sex, not to mention the preceding Thai green curry and red wine, he'd massaged a good half bottle into his whiskers. It had taken him twenty minutes to get the stuff to soak in and by then his big coarse facial hair was so sleek that he left the bathroom looking like Rasputin. He'd rather stick with the itchiness, thanks all the same.

Paolo's phone buzzes inside his jacket pocket. He experiences the usual sensation. It could be the story of a lifetime, it could be his ex demanding an update on his missing child benefit payments, or it could be British Gas, increasingly militant in their attempts to force him into changing energy supplier.

He answers in a stage whisper, cupping his fleshy hand over the mouthpiece. He's got a soft Dundonian accent, made only marginally less lyrical by twenty-five years of living in London.

'Paolo Fergus,' he says, and a few heads pop up from behind computer screens to throw irked frowns his way. He ignores them all with the practised insouciance of somebody who makes a living knocking on the doors of the recently bereaved and asking them just how sad they're feeling.

'Mr Fergus,' comes a voice not too dissimilar to his own. It's rougher, slightly more breathy, but it's pure Scots. 'You wrote to me. You asked me to call you. So I'm calling.'

Paolo takes a moment to ask the secretary in his muddled mind to have a quick flick through all recent correspondence. He sends out a lot of speculative letters. He's always got an idea for a feature or a story or, Holy Grail of Holy Grails, a true-crime book. Who had he been splashing about in recently? Somebody old, somebody Scottish, what had it been in connection with . . . *Oh!*

'Mr Erskine,' he says, quietly. 'Sorry for whispering, I'm at the Archives at present. A good chance some librarian will deliver a spanking if I talk louder than a mouse fart. Can you hear me OK?'

There's silence at the other end of the line, then a long slow release of breath. Paolo can almost smell the cigarette smoke coming down the line.

'I read your article on what happened in Belize,' says Mr Erskine. 'You got a lot of it wrong. You got some of it right as well, which is why I reckoned I'd take a punt on you.'

'You left a comment on the website,' says Paolo. 'Said you were there and that you could give me chapter and verse. I emailed you but no reply. Had to track you down and resort to the old pen and ink.'

'Must be a nightmare for you,' says Mr Erskine, drily. 'You passed another test with that, lad. Finding a postal address can't have been easy. You must have friends in low places.'

'Aye, bottom feeders aren't as territorial as you'd think,' says Paolo, enjoying the conversation. 'As I said in my letter, the story may merit a follow-up but only if there's a new angle or something that moves it forward. I only work for Aletheia now and again, but they don't pay great and all the stories they carry have to fulfil a certain brief. I did pretty well out of the Belize one, as I recall, though it was weeks ago now. What's your own connection? You were there?'

Mr Erskine takes a moment, seeming to weigh his options. 'Would there be any money on the table?'

'Not from me,' says Paolo, who's answered the question plenty of times and knows how best to disguise the answer. 'But if you tell me the basics I can approach a features editor and see what we can work out between us. I'll see you right, of course. You can trust me, though that's probably not a reassuring sentence to hear from a journalist.'

Mr Erskine pauses again. There's a soft crackle as he lights a new cigarette from the burning tip of the last one. 'I'm seventy-nine years old, if you're interested,' he says, quietly. 'Mad age, when you think on it. Not so well, as it happens. The doctor says my heart's on its arse.'

'I'm sorry to hear that,' says Paolo, opening a blank page on his laptop and making a note of the glorious diagnosis. 'Still, modern medicine can do marvellous things.'

'No, no need for platitudes, son. I can hear death sharpening his scythe. It's not a bother. I've drunk a loch of whisky and smoked a forest of fags. Three wives, five kids, a couple of step-bastards who reckon I used to knock 'em about . . . seen most of the world and not just the tourist spots. Can't complain, really. And if it all starts to hurt I won't be hanging about to get too weak to sort myself out. If it comes to it, I'll pull the trigger and save the NHS the money of seeing me off.'

Paolo rearranges himself in his seat. He's really paying attention now. Mr Erskine just got very interesting. 'Are you able to tell me anything now? Your involvement? Your own contribution? I don't have my files in front of me but it started at Kew, funnily enough. Had to make a Freedom of Information request that took up the best part of a day but I got enough on Operation Octopus to make for a decent yarn.'

'A decent yarn?' asks Mr Erskine, with a little smile in his voice. 'Aye, it's that. Bet you were surprised they approved the request, eh?'

Paolo wipes his hand across his mouth. Scratches at his moustache. 'Sometimes you get lucky.'

'They threw you a bone, son. Gave you enough to stop you asking the next lot of questions. What happened in the jungle, that weren't more than the tip of it. My hat's off to you, you've got closer to uncovering something real than anybody else has in all my years as a Quaker, but you fell off the horse well before the finish.'

'A Quaker?' asks Paolo.

'One of the Friends,' says Mr Erskine, slowly, as if it were important.

Paolo picks up his pen and chews the end. A little window opens in his memory. Quakers. Friends. Wasn't that a euphemism? The gentlemen at Century House. MI6 before it moved to Legoland down by the Thames.

'You mean SIS?' he asks, dropping his voice even lower. 'MI6?'

'Give the man a medal,' says Mr Erskine, laughing. 'And right now, if I'm any judge, GCHQ will be listening to every word we're saying. Given that they're about as much use as a sackful of wet mice, that probably means we've got plenty of time to talk, but just in case they're having one of their productive days, I'll keep it brief.'

'Can I record this?' asks Paolo, fiddling with his phone.

'I'd be appalled if you didn't,' replies Mr Erskine and Paolo can imagine the smile on his face. 'Now, listen, and you might just learn something.'

TWO

November 29, 2016
Somewhere on the B6264, Cumbria

Paolo is sitting in the back of a red Volkswagen saloon when the call comes through. The train journey up from London has been excruciating. There was nowhere to sit for the first two hours and when he finally got his ample buttocks on a chair there was no plug to charge his laptop or phone and he'd been forced instead to stare out of the window and consider his thoughts, and that had led him nowhere good.

It's mid-afternoon now and he's on the road from Carlisle to Brampton. A light rain is drifting in across miles of nothingness and the streetlamps are already winking on. There's forest either side of the road and as a seasoned city dweller he finds the nearness of untamed nature distinctly menacing. There are one or two nice houses here and there and there was a pretty little town a mile or so back, but nothing about the landscape has persuaded him that his future lies north of Watford. Even going back to Dundee seems like a ludicrous idea. His mum still lives there and she's a horror who believes her only son to be a wastrel, and ingrate and an embarrassment, all because he quoted her in a story when he couldn't think of anybody else to whom he could attribute a quote without fear of litigation.

The call, when it comes, immediately lifts his spirits. His mobile flashes blue and the number of the caller illuminates the screen. It's from America, and he cannot help thinking that this story will rise or fall based on what he learns.

'Mr Fergus? This is Juan Fernandez from the Asociación de la Antropologia Forense.'

Paolo rearranges himself. He's glad he sat in the back of the taxi. The driver had seemed the sort who might want to talk and right now, all he wants is a clear head and decent mobile service.

'Dr Fernandez,' he says, smoothly. 'You received my email. I've heard a rather fantastical tale . . .'

The scientist is polite and courteous, his accent Latin American but with the softer vowels of somebody who has lived away from their homeland for several years. 'Yes, indeed,' he says, with enthusiasm in his voice. 'It is, as you say, more than a coincidence, perhaps. Sometimes, God intercedes, perhaps.'

Paolo doesn't offer any thoughts on God for fear of offending this clearly spiritual man. Dr Fernandez runs the AAF. In conjunction with the United Nations and several other charities and church groups, he is endeavouring to match the bodies recovered from endless mass graves, with the names of the disappeared. It is a Herculean task but the interviews that Paolo has read all indicate that the doctor and his team of forensic anthropologists will not slow in their undertaking until every last scrap of bone or clothing is cross-referenced against the growing database of the names of the missing.

Paolo had to spend heavily on his last remaining credit card in order to purchase a bogus log-in to the organization's intranet. A hacker friend in a coffee shop in Camden had done the necessary in under twenty minutes. He purchased access to the great unwieldy mass of photographs, maps, grid references and official reports that represented the entirety of Guatemala's war graves. Thousands upon thousands of bodies had been recovered from their hidden resting places. Each body was then painstakingly separated out from those with whom it had been interred. In the pictures Paolo had seen, dedicated young scientists were grimly using paintbrushes and chopsticks to whittle away at dirt embedded in eye sockets, skulls and femurs. Every fibre of clothing, every belt-buckle, eye-glass, training shoe or gold tooth – each were disentangled and individually laid out. Samples were taken. Photographs were taken. And then the blood relatives of the disappeared gave the DNA samples that could allow Dr Fernandez and his team to start cross-referencing. He and his staff have uncovered

more than 10,000 bodies – from villages, from wells, from
under church tiles, from eighty-foot-deep bone pits in a cemetery. Their unenviable goal is to pinpoint causes of death,
identify the bodies and bring the remains back to families
who have been searching for their mothers, fathers, sons and
daughters for decades.

'You want to know about the book, I take it,' says Dr
Fernandez, sunnily. 'I shan't ask you how you know, but it is
certainly something that we have considered asking our press
friends to consider running. Of course, there are many incon-
gruities – this is the right word, I hope? But certainly, a volume
of English poetry, handwritten, inscribed – it has left us
wondering, that much is certain.'

Paolo listens for a while. Doesn't want to spoil the flow
by talking or asking questions. But he hears himself give a
start of surprise when Dr Fernandez confirms the wording
in the opening leaf of the little diary found in a mass
grave in the Guatemalan jungle – the scene of a civil war
atrocity that claimed the lives of dozens of men, women and
children. It had been pure luck that he found any mention
of the book. Erskine had given him some names. And that,
in turn, led to HR #1014. She'd been found along with
eighteen other victims, all women. She'd been buried blind-
folded. Naked, save a golden cross and bracelet. In her hand
she clutched a leather bible. And inside the bible, protected
from the damp earth, was a slim volume of poetry. The
words were unintelligible in places but it was written in
English, in a neat hand, and was filled with half-decent little
ditties about the weather, about people known to the poet;
about cigarettes and grandchildren and grief. It had puzzled
the anthropologists who found it and they intended, at some
point, to start asking questions. Now Paolo Fergus had saved
them the bother.

In his ear, Dr Fernandez is in full flow: '. . . of course
around that time, the paramilitary death squads, they prowled
Guatemala City in unmarked white vans and jeeps, snatching
people off street corners, from their workplaces, from their
houses in the middle of the night. Bodies were often left
mutilated along the roadside or strung up from trees. The

military targeted leftist organizers, Catholic priests and nuns, teachers, university students, trade unionists and the indigenous Maya – anyone deemed affiliated with the Left. Of course, it was the Cuarto Pueblo murders that first truly decided me on what my life's work would involve. Four hundred soldiers ordered the villagers into the square. The men were macheted, shot, the women and children smashed against concrete pillars. The entire village was obliterated – once the last survivors had been forced to dig their own burning pits. The jungle smelled of flesh and fire for days afterwards. When we found the site – my team took forty coffee sacks full of teeth and bone fragments back to the lab. It felt as though we had done something of worth, though there is no celebration in such a moment.'

'We're here, mate,' says the cabbie, from the driving seat.

Paolo looks up from his phone call. They've pulled up outside a nondescript semi-detached house on a sloping road. It has a council estate feel to it. The cars don't look very expensive and the curtains in most of the upstairs windows don't look thick enough to keep out the light. Number 28 has a handrail by the steps that lead up to the garden path. The garden is neatly tended and through the big front window he can make out patterned wallpaper and an unfeasibly large photograph of two boys holding musical instruments and grinning for the camera.

'Thanks for your time,' says Paolo to the good man who's still talking to him about the untold dead. 'I'll call you back.'

Paolo pays on his card, much to the dismay of the driver. Asks for a receipt, just to piss him off. Then he climbs out of the car and lugs his single hold-all behind him.

He stands in the glow of the streetlight. It's deathly quiet on Berrymoor Road. He feels, for a moment, as if he's the priest in the movie poster of *The Exorcist*. Wonders whether he really is on to a story that will make his name, or if he's come all this way to talk to a mad woman.

The front door opens. Standing on the step is a woman he recognizes from her time as head of MI6. Blue eyes, silver hair; an expensive-looking cashmere cardigan worn with a silky blouse and well-pressed trousers. She's slim and fit and looks far younger than the age she admits to in *Who's Who*.

'You'll be Paolo Fergus,' she says, without offering a handshake. 'Bloody funny sort of a name. She'll ask you about it, but don't get sidetracked. She wanders. I presume your dad was Italian or something, yes? No mystery. Why do people always need a mystery?'

Paolo isn't sure what to say. Just stands on the doorstep looking feckless. 'I'm sorry, this is your house, is it?'

'No, Mr Fergus,' she says, withering. 'This is her house, and she won't leave it because she's as stubborn as a bloody donkey. Which means muggins here has to move in and play nursemaid while she's feeling sorry for herself and getting over her latest pretend illness. I, if you must know, have a rather lovely house where she could quite easily live in bloody luxury, but apparently we both need to be here and miserable because she's too much of a home bird to make a move at her time of life.'

Fergus stays silent. A smell of something delicious is emanating from the inside of the house. It gives off an air of cosiness; of comfort. The carpet is loud and trodden almost flat and the little of the hallway that he can see is papered in woodchip. And yet Baroness Cordelia Hemlock is standing in the doorway.

'You'll be coming in,' she says, stepping back. 'She'll offer you the sofa to sleep on but you'll say no. I've booked you in at the pub in the town centre. Better for you, better for her. She'll talk and you'll listen. I've written my stuff out for you and you can have a look when you're good and ready to properly understand. She'll downplay her own part in it and no doubt I've made myself sound like a right bloody halfwit, but the whole thing was such a mess from start to finish that nobody came out of it with any credit.'

Paolo raises his hands, trying to bat away the barrage of information. 'I'm sorry, I'm not really sure what . . .'

'You want the story,' explains Cordelia. 'What happened. The Angels. Bloody Kaibiles running around with guns in

Gilsland. My house. Walt. Cyanide pills and listening devices and Felicity Bloody Goose crawling around in the rafters like a commando in a cardigan. That's what you want, yes? Jesus, when I told Erskine to call you I thought you'd have the brains to keep up. That story of yours – Belize. It wasn't half bad. You seemed like you could write a bit. Did I make a mistake? Did Clive do his Scottish accent? God, he's a ham actor at heart.'

Paolo feels dizzy; feels as though the ground beneath his feet is giving way. 'You asked Erskine to call me? But I called you . . .'

Cordelia closes her eyes. Shakes her head. 'Feckless,' she mutters and leads him into the warm, low-ceiling little kitchen at the back of the house. In the high-backed chair, wrapped in a blanket and looking jolly excited to have guests, is a very elderly woman. She grins, hugely, as Paolo enters the room.

'By heck, he's the size of a hoos-end!'

'This is what I'm dealing with,' says Cordelia, with an indulgent little roll of her eyes. She crosses to the big old Rayburn in the corner and starts moving the kettle around on the hotplate.

'Go on then, Flick,' she prompts. 'Introduce yourself. Make the nice man feel at home.'

'Take no notice,' says Flick. 'She's not really the way she is, if you follow me. Sweet as sugar underneath. My John always said she has a heart of gold, God rest him. Though of course, he went doolally at the end and thought she was the district nurse, so maybe he's not the best judge. Now, tea? Apple cake? Or shall we get down to it?'

Paolo sits down without being asked. Looks up at the two elderly women staring at him expectantly. He feels like he's in a Chekhov play and can't remember his lines.

'Read my chapter first,' says Cordelia, pouring tea into a china cup for herself and a mug for her friend. 'It only makes sense if you read me first.'

'That's true, actually,' confirms Flick. 'She's not putting herself forward.'

Paolo starts to pull out his recorder, his notebooks. Looks

at the teapot and gets nothing. Takes the sheaf of documents
and starts to read. 'So, I suppose . . . it's all to do with what
happened at Gilsland?' he asks, weakly.

'Aye.' Felicity nods. 'Most bloody things are.'

PART ONE

PART ONE

CORDELIA

We'll start in the graveyard. I could start in a dozen other places, but if we're going to get to the nuts and bolts of it all then it might as well be Highgate. Got the right smell to it, that place. Smells as death should, and no more so than when autumn's giving over to winter. Proper end-of-the road smell. Earth, wood, decay – that sickly whiff of fermentation, like there's fruit dying on the vine.

It was December 17, 1982. And Highgate's in London, just in case you're a bit hard-of-thinking. All Gothic and overgrown and spiders spinning their webs between the headstones; the threads catching the light in the way they do, throwing disco glitter into the dark.

I could tell you that I remember it all like it was just yesterday, but if I'm honest with you, I sometimes forget my yesterdays before the paint's had time to dry. Run a hand over the memory and it's all just a jumble of colour and mess and if you're not careful you're nodding like a simpleton and telling people that yes, you'd love to go on a bus to the seaside with a load of old dears. That's age for you. I can see the stuff through the wrong end of the telescope but anything up close is a bit of a blur. The years go by so quickly it feels like you've only just finished 'Auld Lang Syne' when it's time to start singing 'Jingle Bells' again. I'll be eighty next birthday. An absurd amount of time to be alive and I feel every day of it. There are bits of me that hurt and bits that don't work like they should and bits that look like something that lives at the bottom of the sea. It takes me twice as long to recover as it does to get tired.

Don't go thinking of me as some nice little old lady, just before we get started properly. I'm not some scone-cheeked nana with a hearing aid and bunions the size of radishes. I'm not syrupy. Not in that sugary way that Felicity's got. I'm not all toffees and crayons and TCP and I don't buy my shoes at the pharmacy. These loafers are Italian, if you're asking. Hand-stitched, though that seems an odd thing to brag about. Foot-stitched would be a sight worth seeing, wouldn't it?

Anyway, they say I've still got that look about me – that glare that can cause a butterfly to burst into flames if it gets caught between me and whoever's tried my patience. Eighty bloody years old, though. I swear I was twenty-five a fortnight ago.

Birthday coming up, more's the pity. I've warned them all that I don't want a fuss. Anybody who asks me to blow out eighty candles is getting written out of the will. I'm not one of those wheezy old buggers who sound like they've got a popcorn kernel stuck in their windpipe, but the last time I tried to blow up an armband for my granddaughter I ended up looking at the world through fireworks and polka dots and went to bed with a migraine. I swear, another couple of years and I'll need a push just to get my rocking chair going.

What I'm saying is that I don't want you thinking of me *now* when you think of me *then*. The Cordelia in the graveyard in '82, I mean. She'd still be in her prime. She wouldn't thank me for spoiling the picture of what she worked so hard to put out into the world. Keeping an image of me in your head will only spoil it. To be honest if you were to look at her, and at me, you wouldn't think we were anything to do with one another. That was the general idea, of course. No point working in the security services if you can't make yourself into some-body else. I was good at it. Still am. Got so far into my alternatives that sometimes it was hard to come back. And in the winter of '82 I didn't know who the bloody hell I was. You know where you put a straw into your gin and tonic and it breaks as it hits the water and seems sort of dislocated and misaligned? That's the closest thing I can think of to describe how it felt to be me again.

I'd spent months living as somebody else and I'd only just got back into the habit of wearing my own skin. I can't go into it all now, not without getting into more bother than I'll get into for telling you about this, but for the previous eight months I'd gotten damn good at being a subversive. I did the lot. Went full punk. All spit and snot and imitation leather.

Pierced my nose with a safety pin and grew my armpit hair long enough to braid it. Smoked the skunk and downed the scrumpy and took tabs of LSD from the tongues of colourful people with names like Bilbo and Dewdrop and Worm. I was a tapeworm deep in the gut of the anarchist movement; slithering through the underbelly of the subversives. My superiors thought of them as 'the enemy', which gives you an idea just who was in charge at that time. We were looking for rabble-rousing Soviet sympathizers. What we found were nice suburban mums who felt reasonably strongly that storing America's nuclear weapons in Berkshire might not be a great idea. Hippies, mostly. Feminists. Bohemians and bra burners and some goodhearted housewives who brought flasks and picnic baskets and hoped that bringing about lasting change could be achieved without hurting anybody's feelings. A few communists, of course, but communist in that particularly British way where it's more about berets and Che Guevara T-shirts than any passionate desire to smash the system. I went deep cover on that one. Combat trousers, lace-up military boots, stinking fishtail parka and a buzz-cut with a feathery bit at the back of my neck. I blended in like a grain of salt in a sugar bowl and I'd wager a pound to a penny that there are plenty of women of a certain age who don't know that Gwendoline, one of the movement's senior figures, was reporting back to the security services the entire time we clung to the chain-link fence outside the military base and sang our jolly protest songs.

I sometimes wish I'd gone full native. If I'd really committed to CND and the Peace Convoy I think we could have actually achieved nuclear disarmament and got rid of Thatcher by the mid-eighties. Unfortunately the rest of the movement were too nice by half. Wishy-washy and well-intentioned but if they put a gun to your head you'd know they had no intention of pulling the trigger. If they'd been handed power they wouldn't have known what to do with it. So I did the job I was there to do, spying on people I liked and reporting back to bastards I couldn't stand. That's the eighties for you.

By mid-December I'd been myself again for a month or so. I was wearing the blonde-brown wig and had removed my tinted lenses to again peer out through naturally blue eyes. It still didn't feel entirely comfortable. I was moving around inside my own life like a burglar, rattling door handles and peering in cupboards, constantly alarmed by my own reflection. I'd been medically cleared for whatever operation might need my services, but in the interim I was damnably deskbound: a grey smudge of fag ash and manila festering away at a borrowed desk in HQ. Eight-hour days with an hour for lunch. Barely a soul to talk to and going slowly mad, poring over reams of paperwork, red pen hovering above a great blur of reports, transcripts and internal memorandum. Intelligence Analysis only became fun when you found something, which meant most of us poor buggers spent our days eagerly trying to unearth evidence of mendacity, duplicity or imminent global threat. There weren't many people to talk to in our little section of the office and I can't pretend I was a known quantity. I got mistaken for the tea girl so often that I found it easier just to go along with it. I knew I was only killing time until I was able to be put to a proper use, but I could feel myself going a little mad in the silent stillness of those close little rooms. If I hadn't picked up the call on the Pandora line I might have been sat there for months on end.

Sorry, didn't I say? Pandora line, so-called after the locked box in which it's kept. Big black telephone encased in a rectangular tin and the joke goes that if you open it you should be prepared to let all the evils of the world flood out the receiver. It's the line used by people from the old days – the real Cold War faces whose connection with the Service went back to the dark ages. It was a dull grey Tuesday and I was counting the minutes until I could throw on my coat and head for the bus back to my flat in Chelsea. We had a house in Knightsbridge but Cranham had that weeknights and the flat was more in keeping with the me I was trying to be. There were three or four bright young things in the office: floppy hair and nice suits and the right accents, but they still looked to me when the phone went off in the section chief's office and boredom alone made me act like the departmental secretary. The key for the lockbox was on a string attached to a nail in the central pillar of the office. It had rung eight times before I got the key in the lock, checked the duty log for the day's code word, and finally raised the receiver to my ear. And that's when a cheerful voice I hadn't heard in an age addressed me as 'bonny lass' and told me that he had something to share that was so hot, so fresh and so damn delicious that he couldn't think of anybody to share it with but me.

CORDELIA

S orry, I did say we'd start at the graveyard. That's old age
for you. I have a chronic fear of becoming one of those
people who ramble. Felicity says I haven't adjusted to
old age yet and that I could still give Helen Mirren a run for
her money, but Felicity has started putting her tongue out
before her spoon reaches her mouth so she has absolutely no
right to give opinions on anything any more. I'm not old. Not
properly. Felicity bloody is. Eighty-eight in August. Eighty-
eight! Mind's still sharp as broken glass but her body's a real
butcher's shop of a thing. There's barely a bit of her that isn't
breaking down or eating itself or dropping off. She doesn't
complain, of course, though she has a way of not complaining
that sounds like a Sicilian widow has just stubbed her toe.

Anyway, Highgate. Dark as misery. And it's some time not
far off eight p.m. It's cold, I know that much. It rained earlier
in the day and the piles of raked leaves have formed a slimy
mulch at the edges of the overgrown paths. There's a muddy
gravel beneath the soles of my shoes, but I can promise you
I'm barely making a sound as I pick my way towards the
moss-slimed tomb at the apex of two twisting paths. It's half
covered up by overhanging branches that dangle down from
the nearby elm. This is the oldest part of the cemetery and
the headstones stick up haphazardly; the writing obliterated
by rain and lichen and time. There's a body of a Ripper victim
somewhere nearby, the headstone paid for by public subscrip-
tion. Guilt, I reckon. We're good at that, the British. We'll let
people suffer the torments of Job while they're alive, but we'll
make a bloody great fuss of them once they're six feet under.
It's a spooky sort of a place to be on a cold, blowy night,
especially when you're not yet feeling yourself and you're
doing something that you know, in your bones, you shouldn't
really be doing. I keep turning the shadows into people and
the people into monsters. Every tree root is a serpent, each

creeper intent upon fastening around my ankle and tugging me into the soft, meat-scented earth. It feels as if I'm walking deeper into darkness; as if I could turn back towards the hazy lights of the road and find that every last one has been snuffed out while my back was turned.

A twig yanks the wig askew and I'm in a fighting pose and thrusting out a kick at nothing even as I'm laughing at myself and trying to rearrange the damn thing. If this were a training exercise I'd already have failed. I feel as if I'm getting twisted up in spider-silk as I push further through the tangle of spindly branches. I start hearing an unsettling sound, a keen-edged rhythm: like a saw finding purchase in wet wood. It takes a moment to realize that it's me, getting myself scared, softly hyperventilating, making up spectral dangers when I should be fixating on the one very real danger that could be hiding nearby. I look left and right, horribly aware that each of the weathered headstones could conceal a threat. Ghosts of warm breath gather in the black air around my face, drifting away to mingle with the mist and the cold night air. I want to stop and light a cigarette, to pull out my lighter and gaze for a moment into the crimson flame; to cup my cold hands around it and suck in a breath of red fire. I feel as if I'm spiralling into a photographic negative. Nobody lays flowers here. Even in daylight there's no colour to be found amid the greys and parchment whites. It has a fairytale feel and it's hard not to start telling myself stories as the spindly black branches catch the breeze and start writing invisible script upon the low, breath-fogged dark. I think upon my children. Thinking, before I can stop myself, upon the twins. See myself on my back, my arms around the both of them, holding a big hardback book open in front of me. I'm reading fairy tales but I'm improvising; making up little sub-plots and giving the characters better motivation. Everybody has a distinctive voice and I'm damn good at pretending to be the evil witch, dropping down to a whisper and then erupting in a shriek, grabbing them both in a fit of tickles and laughter as they kick their legs and mummify themselves in blankets and bed sheets. They're happy memories, though I wish they'd make themselves scarce. Thinking of Louis and Tamara inevitably causes me to slip into recollection of Stefan. He didn't get past two years old and he'd been dead fifteen years by '82, but the grief has never left me. Hadn't then, hasn't now. I don't want it to. Grief's something to cling to, isn't it? An anchor or a lifebuoy or a big blue plaque. A connection. Nobody's really gone when you'd give your own heart to bring them back. And it was the graveyard that did it. He used to love the little cemetery outside the tiny church in the village where he spent his short little life. I was a different person then, too – wife of a minister and lady of a manor house I didn't know what to do with. We treated consecrated ground like our private play-park and it was there, amongst the gravestones and the wildflowers where I scattered his ashes when meningitis took him away from me and dimmed the light in my eyes.

So I'm wiping tears and sniffing back snot and wishing I'd never answered the bloody phone as I reach under the loose kerbstone and find the shiny brass key that unlocks the gates to the O'Farrell mausoleum. I should be checking my perimeter and doubling back on myself, but instead I'm off in my own little world, thinking of a place 200 miles north where I experienced something a little like happiness and made the only real friend I've ever had.

The key slips into the lock as if it's been buttered. I detach the lock from the big black chain and slowly uncoil the links from the rusty iron railings that serve as sentry to the black mouth of the tomb. The chain is new but care and attention has been taken to make it look old. So, too, the railings. It might seem as though a well-placed kick would detach the metal from the brickwork, but the hinges are sunk deep and anybody aiming a boot at the metal would end up with nothing more than a pained knee.

I pull myself together once I'm inside, slipping between the two halves of the railings and moving forward into the absolute black of the mausoleum. There are two thick wooden doors a little way ahead. The key is somewhere by my feet, hidden beneath the carpet of dead leaves and broken bottles, an installation piece of artfully arranged debris. I find it without cutting myself and manage to locate the lock, turning the big brass handle; the blood smell of rust rising above the bass-note reek of damp earth and softening flesh.

I step into the darkness and close the door with my foot. The blackness is absolute. I know there's a torch somewhere to my right but I can tell already that the man I'm due to meet has already arrived and is standing, silently, in the ink-black recesses of the circular tomb. He smokes nasty little cigars and favours spicier foods so even with the absence of light I can pick out the blob of darkness where he lingers.

'There once was an ugly duckling,' I say, softly, wiping the sleeve of my overcoat across my nose and cuffing away any tears that might have slipped, unremarked, from my eyes.

'Feathers all yucky and brown?' comes the reply, rising at the end as if the speaker isn't entirely sure he's remembered the snippet of code correctly. 'Maybe it's "mucky". Gosh, my memory. I've been repeating it to myself over and over and I've still buggered it up. Who'd be a spy, eh, my bonny lass?'

'I'll forgive you, Hinny,' I say, a smile in my voice. 'Nobody else sounds like you, Walt, my pet.'

I hear a little snuffle of laughter. He's always made gentle fun of my north-east roots; a discord to the Home Counties newsreader accents of everybody else in the Service. I've always amplified my Geordie in his presence.

'When the boat comes in,' he laughs, in the worst Newcastle accent I've ever heard. 'A fishy on a little dishy, eh, sweetheart?'

I'm grinning, my mind full of memories both good and bad. And then I'm wincing, holding up a hand to shield my eyes as Walt flicks the torch into life and steps out of the shadows as if he were Rumpelstiltskin come to life. He's aged poorly. It's been a few years since we last shared a gin and a chinwag but they've been harder on him than on me. Walt is a tubby little chap: conspicuously gnome-like in his red-cheeked, white-bearded jolliness. There's a gumminess to his mouth now: a suggestion that his big white teeth no longer fit his shrunken gums. He's not fat, not exactly, but there's something about him that puts a person in mind of a painful mosquito bite, as if his skin is stretched tight over some irritating infection and that a shaving cut could cause him to burst. The lenses

of his eyes are the yellow of a harvest moon. He's dressed for
the weather: his boilerman's cap pulled down so low that it
nearly touches his big pink ears and his short Alpine jacket
looks to still be damp from this morning's downpour. Beneath
his coat he wears the grey suit and loudly patterned jumper
that were his trademark when he was a senior figure near the
uppermost reaches of the Service. His glasses, I notice with
a whiff of nostalgia, are as filthy as they were when he first
introduced himself to me as a new recruit in the spring of '68.
I wondered then, as now, how much of his appearance was
affectation. He looked so very unlike a spy. And yet he
was the best of all of them: clever, cunning, witty in his way.
He was the last of the old school; the last of the Cambridge
intelligentsia with the old-England surname and a reputation
for causing the right kind of mischief. Whether he achieved
greatness or missed it completely depends entirely upon whom
you ask. But in '82 he's long since been given his marching
orders after one row too many with his Whitehall overlords.
He wasn't, as they saw it, a company man. He either saw the
bigger picture, or didn't see the same one that everybody else
at the table was looking at. He had an annoying habit of trying
to do the decent thing in a merciless business. There was some
sticky business involving a botched buy in Nicaragua and I
know he took the loss of one of his agents hard. Not much
leaked out during the ensuing autopsy but it became clear, as
these things do, that Walt was no longer one of us and that it
would be better for those with an eye upon advancement, to
start making fun of his memory and mocking his outdated
little ways. I, as something akin to a protégée, was lucky not
to be tarred by association. It still sickens me how little I said
or did in his defence. All the things I've done and not done
and that's what I feel the most shame about.

He gives me that smile of his – the one that says this is all
jolly good fun and a little bit silly but he's happy to play along
with it if it means he gets to continue thinking of himself as
someone who's considerably more interesting than he looks.
He pulls a little cigar from an inside pocket and lights it with
a match from a damp box, sucking on the foot of his smoke
like a baby with a teat. He looks at me as he does it, though

it's more out of a sense of good manners than anything
suggestive. He's a funny little man but he's not a lech. I think
he's probably sexless, though that hasn't harmed his marriage
or his relationship with his kids. Walt's a man of duty.

'You hear it?' he asks, when his cigar is lit and the air
between us is full of greasy grey smoke. He moves to the back
of the tomb where what remains of a fresco has turned into
a dull swirl and smear of misshapen nymphs and deformed
cherubs. He puts the torch on top of an alabaster casket and
steps into the circle of light as if walking onto a stage to
deliver a reading. 'I heard it. Straight from the cowboy's mouth.
Stood there beside him at the podium and looked out at the
world and said it straight out. "A man of integrity. Of unim-
peachable moral character. Standing proud against a sea of
Reds".'

I found a more comfortable spot on a coffin. Pressed my
back to the cold stone. Gave him the nod that he took as
permission to keep talking. Neither of us checked the
other for a wire or a weapon. To do so would have been
the ultimate in poor manners.

'I see you haven't changed your attitude towards our chums
in Washington,' I said, suppressing a shiver. I looked again at
his complexion and thought that there might be a whisper of
a white line around the arm of his spectacles. He'd been abroad
recently. Had let some sun upon his skin then brought it back
to London in December.

He lets the smile leave his eyes. It stays on his lips but he
doesn't make the effort to keep the jollity in his voice. 'You
have to ask yourself how bad the real enemy must be if our
allies are Reagan and the bloodthirsty monsters he feeds by
hand. You know he's going back to Congress to ask for more
money for his brave comrades-in-arms, yes?'

'He probably wouldn't use the word "comrade"?' I say, if
only because I know Walt of old and it unnerves me to see that
there is a tension vibrating inside the ridiculous, relentlessly
chipper demeanour.

'He'll get it too,' says Walt, ignoring me. 'Whatever they
want, Congress will stump up. They'll keep doing what they're
doing.'

I feel cold, suddenly. It feels as if a chill is rising up from the floor of the crypt: an icy miasma of pestilence and sickness. Suddenly I feel an urge to shiver; a queasiness in my gut. Beneath my clothes I can sense the hairs on my arms rising up like sails. I'd known that this was what Walt wanted to talk to me about but now I'm here, in his presence, I don't want to hear it. He's going to put something in front of me that is too much of a responsibility. He's going to task me with doing something that is more about decency than duty and I know for a fact that I'm not going to have the strength of character to pick a side.

'They have their own intelligence services, Walt,' I say, as if explaining it to a child. 'They know precisely what they're supporting. They know what the military is doing and they don't care. It's the price they pay to stop the Communists getting another foothold in Central America. They have to work hand in hand with bad people.'

He looks at me as if I've sorely disappointed him. He was my boss, once. I don't know what he really is at this moment in time. He's an asset and he's very well-informed but he's not officially MI6, for all that he seems to know far more about world events than I ever do. He seems to think that I'm cut from the same cloth as he is – that I'm more interested in doing the right thing than that which is politically expedient. Such an approach has derailed a stellar career. After fourteen years in the intelligence services, my own star is continuing to rise, albeit irredeemably tarnished by my deeply selfish decision to take a year off to have the twins in '72. I keep hearing the voice of common sense prattling away on my shoulder, telling me that I shouldn't be here, that I've only come because I feel like I owe a favour to an old friend.

'Is that our excuse too? We have to work with the Americans because of our . . . what did we call it? Ah yes, the "special relationship". Yes. I once watched a terrier rape a squirrel in one of Her Majesty's parks. Held it down and properly gave it a seeing to. Held its neck and walked away afterwards with a proper strut in his step. I always return to that mental image when I think upon the special relationship we have with our friends across the Atlantic.'

I pull a face. 'How long were you watching for?'

He doesn't smile. 'At what time do we ask ourselves whether the price we are paying to preserve our way of life is one actually worth paying, Cordelia? The things we've done – the blind eyes we've turned. Is it really about security if we're trampling over the liberties of half the world's population? Is there a greater good to be considered when our allies are slaughtering innocents in their thousands?'

He shakes his head. Looks at the tip of his cigar and swallows as if feeling nauseous. He presses his hand to his chest, suddenly looking unwell. He presses the tip of the cigar to the sole of his damp grey shoes and slips the butt into one of his many zip-up pockets. When he looks at me again I'm horrified to see that his eyes are damp.

'Walt,' I say, in a voice that fairly dribbles with regret. 'I'm not who you think I am. I know you think of me as the northern lass who loved to read George Orwell, but for all that fight – all that I was, that sense I was changing the world – I'm just an analyst. Your old networks, your contacts, they don't talk to me the way your people talk to you. The people upstairs don't listen. They don't want to hear things that deviate from the party line. It's all political.'

He wipes a drop of moisture from the end of his nose. Blinks, slowly, and lets some cheer bleed back into his features. 'If I had something . . .' he says, cautiously. 'Something real. Something that would actually make people stop and say no, we can't do this, we can't support people who do these things . . .'

'People don't care, Walt,' I say, and I regret it at once. He looks at me as if I've just held up a picture of the two of us together and ripped it right down the middle.

'People do care,' he says quietly. 'Perhaps they care about the wrong things but they deserve to know what we are doing. We're supposed to be a land of integrity. Does nobody think of shame any more? Is there no honour left anywhere? Yes, of course we have to resist the threat of Communism but Reagan is standing next to a genocidal maniac and we're colluding in the pretence.'

'It's an ugly business,' I say, quietly. 'You told me that when

I was starting out. You said I would have times in my career when I wouldn't be able to face myself. There would be times when I'd be offered medals and I'd prefer a gunshot to the head. It wasn't much of a pep talk but you've been proven right. I've done things that make me feel sick but I cling to the idea I'm helping stop things getting any worse. We've done some good, you know we have.'

He sags a little, as if some fight has gone out of him. I wish I could just give the old sod a hug. He just looks so pitiful and ridiculous, this washed-up spook in his ill-fitting clothes and his dirty glasses, imploring me to see the world his way.

I pull a face, already unsure if I'm making a mistake. 'Something real,' I say, quietly. 'What do you mean, something real?'

He looks up. The light of the torch flickers for a moment and in the sudden strobing darkness it seems as though each of the dancing shadows is suddenly alive: each raven-dark silhouette the outline of one of his past incarnations; one of the many likenesses and aliases he has stepped into and out of during a career that began before the end of the war. He reaches into the zip-up pocket of his jacket and retrieves a small silver case. He slides it open, soundlessly, and from within he removes a strip of photographic film, he pulls at either side of the case and it extends in the middle: a magnifying viewer suddenly visible in the base of the box. He hands it to me without a word. I take the torch and arrange myself so I can examine the film through the viewer.

'What am I looking at . . .?'

He doesn't speak. Waits until the image comes into proper focus and my mind fills in the gaps in the dark, grainy image. I see children. Flame. A man with dark eyes holding a naked little girl by the ankle.

'When?' I ask, my mouth dry. 'Where?' I stop myself, focusing on the most important question. 'What am I supposed to do with this?'

'I have a source,' he says, quietly. 'Absolute proof of what we suspect to be happening. Willing to talk. Willing to spill their guts about what our dear friends in Washington are willing to condone. The scale of it, Cordelia – a silent extermination and the world is just looking the other way.'

'The world's changed,' I say, repeating a mantra that I've been hearing daily. 'It's not about righteousness and villainy any more. They care about expedience. Pragmatism. About maintaining our friendships and having a big old pal we can point at if anybody glares at us.'

'There are still decent people at Millbank,' he says, as if I'm muttering nonsense. 'People who will do the right thing if they see this – if they hear what we're doing . . .'

'There's a chain of command,' I say, half pleading for him to stop making me defend the indefensible. 'It's all changed, Walt. If I even try to get anybody to look into this or to clear an operation, then I'm going to have to go up every rung of the ladder – by the book, all above board . . .'

'While innocent people are murdered by our friends,' he says, and there is a flash of something in his features that I would have called 'desperation' in a lesser man. He recovers himself quickly. 'All I'm asking you to do is listen. I don't want to have to resort to Plan B.'

I don't ask what Plan B is. I presume he means taking his information to another friendly source within GCHQ. I should have asked, I think. Forty years later I feel like reaching into the memory and dragging myself out of that place, telling that silly slip of a thing not to get involved. If ignorance is bliss then knowledge is torture and I swear to God I would give anything to have stayed in the dark. But I couldn't help myself. It was guilt and ego and a desire to impress an old friend, and within a fortnight I would be hanging from my thumbs in a different darkness, listening to the screams of the dying and the sobs of my oldest friend.

'OK,' I tell him. 'Tell me all of it.'

FELICITY

. . . that's a fancy looking one, isn't it? Where does the tape go? Will it pick my voice up? I know I'm a bit raspy. It's my jazz-singer voice. Have you got what you need? Was she nice to you? I know she comes across as a cold fish but she's got a heart of gold underneath it, I swear. Is it warm enough for you? I can't tell. Always too cold, me. John used to say I must have slipped and come down hard on an icicle. How's that for cheeky? He doesn't make those jokes any more. Doesn't know who he is half the time, poor thing. I half thought the flu would finish him off but we've all got lucky, touch wood. Go on, touch it. The bread board, just next to you. He doesn't know me from Adam these days, but they're all still fighting to save his life, as if he's even in there any more. We might make seventy years married if he hangs in a few more months, though I doubt we'll cele-brate. It's been five years since he even got my name right. Sorry, can we stop a second? It creeps up on me, with John. I think I've got myself all settled and then there are tears running down my nose and landing in my lap and I don't want to make you uncomfortable – not with what you've seen. Could you . . .

This house, it were. This kitchen. Me, there, standing by the sink, giving the dishes a wipe with a tea towel and listening to the wireless. There was rain on the way, according to the weatherman and my chilblains. I had the curtains open and with the dark outside, the kitchen window served us like a mirror. I'd got used to it by then, of course. It was 1970 when we moved in so I'd had time to get a feel of the house and the street and the people. Council property but good and sturdy. John was Brampton born so it was nothing unusual for him, but we'd spent most of our married life out at Lower Denton, near Gilsland, where you'd be lucky to see anybody other than the postman for days on end. We had to move, though. No doubt about that. There'd been bother. A rumpus. 1967 it was. That was when her ladyship and me first became friends. I'd tell you all about it but I've promised that story to Cordy's grandson and it makes me get the shivers when I think about it.

Sorry, I do prattle, don't I? Proper cure for insomnia, so they say. Cordelia used to have me ring her some nights and start telling her about what I'd been up to, just to help her drift off. She'd put the phone on the pillow and then pretend to snore. Cheeky so-and-so. You won't know that about her, of course. You won't know she's a bit of a joker and that she'd give you the skin off her back if she thought you were cold. She hides all the sweetness. And there I go again.

So like I said, I was at the window, doing the pots. Can't have been much after seven. John was sitting where you are now. We've redecorated twice since then but it's not going to take much of a leap of imagination to picture it. I've got photos if you're struggling. Little sofa on wooden legs, a couple of nice armchairs and that drop-leaf table with the fruit bowl against the back wall. Same fruit bowl, if you'll give it credence. Wedding present, that was. There'll have been a bit of a fog around our John. Smoker, our John. Was when we met and he would still be now if the grandson hadn't given him earache for it. If you want to get it right, he'd have been sitting in his vest and pyjama trousers. He'll have had the cardigan on – the mustard-coloured one with the harlequin pattern on the front. It was his favourite and the pocket was just the right size for his packet of John Players. He'd have been a few months shy of fifty. Bald since not long after we said our vows but he still had a little horseshoe of grey hair around above his ears and down the back. He always said it was me who did it – that marrying me put years on him. He used to tell people that he'd torn it out by the roots with me nagging. It was only a joke, of course. I wasn't a nag.

Sometimes I said what had to be said but I was a worrier
if I was anything. Still am, when it comes to the family, though
I've given up getting myself in a state. I'm not far off eighty-
nine so most of my problems are behind me, I'd say.

Anyway, John's there, smoking away, little cloud of yellow
and grey circling him like his own private raincloud.
He'd been off on the sick for the best part of three months
and we'd just about had enough of each other. I did the
nursemaid bit and he really wasn't one to complain, but it
was draining seeing somebody that matters to you suffering
like that. He'd had his kidney out, did I say? The left one.
Apparently it was going to make him fit as a fiddle in time,
but we hadn't seen much evidence of that by mid-December.
The scar went right the way around from the front to the
back and I was changing bandages three times a day and
trying to get some food and drink down him was a bloody
nightmare. I think he got an infection. Had a high temperature
and went a bit odd a couple of times – shouting out in his
sleep and getting himself in a proper lather about this and
that. He'd never talk about it when he came to and I knew
better than to ask. Saw some sights during the war, did John.
He was Navy. Didn't like to talk about it, so nobody asked,
and then when he did feel like talking about it no bugger
was interested any more.

He was talking about Cordelia, as it goes. He was always
making his little digs, though there were no meanness in it.
He liked Cordelia plenty, though I did have to put myself
between his eyes and her backside a few times during the first
few years we were pals. Not that I blamed him. Always a one
to catch the eye, is Cordelia. Even now there's something
about her that makes people's gaze linger. I'm just the batty
old woman in the wheelchair beside her, though that's been
the way of it for fifty-five years. She's got the razzle-dazzle,
or whatever you young ones might call it. I'm just a mam
from Brampton.

Anyways, there he was, making fun. I'll do my best to get
his voice right, if it helps, but don't go laughing if I sound
like I've gone soft in the head, OK? Cordelia's told me that
she wants this all done properly so I'll tell you what was said

and what I remember and where I can't be sure I'll do my best. So like I said, he's off work. Bored. Getting a bit niggly. He's not earning, which puts him in a grump, and I've had to go back to doing some cleaning jobs here and there to bring in a bit of cash while he's getting better. Worked his whole life, our John. Worked up at the rocket place, though you'll know that if you've done your homework. RAF Spadeadam. They tested rockets there in the sixties and seventies. You probably won't even know that we were in the space race. Most people don't. Massive great place it was and it brought no end of money into the area. Gilsland did bloody well out of it all and our John worked on the base. It was a good job for a plumber, getting a job with Rolls-Royce. They used liquid oxygen so it was all a bit dangerous and it was a bit of a pat on the head for our John to be able to say he was part of it all. Got the push when they sold it on to the military, of course. Worked here and there but not long enough to get much in the way of holiday pay so when his kidneys packed up it was proper tightening of the purse strings for the pair of us.

'She is, you know. I swear it. Jane Bone, that's what they'll call her. Moneypenny, if not.'

I'll have been enjoying it. He always had it in his head that Cordelia did something in the security services though I swear to you I didn't know the truth of it at the time. She said she worked for the United Nations – some boring office job reading reports and whatnot. It meant she was away a lot but that made plenty sense to me. You can't unite nations if you're going to stay home, can you? And she and Cranham – that's her late husband, you don't need to check your notes – well, they'd been living apart as long as I'd known her, but he wasn't ever stingy with his money and he made sure that the twins were well looked after when she went away. Nannies and what-do-you-call-thems? Au pairs. Boarding school, once they were old enough, though that broke my heart a bit. I'm Tamara's godmother, do you know that? She's a film director in America now. Always struck me as funny that Cordelia picked me to be godparent to one of the twins and Cranham picked that snooty chap he was at university with. He ended up Foreign Secretary or Chancellor or one of those jobs that doesn't seem

to mean anything. And Louis does joke that he'd swap with
his sister in a flash.

'That'll be Gwen,' he said, and I looked at him in the
reflection like he'd gone daft. My ears were getting bad and
I could tell he'd already said something a couple of times
and was getting annoyed with me. He was nodding at the wall
like Muffin the mule. I heard it soon enough. Gwenny, God
rest her, was our neighbour the best part of forty years. Lovely
woman, though she was a martyr to her bowel. She had a son
in the Army who'd just been dodging bullets in that silly war
Thatcher got herself all excited about, but him being away
meant Gwenny was always a bag of nerves and had this great
fear of seeing a postman coming up the drive with a letter
telling her he's been hurt. So she had a phone put in – that's
what I'm getting at. We didn't get a phone for another three
or four years after but as John said, we didn't need one. We
knew where everybody was, near enough, and the last thing
he wanted was to come home from work to listen to me having
half a conversation. But we gave out Gwenny's number to use
in emergencies. My eldest was living in Carlisle with his
wife and their own little lad and whenever I got a knock on
the wall from Gwenny I expected the worst about one of them.
He was a sickly lad, our Peter, though he's doing all right for
himself now. London, like you. Shoreditch, is that right? What
an ugly word. The youngest, he'd already passed away by '77.
Never was quite right for the world, God rest him. I don't
know what comes after but I hope he's found peace wherever
he is. I know I haven't been proper whole since he left us,
but, well, let's steer off all that sadness, it's not why you're
here.

Anyway, look, I know that while I was washing the dishes
and listening to the wireless and thinking all my little
thoughts, stuff was happening in other places that was all
going to impact on my life. I know that now, yes? But I
didn't know it then. I don't think I'd have answered if I did.

'I'll go, if you like,' said John, making no effort to move.

I gave him that smile of mine, telling him not to worry
himself on my account. Dried my hands, no doubt. I'd have
had my pinny on, I shouldn't wonder. Then out the back door

and the passage past the woodshed and the coal store and the wash house. Out the back door and up the path. Cold and dark, I can tell you that much, though if you're wanting more colourful descriptions than that you might have to give me a while. There'll have been coal fires burning, and I've no doubt the family three doors down will have had their Christmas decorations up already, so there might have been a couple of lights down the way past the sheds and the rhubarb patch.

She was standing at the back door with the phone wedged up against her ear – the cable pulled so tight it looked like it could cut your head off if you ran at it too fast. The way she was talking, with her accent all proper, I knew it was Cordelia she must have been talking to. It was always a source of amusement for the ladies at our WI – me and my London pal; her married to a minister; her who turned up for my birthday with a fruit basket the size of a rowing boat and who took me out to Crosby Lodge in a chauffeur-driven bloody Rolls-Royce. And Gwenny was all but bloody curt-seying as she stood there, wrapped up in her housecoat, four foot eight in her slippers and with her curlers half in, half out of her hair.

I pushed Gwenny back down the passageway, eager to be out of the cold and worried the phone cord was about to ping out of the back of the phone. She said her goodbyes like she was talking to the Queen Mother, half curtseying as she handed me the phone and scuttled off back towards the parlour. I followed after, winding up the phone cord and didn't say hello to Cordelia until we were in the warm and Gwenny was able to start fussing with the kettle and cups and shovelling a scuttle of coals onto the fire of the big old Rayburn in the corner.

'I've told you before, it's not fair to be using Gwenny's phone and expecting her to be my secretary . . .'

She laughed at that, genuinely laughing out loud at the very suggestion of me with a secretary. 'You sound breathless, Flick. Did you run?'

I preen a bit whenever she uses my nickname, even now. I like being a Flick. I'd been Felicity Eagles, then Felicity Goose, and the closest I got to an affectionate little name was when

John called me Phyllis for a fortnight, but Cordelia had called me Flick from day one and it made me feel like I was somebody other than I was. When you're a man and a wife and you clean schools and other people's houses, there's something nice about the idea that you might just be pretending.

'How's John? Is the scar as bad as you thought it was going to be? I did plan to send him some of those cowboy books he likes but I forgot the name of his favourite writer and then I couldn't be sure which ones he's already got, so I suppose I've ended up doing nothing, but do tell him I've been thinking about him.'

I could tell from the way she was talking that something wasn't quite right. We've always been able to spot those little things about one another that speak volumes if you really listen. Her accent wasn't there at all – she was doing the whole BBC newsreader thing, thought it wasn't easy to make out what she was saying, what with my bad ear and that persistent crackle on the line.

'He's being a nuisance, that's what he is. Barely touched his tea tonight. Mally Foster brought us a lovely bit of rainbow trout and I had some potatoes left over but he just pushed it around his plate. Didn't hang about with the pudding though. It's not easy, seeing your husband sat there in front of you eating a bowlful of blackcurrant jelly and three scoops of raspberry ripple. Not when he's left his teeth by the bed, any road . . .'

She cut me off before I could start a proper chinwag. Asked me straight out if I could do her a favour. She knew it was a real pain for me and it was no doubt going to ruin my plans but she was absolutely desperate and wouldn't ask unless it was an emergency. I didn't even think before I told her that whatever it was, I'd be only too happy to help. I meant it too. Cordelia doesn't ask many favours and God only knows how many times she's done little things and bloody big things for me and mine, and as it turned out, it wasn't even that much of a thing she wanted me to do.

'Will he be able to drive you, do you think?' she asks, sounding jittery. 'Oh Flick, I wish you'd just get over this silly fear and get yourself some driving lessons. It's so silly that you're reliant on your husband if you want to go anywhere. So silly . . .'

'That's three sillies,' I warned her. 'And you're asking me for a favour.'

'The house,' she went on, as if I hadn't spoken. 'My house, I mean. Cranham's house. There are people going to be staying there for a little while. Friends of friends, I suppose you'd call them, and, well, I haven't so much as asked anybody to run a duster over the place since the last time I was up home and I've got papers and books and, well . . . personal things, and I can't get there for at least a couple of days, and . . .'

I made some clucking sounds, telling her it would be my pleasure, which was a bit of an exaggeration but not much of a one. I still felt like she had made some terrible mistake when she first became my friend. She was cleverer and prettier and more worldly than me but she seemed to think there was something in me worth being around and after fifteen years of being bosom pals I still got a bit of a kick from being her confidante.

'Flick, you're probably going to do your nut but can you go tonight? It's just, well . . . Flick, there are things there that people shouldn't see. Least of all these people, if you catch my meaning. And, look, don't say any more, OK? And if you could get in and away before they arrive, well, that wouldn't be the worst thing. It's all a bit hectic this end. A work thing. But, look, I know there might be some bad memories for you, but you're over all that fretting stuff now, aren't you? If you see anybody up there, well, don't even bother, just head on back, but if you could get Stefan's blanket and some pictures and maybe those papers in the bottom drawer. Honestly, Flick, you're really saving my life here . . .'

I hung up not long after. The clicking and buzzing on the line was making my head hurt and it made me sad to think upon her Stefan or the way her eyes went whenever she talked about him. We'd have to get a shift on if we were going to beat the rain and get there before her mysterious guests. John would grumble but his heart wouldn't be in it. He hadn't been out in the car for weeks and it might do him some good to get out of the house. He'd do anything for Cordelia, within reason. Life wasn't offering us much excitement at that point and a chance to drive out to Gilsland in the dark and let ourselves in to Cordelia's big spooky house was actually quite an offer. I told her we'd be on our way in no time and that I'd be quiet as the grave.

Looking back, it was probably a poor choice of words.

CORDELIA

I made the call to Flick from a phone box just off Tottenham Court Road. I can still see it if I close one eye. There were little business cards and postcards showing off women in red suspenders and big hair, offering their services to anybody looking for a good time. It stunk of ammonia and petrol and somebody had pushed half a Scotch egg into the little slot where the coins were supposed to be returned if nobody answered the call. I remember looking into the brown eyes of an exotic beauty in some kind of mesh leotard and pink eyeshadow. She was bending down and looking back at the viewer from between her legs; red-nailed fingers splayed around her flexed calves. She was willing, according to the card, to be pissed on for an extra five pounds per hour. Good on you, I thought, bitterly, as I pushed open the door and stepped into the cold, blue-black air of London. At least one of us was making a living out of being treated like a pub urinal.

The traffic was all hisses and groans behind me and I barely heard the ringing from the neighbouring phone box. I pulled open the door and cursed the rain, worming my head into my collar and nipping past the puddles to the next big red box. London was reflecting back from the dirty water – fragments of neon and shimmering silhouettes; the images disrupted by footfall and bicycle tyres, pecking pigeons and little waves of water splashing over from the road. I was out of breath by the time I was inside, sucking in a lungful of the same pissy air I'd just left.

'He said no,' pronounced Walt, that little laugh in his voice that suggested that everything I was about to tell him was already old news. 'Suggested that the best thing you could do was clip-clop away in your kitten heels and leave it to the grown-ups, yes?'

I'd met with Talbot at two thirty p.m. The thinking was that after lunch he might be more amenable, or at least less likely to turn purple and tear his hair out over what I had to tell him. It had cost me a couple of hard-won favours to get myself a slot in his diary. His secretary was one of those particularly outdoorsy women who look as though they spend their spare time drowning puppies in sacks and putting arthritic Fell ponies out of their discomfort by hitting them with a spade. She wore these god-awful ruffle-fronted blouses with tweed jackets. Big messy pile of dyed brown curls and hairpins. Always a cigarette between paper-cut lips. If you were drawing a caricature you'd start with a bullock and work out from there. But she'd fitted me in, if only for the pleasure of seeing me beg.

Edric Talbot was my section chief, head of the division that most of us referred to as the bran tub. It was a mixed bag of different specialisms: covert surveillance, information analysts, intelligence assessors and archivists. Talbot wasn't quite top-table but he was well on the way. He'd been Royal Navy before he drifted across to intelligence work, reaching us by way of Special Branch and GCHQ. He hadn't had a great deal to do with me, but that didn't mean he didn't know every last indiscretion in my file. He was very much an arm's length kind of a boss but he was an absolute stickler for chain of command and if I wanted what Walt had shown to me to be of any use at all, Talbot would have to give the nod.

I'd arrived in good time for the meeting but the harridan kept me waiting just long enough for me to be ushered in five minutes late. Talbot was sitting in a captain's chair, low-backed and leather-studded and mounted on casters. He'd pushed himself away from the desk and was sitting in the centre of the high-ceilinged office; a row of books and files along one wall and three large filing cabinets against the other. There was a small window across which he had installed some dark blinds and the walls were painted in an unpleasant shade of green. It didn't have much personality, but then, neither did its occupant. He was stick thin, and his thinness was further emphasized by the penchant for pinstripe suits and the curious sucked-in nature of his gaunt, angular features. He had a sort of jaundiced look about him – a yellowness to his skin and a darkness beneath the eyes. He always seemed to have unnaturally wet lips; two slivers of fresh liver twisted into a scowl upon the taught parchment of his skin. He was wreathed in cigarette smoke, one hand warming a brandy, the other holding a sheaf of shiny, crinkled paper, his eyes moving over line after line of something marked 'Top Secret'. He gave an audible tut as I entered. Motioned towards the desk with a slight inclining of his head. The light reflected off his scalp, winking through from behind prison bars of dyed black, swept-back hair. I followed his gaze to the brandy bottle and the glass beside it. Politeness dictated I join him in an afternoon livener so I poured myself a humble measure. I turned to find that he had extricated himself from the chair and was standing uncomfortably close – several inches taller than me and his eyes still lingering on where my backside had been a moment before. He showed no signs of embarrassment. He had no reputation as a ladies man but I do seem to remember some unpleasantness with an Embassy secretary that proved expensive. He wasn't the worst of them, not by any means, but there was still an unspoken feeling among most of the men at HQ that the women were there to be looked at, pawed at and competed over.

'You've been playing away,' he said, adopting a headmasterly tone and wagging his finger at me. 'I'm sure you've got it all prepared in your mind, my dear, but we can save ourselves a lot of time if you accept that "no" is the best response you're going to get here today.'

He glanced down at the document in his hand. It had been marked for his eyes only and contained the merest details of what Walt had told me in the crypt the night before. The way he held the paper suggested that he didn't even like to be touching it.

'Guatemala,' he said, tasting each syllable and pulling a face. 'Not your remit. Not your area. Not mine. Not, may I add, very much of your business, my dear.'

I'd been in the Service for fifteen years. I'd proven my mettle, my quickness and my gift for tradecraft. But I still hadn't learned much in the way of diplomacy. I hadn't ever really learned to play the game. I still had that naïve belief that those who didn't agree with me simply hadn't understood what I was trying to tell them. So I tried explaining myself again, my manner becoming more animated, my tone more earnest – completely failing to notice the change in the colour of his cheeks or the vein in his temple that began to twitch the longer I spoke.

'There's no room for doubt, sir. These incidents are happening almost daily. The Americans are not just turning a blind eye to genocide, they're actively funding it, enabling it and demanding our complicity. If the minister were made aware, then at the very least there would have to be questions asked. We are being asked to look the other way while a silent genocide is carried out on the doorstep of a colony we have given our word to protect . . .'

He laughed at me. A proper bark: one harsh syllable flecked with tobacco and spit. His features split into something that wasn't just contempt but open disgust. He seemed as though he was trying not to throw something delicate at a wall.

'If the minister knew?' he asked, dripping scorn. 'Good God my girl, do you think he isn't aware? Do you not think the prime minister is painfully clued-in on the reality of the situation? Do you think that this is the first we are hearing of these unfortunate allegations?'

'Unfortunate?' I asked, unable to help myself. 'The Kaibiles are wiping out whole villages. Thousands of people . . . entire communities . . .'

'Your idea of community and mine are clearly not in alignment,' he scoffed, turning away and returning to his chair. He had a strange way of walking, stiff-backed and his legs barely bending. It was like watching a mannequin on invisible strings. He folded himself back into his chair, licking his wet lips and muttering to himself. He fiddled in his pocket and produced another cigarette. Lit it from the stump of his last one. I took a deep swallow of the brandy. It burned. Cheap stuff in a crystal decanter, just like the rest of us.

'Community,' he said again, testing the edges of the word and still finding it ludicrous. 'They are Mayans, I believe, yes? Not much more than cavepeople. Blow darts and tree frogs and ritual dances to the tree gods, that sort of thing? The last departmental memorandum warned that we cannot use certain words any more but if the price of freedom is the death of a handful of . . . let's be frank here, savages . . . then I will not fall to pieces. Look at the Falklands, girl. Look what we have to do to stand against our common enemy. The Americans are our allies and they would not thank you, or me, or even our sainted prime minister, for putting down on paper that which we would all rather not know.'

I finished the brandy. Looked through him. 'I have a source,' I said, quietly. 'A genuine source. Willing to tell us what they saw. I have the promise of footage, sir. The frame I attached to the briefing document . . .'

He reached into a pocket and pulled out a strip of film. Four negatives in a row. Walt had given it to me as a gesture of faith. He knew that the Service would need proof that what he was selling was worth the purchase, even if only to burn the thing before it caused any trouble. 'Too dark to make anything out,' said Talbot, shrugging. 'I've had it to my eye and it could just as well be one of Attenborough's blasted nature programmes as a clip of a massacre. It's jungle and darkness and a couple of shanty huts. Really, Hemlock, I had thought of you as a realist. A pragmatist, even. God knows, your arrangement with your husband suggests that you know the value of a don't-ask-don't-tell approach to matters of discretion.'

I couldn't reply. My throat felt dry and there was a tingling in my skin. My husband had been moved up to the House of Lords eighteen months earlier and he had some vague oversight brief regarding the intelligence services. We weren't yet divorced but we lived separate lives – his permitting him to continue his endless succession of romances with waiters, gym instructors and swarthy young chaps from North Africa. He had the highest possible clearance level and yet I'd never told him I worked for the Service, happy to continue with the lie about the position in the United Nations. There's no doubt that he knew, but he, in turn, had no enthusiasm for altering a status quo that permitted him to move through life as a family man. For it to be thrown in my face during an operational briefing had felt like a punch in the throat.

'All I wanted . . .' I began, my throat hoarse.

'I know what you wanted, girl,' he said, unpleasantly. 'You say it right here, in this bloody silly briefing note. You've asked to requisition the house near the Heath. Three operatives. Full de-brief, finder's fee. You go to the trouble of costing the whole endeavour, all so that we have the honour of telling our friends in Washington that we'd really rather they stopped being so chummy with the good general as his soldiers are being beastly to the Mayans. Good God, I know Walt Renwick was a bit of a father figure to you, but it's like the silly little man never got his marching orders. This has the whiff of him all over it. You shouldn't even have Central American contacts, let alone be fiddling around making operational, nay political, suggestions. I did promise myself I wouldn't read the riot act but you do have one of the most slappable of faces, regardless of how pretty it might be.'

I think it was that last little bit that made up my mind for me. I've been told plenty times in life that there's something objectionable about the way I hold my lip. There's something about me that makes a certain type of man ball his fists. He really did look as though he thought that giving me a crack in the mouth would serve me well, as if I was a hysterical woman in a movie who needed two brisk slaps across the cheeks. I swallowed it all down. Made my decision without even registering that I had moved from one mental position to another. I'd proceed with what I knew to be right, and damn the bloody consequences.

'Chain of command,' laughed Walt, in my ear, over the crunch and sizzle of the traffic. 'If you'd only gone straight to the top . . . I still have some friends, some clout . . .'

I didn't contradict him. If it were true, he wouldn't have come to me. If he had any way of getting in touch with the top table, he wouldn't have needed an ally inside the Service.

'I've taken steps,' I said, quietly. 'I have a place. Your source – they can stay out of the way until I've got my thoughts in order. I know Talbot isn't going to bend but your Joe deserves better than to be sent packing without so much as a handshake or a pocket watch. I have a horrible feeling I've stirred the wasp nest. You'd have been better served if you'd never involved me.'

'The house in the north, I presume,' said Walt, silkily. 'If they do get wind of what you're up to it won't take them more than a couple of metal jumps to work out where you might be hiding.'

'I'm on leave,' I said. 'Talbot thinks I'm still burned out from my last deployment. Told me to get some good air and to stop thinking about things that might cause me to become distressed. I swear, if there ever is a revolution, he'll be the first I put up against the wall.'

'Is it ready?' he asked. 'We can go straight there?'

'I have a friend making preparations. Will you be taking the train or driving? I've booked two sets of tickets in different directions for myself, but the sleeper should get me close enough to drive the last leg. There's just the two of you, yes? I can arrange a vehicle . . .'

'We're already on the motorway,' he said, with a smile in his voice. 'Tell your friend to cater for four, as it happens.'

'Four? Walt, I need you to tell me . . . sorry, you're already on the way? How did you know which way . . .?'

That laugh again, and something affectionate in his tone. 'I can still read you like a pop-up book, Hinny, don't ever forget it.'

I hung up, feeling jittery. Unnerved. I had so much time for the Walt who had first identified me as somebody worth his time, but the old, sickly-looking man who had handed me a strip of film and promised to provide evidence of a massacre was proving harder to trust. I had questions aplenty but I could tell he was only going to answer them when they served whatever purpose he had identified as the real goal.

I stepped back out into the bustle of the city and pulled up my collar against the wind. I was involved in something that felt like it mattered more than anything had in years but I couldn't even work out what I wanted to happen or how the world should reshape itself to my satisfaction. I'd been made aware of something that was irredeemably wrong. I'd been made a witness, by extension, to acts of genuine evil. And to all extents and purposes, if I wasn't to oppose it then I could only be complicit and that was something I couldn't stomach. In a choice between conscience and country, I know what matters more. If you don't, it's not up to me to help you.

I didn't see the sod on the motorcycle. All those training courses, all those lectures in evasion and counter-surveillance and I was too caught up in the moment to even look in the mirror of the black cab as we headed for King's Cross. I'd come to regret that. I'd regret far more, before all was said and done.

FELICITY

Transcript 0020, recorded November 30, 2016

D ark as pitch on the Gilsland road; a few little spits of rain now and again and wind lashing across from every direction. It's a place at the edge of things, is Gilsland. Proper Borderlands. It's not much of a leap to the Scottish border in one direction and then you've got the boundary between Cumbria and Northumberland running right through the middle of the village. As if that weren't enough there's the scraps of Roman Wall cutting through people's back gardens and farms. It's a big old cobweb of ley lines and most of the history is written in blood and dirt and cow muck. Stick your shovel in the ground and you'll pull up bones or sword hilts or musket balls. Pretty to look at, though; just miles and miles of wild nothingness, all these bare fields and little dark pockets of wood. There's a ruggedness to it: a toughness. Always makes me think of some old warrior with stitch marks and scars all over his skin. John says I talk daft when I'm trying to be poetic, which is rich, given that he once spent three hours trying to find a rhyme for 'seagull'. Fairly near to wetting ourselves when he finally finished the ditty and he'd plumped for 'giggle' but in a funny voice. Were a good afternoon, that.

The Zealand place, as we still called it, was at the top of a slope about half a mile from the village itself. Three storeys, lots of chimneys, big rectangular grounds but it looked about as inviting as a crocodile's mouth. Never had known much joy, that house. The little square windows were eyes that had looked down on a lot of sorrows. I always felt as though the tears Cordelia shed after her boy was taken had somehow bled into the walls. I got a shiver when I stepped inside.

'You all right?' asked John, as the car slipped and slithered over the muddy track to the back entrance of the house. We never felt right going to the big front door. It was the kind of door a butler should open. We went in by the old farm track, a narrow little curve of rock and mud that you could only find through a gap in the neighbouring field. It was screened from the road by a line of trees, but I still felt like we were burglars as John nosed the car down the lane and we crunched into the back courtyard where the kitchen staff would once have greeted butchers and bakers and their ilk. John had to ask me his question another three times before it registered.

'All right?' I asked.

'You get jittery when it comes to this place. Your nerves. You fret.' He shrugged, not uncaring but just not having the right words.

'I'm fine. Are you hurting?'

He shrugged again – a different shrug this time. It meant that he was hurting, but wasn't going to moan. He still had his pyjama trousers on but he'd changed out of his slippers and into his gardening boots. He had a donkey jacket on over the cardigan and a nice blue flat cap on his head. With his cigarette hanging from his lower lip and his eyes looking a bit misty from the painkillers, he did look a handsome chap. I had to tell him to stop whittering on or I might have gone and embarrassed myself by saying something nice.

'Let's mek it quick, eh?' he grumbled, as he pushed open the driver's door. 'Grab what you need and we'll be away.'

I stepped out of the car – my foot going right in a mucky black puddle. It went over the top of my shoe and soaked my sock before I could jerk back. I said a bad word and looked across the bonnet of the car to see John laughing at me, shaking his head in that way husbands do when they're asking themselves just what they've gone and married.

I limped towards the back door, soaking wet and cross with myself, trying to pull my anorak around my middle. I had my vest tucked in my knickers so I know Mam would have been proud, but it was always that little bit colder up on that hill than anywhere else and I was shivering as I nipped up the steps, my hands in my coat pocket rummaging for the key.

'Nip of fox in the air,' said John, jerking his head in the

direction of nothing in particular. 'You smell it? Meat and vinegar smell – you never forget it.'

I made a show of sucking in a gulp of air through my nostrils. It serves to humour a partner, doesn't it? I was more interested in finding the right key than I was in him and his silly outdoorsy nonsense. He'd be pointing out trees and birds and telling me the names of different farms if I let him ramble. So it was a shock to actually get a whiff of it. To get that little trace of something that didn't seem right.

'Fox?' I asked, my hand on the iron doorknob, the key in the lock. 'It's earthier than that. It's like chicken gone bad. Do you think somebody's left her a gamebird and the maggots have . . .'

It seems a silly thing to say, looking back. Seems a silly picture to hold in my memory. But I'm there, on the back step of the big old house on the outskirts of Gilsland, one hand on the door, one foot soaking wet: a bag over one arm and my hair tied up in a scarf. John behind me in his pyjama trousers, trying not to show that he's suffering; making sure I know that this is a pain for him, but he's got no bloody choice because that's what husbands do.

I suppose I remember the door bursting open but I can't picture it properly. There was just a sudden rush of movement and a sensation that the darkness had changed shape and then the door was smacking into my face like a fist and I was pinwheeling back down the stairs and my head was smacking into John's teeth and then we were both on our arses and seeing stars and staring up at the star-speckled blackness, fighting for breath, fear gripping every bloody bit of me.

And then there was somebody above me, a boot either side of my head. I think I noticed dark eyes. Maybe there was a whiff of some nasty-smelling cigar; perhaps the gleam of a funny green wristwatch.

But all I truly saw was the glint of the shovel, its blade angled downwards, pointing at my throat like I was glaring up at the guillotine.

CORDELIA

I t was one of the old trains. It had been tarted up around the edges and given a lick of paint but it still sounded as though it was in pain and the windows were either locked open or welded shut. The fabric on the seats was a horrible mixture of rough fabric and old imitation leather and the chap who clipped my ticket had the look of somebody who'd been sentenced to do the job as a punishment for some hideous crime. There had been half a dozen other people in my compartment when we hissed and shuffled out of London in the rain-stippled darkness but by Peterborough I was alone.

It was pushing ten p.m. before I did more than glance up from the big sheaf of papers on the plastic-topped table. I'll admit to feeling halfway between a maverick and a bloody fool as I sat there. I didn't know whether I'd got into something important or irrelevant so it was hard to know whether I was engaged in an important operation or on my way to humour somebody I'd once been fond of. I'd got soaked on the mad dash across London – doubling back on myself and twice changing clothes in pub toilets before slipping onto the train at Waterloo: an artsy-looking woman in her late twenties – short ruffled red-brown hair, plum-coloured raincoat and a flowery skirt stopping an inch or two above the knee. I'd added a nose stud and some big bangles and was carrying a thick carpet bag. I looked like somebody heading home from the city to see aged, parochial parents. Nobody tried to talk to me. It would have been clear at a glance that I was absolutely transfixed on the reading material on the table.

Now, listen to me for a moment, will you? Listen properly. You probably think that the intelligence services are properly named. You might have a presumption that MI5 and 6 and Special Branch and GCHQ and all of our opposite numbers all over the world are absolutely clued up as to what is secretly going on behind the scenes. You might think that there's a big pot of highly trained men and women with white-hot intelligence and charm manipulating world events and forever staying one step ahead of the various agents of chaos trying to harm our way of life. I envy you that. When you've been in the Service, when you've been near the top, you don't get to have that reassuring thought any more. You know that half the time we don't know any more than any bugger else. There are half decent regional newspaper journalists with more of an idea of what's actually happening in the world than the top tier of our sainted spymasters. We know bits, of course, and we're very good at probing for weaknesses and gaps in the intelligence capabilities of the other countries involved in the game, but the majority of the Service is staffed with people with old-fashioned surnames who weren't clever enough to make it as a stockbroker and not dishonest enough to become a politician. What I'm trying to say is that if you think I knew any more about Guatemala or Belize or very much more about Central America than the average bugger in the street, you'd be wrong. And I hated not knowing this. Hated it then, hate it now. So I was damn well going to use my time on the train to change that. The document in the beige folder was property of the fourth-floor archive Century House. I'd checked it out on my way out of the building, tucking it into my coat on the off-chance that I didn't look too obvious if today had been selected for one of the random internal security spot checks. I could probably have talked my way out of it if called upon, but as it happened I left the building without so much as a wave from the door staff. The report had been compiled from different clippings, research papers and a handful of recent university essays and did a serviceable job of breaking down the political situation in Guatemala into something more easily digestible. I was thoroughly immersed in it, fingers in my ears, occasionally closing my eyes to allow the most important bits to really take. People have told me that when I read it looks like I'm chewing and swallowing, chewing and swallowing. I know that what I was reading was starting to make me feel sick. Although the report was littered with the words 'allegedly' and 'unsubstantiated', it was clear that what had been happening in Guatemala these past years amounted to little less than genocide. Successive governments had pulverized the indigenous Mayan population. For twenty years the country was immersed in a bloody civil war, pitting the army against Left-leaning guerrilla groups. The native Mayan population was deemed by the government to be harbouring these 'terrorists' and operation after operation had been mounted to terrorize them into giving them up. Reading between the lines it was clear to see that the fight was ludicrously unbalanced. The 'guerillas' were poorly equipped and few in number, while the Guatemalan forces were backed, trained and equipped by overseas allies who were willing to turn a blind eye to their extreme tactics in exchange for not letting these potential Communists get a toehold in the region. Things had escalated the year before when the military seized power and placed General José Efraín Rios Montt in the presidential hot seat. And Rios Montt, it was clear, was a madman.

The train juddered as I read. Jolted forward. There was a squeal and screech and then we were rolling again. I looked up from the page, a pressure headache pressing into my temples like knuckles. I screwed up my eyes, feeling bone-tired suddenly. The adrenaline had worn off. Much as I tried to fight the feeling, I was growing increasingly irritated. Walt had brought my attention to something that I was happier not knowing. Does that sound dreadful? I suppose it does, especially when you know what you do about me and what I later became. I've never been sure which of my critics to believe, you see. Am I really too fond of myself by half? Arrogant, all-knowing; a sense that if I don't save the world then nobody else will? Or am I the quite-clever girl from Newcastle who grafted her way into a posh university, seduced her professor, got knocked up and lucked her way into a sham marriage and a comfortable life? I'll be honest with you, I've never been sure. But neither of those personalities were particularly feeling benevolent towards Walt as the train rattled its way towards Sheffield and the rain began to hit my reflection with the sound of hoofbeats on tin.

I was so caught up in feeling sorry for myself that it took longer than it should for me to notice the newcomer in the carriage. He was sitting three rows back from me, facing the same way. The windows all served as mirrors and from where he was he could see me a damn sight better than I could see him. Not that he was looking, of course. He was sitting there with his eyes closed, arms folded, head lolling back to his right. I got into character – the ditsy, creative type, forever forgetting things and spilling her tea. I made a show of reaching over for my bag, rummaging through the contents and changing my angle so I could look at him properly without him registering my eyeline. It sounds paranoid, I know, but I've no problem with that. Paranoia has saved my life less often than it's made me look over-cautious, but I'd rather look daft than dead.

He was a bulky specimen – one of those men who looks fat until you give them a punch on the arm and realize that everything under their coat is as firm as a roll of carpet. He had a round head, broken nose and a moustache split by an old scar. He was wearing jeans and a bomber jacket; a little sliver of gold at his broad neck where a pendant on a chain disappeared into his collar. It was his boots that concerned me. The boots and the lack of rain on his clothes. The boots gleamed. The laces were triple knotted and there were little rough patches on the toes, but they had been polished with a precision and devotion that reeked of military training.

I sat back in my seat. You wouldn't have known I was worried to look at me, but there was a definite jitteriness taking hold, settling on me like seed pods and dandelion seeds on a hot day – little irritants that wouldn't let me settle. I tried to read the document again but I couldn't focus and I became increasingly aware that if my new companion was here for me, the report was a big red flag. I put my papers away as quietly as I could, slipping the folder back into the bag and making a show of settling myself, hands folded in my lap, closing my eyes as if preparing for a little nap ahead of the next leg of the journey.

I found myself cursing Walt afresh. What did he actually expect me to do? What did he have for me? I tried to get my thoughts in order; tried to work out my own reasoning and motivation. It sounds daft but sometimes we get caught up in momentum, don't we? We do something because it's more interesting, more entertaining, than not doing it. I met up with Walt because I was feeling lost and he was a figure from the past who gave me a fleeting sense of stability. I agreed to help him out because I felt a bit sorry for him and because I was bored. When he gave me the little he was willing to share, I saw an opportunity to impress my increasingly distant bosses and perhaps be permitted to investigate further, curtailing my work with the Greenham Common protesters and permitting me to stop feeling like a cad whenever I had to look at myself in the mirror.

And now? Why had I given Walt permission to use the old house, far to the north; to hunker down with whoever the hell it was he was so desperate for me to see? Why had I dispatched my only friend to make sure it was up to his standards and to hide away those few precious trinkets from another time, another life? It was because it was exciting. It was because Talbot had been rude to me and I wanted to stick my thumbs in his eyes in some way or another. Why was I heading north to join Walt? It was to get away from London – to return to a place where I had once been a different person entirely and where somebody I loved was going to help me make sense of myself again. That was it, I realized. Everything else was just some elaborate construct that permitted me to go home and see Felicity. I didn't like who I'd become. I knew that life didn't provide absolutes and that few fights come down to good against bad, but I was spending too much time in a murky shadow-world where pragmatism and compromise were seen as justification for looking away while terrible things went unpunished and unremarked. I was supposed to be a cog in a machine, part of an unwieldy but effective apparatus that kept people safe and stopped the Cold War from freezing too many people to death. But politically, philosophically, morally, I'd never been any more in favour of Capitalism than Communism and if I hadn't been sent to the Peace Protests as a spy I'd have been there as a civilian. I was sick of spying on good people. I was sick of putting the needs of the state above the needs of its people. And Walt knew it. That's why he picked me. I was the new recruit who didn't think it would be a good idea to hide their love of George Orwell or stand when the national anthem played. I was the outsider – the northern lass with the trace of a Geordie accent; the politician's wife who would sooner go to a Led Zeppelin concert than take tea with the queen. I was wrong for the intelligence service, but also exactly what it needed. I started shaking my head at myself, giving little tuts of annoyance, working myself out, picking myself apart. What the hell was I meant to do about acts of evil happening thousands of miles away? Britain had just won a war, for God's sake. Maggie's popularity was at an all-time high. Huge swathes of the public had got into the old Blitz spirit and celebrated every dead Argentinian as we trundled our way through the Falklands conflict and reclaimed a few square miles of inhospitable rock. What were we going to do? Invade Guatemala and tell the president to stop being beastly? It was a bloody joke.

I thought of Felicity and felt a real swell of regret. What was I thinking? Supposing she started giving the house a proper going over, cleaning up, polishing, making it lovely as a nice surprise for my guests. God, she could still be there when Walt turned up with his source. She was a panicker. She'd say the wrong thing, or the right thing, but she'd get herself in a tizz. And John. Poor sod not long out of his hospital bed. I needed to be there. Needed to get hold of things. Take charge.

I didn't hear him move. I didn't register anything at all until he plonked himself down in the seat opposite – the bulk of him somehow making my own seat bounce. I jerked my head up. He gave me a smile. The place where his lip had been stitched looked more painful close to but there was a certain rough-hewn handsomeness about him. He looked as though somebody had started sculpting a really handsome man but stopped before doing the fine detail. Although he had a round face his features seemed blocky. I thought of footballs: a sphere made of up of stitched hexagons.

I reminded myself I was an arty young woman on her way

home. I was pretty. I was alone. He might just be trying his luck. He leaned forward, enfolding one big pink fist with the opposite palm. There were patches of glistening pinkness on the knuckles: grafted skin. A wedding ring glinted on the wrong finger of the wrong hand.

When he spoke, it was with a thick Glaswegian accent.

'You looked lonely, love. And I know I was. I've half a bottle of Whyte and Mackay if you're thirsty. A listening ear, too.'

He was friendly in his manner. If it was a come-on, it wasn't the creepiest I'd endured.

'I was dropping off, as it happens,' I said, mirroring his manner. 'Two glasses of wine at a leaving do. I feel blotto as it is.'

'Somebody picking you up, are they? We can split a taxi if we're heading to the same place. You carrying on through to Edinburgh?'

I gave him a querying look. Picked at my nails, distractedly, glancing at my reflection again to see if I was looking as unnerved as I was starting to feel. 'Why Edinburgh? Why not Glasgow?'

'You look Edinburgh,' he said, shrugging his big beefy shoulders. 'Poet, or something. An artist.'

'And you look Glasgow,' I said, waving a hand at his general air.

'What does "Glasgow" look like?' he asked, and he seemed to be chewing on something with his back teeth; the hinge of his jaw pulsing in his cheek. 'Knackered? Old? Gone to seed?'

'Formidable,' I said, picking a word that covered a multitude of sins and seemed the sort of thing this lady would say. 'I went once. Such character.'

'Character,' he said, shaking his head. 'That's what the English always say to describe a shite-hole. Pardon the French, and all that shite.'

I didn't reply. I figured that an awkward smile would probably do the job. He'd embarrassed me. Sworn when he shouldn't have. I was a nice middle-class lady who didn't have much experience of his coarse, Caledonian ways.

'You never answered,' he said, his eyes on mine. 'Shall we split a cab to wherever you're going?'

I was getting cross. He was hitting on me and he was doing it in a way that would have scared this poor woman half to death if she'd been real. I wanted rid of him.

'No,' I said, more firmly. 'I'm off at the next stop, thanks all the same . . .'

He closed his eyes. Looked for a moment as if he were counting. Opened them again and his pupils were huge: black tadpoles devouring the lenses of his eyes.

'You're not,' he said, giving a little shake of his head. 'You've got a ticket to Carlisle. Then you're heading to Gilsland.'

I didn't let the fear show. Forced myself not to react at all. Didn't glance around to see if there was anybody nearby who might be keeping a watchful eye on proceedings. I told myself, again, that he might just be a bloke – no more of a risk than the thousands of macho men who thought that it was their right and responsibility to bang as many women as they could before the grave. But I wasn't fooling anybody. He knew who I was. Knew what I was, too. There was a twinkle in his brown eyes; a glint of something that said he had only been playing along.

'I'm engaged,' I said, trying to sound apologetic and jolly English about the whole thing. 'Fiancé is picking me up at the station. I don't think I know Carlisle. Sorry if you've got me confused with somebody else. Actually, look at the state of me. My eyes look like a tramp's. I'm going to go and put on my war paint, if you'll excuse me . . . bit of lipstick, take the tiredness out of my eyes . . .'

He shook his head. Looked momentarily disappointed in me, as if I were acting in a way that was somehow beneath me. Then he sat back in his seat and reached inside his jacket. He pulled out a packet of cigarettes in a battered yellow packet. Flicked the case with his index finger and deftly removed the unfiltered cigarette that shot out of the top of the packet. He offered it to me and I shook my head. That look again, dissatisfied with me, perhaps momentarily unsure of himself. He seemed to come to a decision. Reached into the packet and pulled out a strip of negatives. He put it on the table in front of me. I glanced down. Fire and forest and pale, dead skin.

He proffered the cigarettes again.

'You should try them,' he said, lighting his own with a gold lighter. He gave a little smile; a gold tooth lustrous in his upper row. 'They're Guatemalan.'

FELICITY

Transcript 0021, recorded December 1, 2016

I could hear John somewhere nearby, swearing like he worked on the dust cart. I was flat on my back, shivering like a damp dog; no breath in my body and a strange drunken feeling, like I'd had a Bucks Fizz too many at Christmas. I think I'd smacked my head on the ground when I clattered down the stairs. I know my teeth had knocked together at the back. They'd slid right off the gum and there was a nasty chemical taste at the back of my throat.

'I'll break your fucking bones . . . you touch her, you touch me . . . I'll bite your eyes out of your head, you dirty fucking . . .'

Honestly, I felt like apologizing for him, I really did. But the shovel blade was only inches from my face and I didn't know what the hell had just happened or who had barged into me. I squirmed around, feeling the wet soak up through my overcoat. The blade retreated an inch. I shot a glance upwards into the dark, but I couldn't make out more than the shape of him. And it was a *him*, right enough. Big and sort of sporty-looking, with that wide-legged stance that all the confident people have.

'Don't you touch her . . . don't you . . . *bastard*!'

I heard him make the sound that he gives out when something's proper hurt him. I didn't give a damn about the spade, I wriggled onto my side and looked around desperately, trying to find my voice, to offer some kind of apology, some explanation, some plea.

He was on his knees. Two big lads were holding him. They were both dressed in the same dark colours as the big man standing over me. One had John's hand up his back, pushing his head forward. The other stood beside him. He had John's coat in his hands and was going through the pockets.

'You leave him alone,' I shouted, though there were more tremble than rage in my voice. 'This is my friend's house. I don't know what you want but she'll have your guts for garters if you hurt my John. He's just out of hospital. You should be ashamed.'

Then there were hands on me. Before I could get another word out he'd rubbed his hands right down my sides and inside the coat, down both sides of my legs and even over my backside. I was too shocked to say a word, just froze up like I was a nipper and Dad would smack my legs for being cheeky. I just went small and scared and then I was being hauled up from the ground. My head was proper spinning and I had this horrible feeling I was going to wet myself and then he had my arm up my back just like the other bugger had done to John. There was a shove in my back and I heard the sound of John growling and his feet scraping over the gravel as he was dragged up and hauled after me.

'Say something then,' I whispered, teeth chattering, as I tottered forward. 'If you're burglars there's nowt worth having, I swear. She's got a fancy place in London, her husband's a politician and he's rich as they come, but this place is bust books and some old furniture and a few keepsakes. It's half falling down, you've just made a mistake, just go . . . I swear. I'm only here to clean . . .'

He yanked at my arms. Hauled me backwards and spun me to face him. That was the first time I got a proper look at him. He was well over six feet tall. You could tell he was tanned, even in the dark. Brown eyes, big unlined forehead with a neat side-parting in his black hair. He had one of those Roman noses: a big shark's fin in the centre of his face, but he was handsome, sure enough. A film star look about him when he smiled, showing off such perfect white teeth that it seemed like the moon had come out from behind a cloud. It made it all the way to his eyes, too – a proper smile, not a nasty one, not a false little grin the way you'd think a snake might as it tightened around something fluffy. No, he was smiling at me like he found something really funny.

'You're the cleaner?' he asked, and he narrowed one eye

and scrunched up his cheek as he said it. 'Mary and Joseph, you had me worried.'

He let go of me at once and I felt those same hands that had patted me down give me a gentle squeeze on the forearm and hip. He suddenly looked as if he couldn't do enough for me and the transformation was so complete that I couldn't think of a damn thing to say. I looked past him to John. The other two men still had him, his arms behind his back. There was mud on his trousers. A big pee stain too, the poor sod. He was looking down at the floor, his features all grey and saggy.

'Let him be,' said the man who'd been holding me. I darted past him and grabbed for John as his legs buckled and he folded in on himself towards the floor.

'John . . . John, I'm here, is it your stitches, have they hurt you . . .'

I wasn't making sense, I know that. I just wanted him to be OK, to not be hurt, to not be embarrassed or feel like he'd done anything that he needed to be ashamed of. I tried to get his arm around my shoulder but I couldn't get him up and even if I did, where was I going to take him? I couldn't drive.

'Call an ambulance,' I said, and when it didn't come out loud enough I said it again, letting my anger out, shouting and bawling until the nearest bloke lost his patience and told me to shut my mouth.

I didn't even try to make sense of what was happening. There were bad men at Cordelia's house. Cordy had asked me to come and grab a few personal items before her visitors turned up. Were these men who she was expecting? Were they early? Could they really be the sort of people Cordy would invite to stay in her little bolthole? And why had they suddenly let go of me? I needed to know what was going on but I couldn't do a ruddy thing until I'd checked John over. I looked back to the one who'd been kinder to me. He was standing where I'd left him, leaning with both hands on the handle of the shovel. He looked like a golfer watching somebody else take their shot. He smiled that weird little smile again and then shot a glance to his companions.

'I think this gentleman needs some assistance,' he said,

and this time there was no mistaking the accent. It was subtle, but there was a distinct American lilt there, the way British actors get in interviews when they've been too long in Hollywood. He turned his head to me. 'You said he'd been in hospital?'

'Kidney removal,' I said, from under John's armpit. 'He's still healing. Only drove me up here because I couldn't get a bus at this time of night . . .'

The men nearby shook their heads, growling at one another, as if something had gone properly wrong. They shot hard glances at the other man and he gave them a shrug that said there wasn't much that could be done about it now.

'You mentioned Cordelia,' said the tall man, looking at me. 'She's the owner? Her husband's a politician, you say?'

'Cranham,' I gasped. 'He's something important but I don't know what. I've only met him a couple of times. Cordy's my friend. She said to come and get the place ready . . .'

'To clean,' he said again, emphasizing the word as if it's significant. He shrugged again. Pursed his lips and blew out a long thin plume of grey air. 'Lordy, this is a pickle.'

'Nothing on him,' said one of the other lads nearby. He sounded British enough. Sounded royally miffed, too. 'No weapons, no paperwork . . .'

'No weapons?' I asked, feeling like I'd been reading a book and turned over three pages at once. 'What are you talking about . . .?'

'Come on then,' said the man I took for the leader. 'Best get in out of the cold, I suppose. We'll get the kettle on. Have a little chat. See if we can't all make friends. Morgan, Bench . . . try and be gentle, yes?'

They did as they were told. Hooked their arms under John's and got him to his feet. Moved us towards the house while I wittered and fretted and tried to dust the muck and the pee off his front. He was sweating. Shivering and sweating and already there was a smell coming off him that said he was running a fever and something inside of him had gone wrong.

The man in front went to the back stairs and opened the big door, pocketing the key that I'd left hanging in the lock as I clattered backwards down the steps. He held it open for me and I ducked under his arm, turning to see the two men manoeuvring John through the doorway. There was the sound of a match striking against a rough surface and then a soft light was filling the old parlour. The man in charge was holding a big fat church candle near to his face and it made everything look all eerie and off balance. I didn't know why he didn't just flick the light on. I was pretty sure the system must still work because Cordy had been there herself not more than a few months before and never said they were having difficulties. Then the other two were pulling out little torches from zip-up pockets. There were circles of yellow light spinning and flashing on the flagstone floor and up over the beams in the ceiling. It was like being in an air raid. I was trying to get my bearings, stumbling over to where the kitchen table should be, reaching out for a chair for John, wondering if the phone would still work, whether these people were going to help me or make things worse.

I half squealed when I saw the others. A man and a woman, arms around one another, thick black hair and eyes white as winter moonlight. Beside them sat a small, thin-limbed little man, thick glasses and a goatee beard. His face was like a caricature: like somebody had doodled some vague features on a scrap of paper. He gave me a look that was almost apologetic, flashing something between a grimace and a smile. His teeth were the sort you'd see in a dug-up skull – three or four missing at the front and the others all crooked, as if they were trying to plug the gaps. He was wearing a thick sheepskin coat and a silly hat with ear-flaps. It took a moment before he glanced down at what he was holding in his hand and then back up to me.

I didn't say a word. Just stared at the little black gun in his hand.

'The cleaner, apparently,' said the man in charge. 'And I presume this is her husband. If poor timing were an Olympic sport they'd be medal contenders. He's sprung a leak. Not long out of hospital. I'm going to mentally file this under "unforeseen circumstances".'

He said something in a language I didn't understand. Directed it to the two who were sitting next to him. The woman raised her head. Gave me something that might have been a smile.

I looked back to John. The other two had plonked him on a kitchen chair. They were lounging against the big enamel sink, stretching out their necks, checking their watches with a weird kind of symmetry of movement, torches in their mouths.

'Please,' I said, to nobody in particular. 'I don't know what's happening. Just take what you want and go. Cordelia will be here soon . . .'

The little gnome gave a real grin at that. Smacked his lips together as if savouring something delicious. Glanced past me to the door that led through to the main body of the house. I followed his gaze. There was another fellow in the doorway. He was perfectly still: just an outline, shoulders almost touching the frame. A perfect red circle glowed for a moment and then a drift of grey wafted across the kitchen like a cloud. I smelled cigar smoke. Smelled sweat and oil.

'Please, I just need to call an ambulance . . . I'm only here to . . .'

'To clean, yes,' said the man who'd led us in. He shook his head. 'Jeez, you do repeat yourself.' He looked to the small man. Looked to the two dark-haired strangers, huddled up against each other as if sheltering in a doorway on a bitter night. He gave a shrug. Looked to John and then to me and then back to the little man. 'It might be quickest . . .'

And right then, right in that moment, like a train pulling into a station, realization finally hissed and clanked into my head.

We were going to be dead before the dawn.

CORDELIA

I smoked his cigarette right down to the filter before I spoke again. We were a couple of chess masters playing out the moves in our heads before daring to put a finger and thumb on a pawn. Or maybe we were a couple of alley cats staring at one another and hoping that something or nothing would happen before either of us had to make a decision. He didn't revel in the moment. Just smoked his own cigarette and stared through the smoke and watched me as I stared through my own face into the darkness outside and tried to work out whether I was in danger. I wished I had a cover story to rehearse. Wished that Walt and I had come up with a legend for me in case anybody enquired about my business. I should have a name and a backstory, not just a costume and a wishy-washy idea about going home for the weekend. I tried to keep hold of myself. Had I done anything wrong? I'd been contacted by an ex-agent, been given a lead on some good intelligence and I'd reported it to my superior through the proper channels. I'd kept Walt's name out of it because he'd suggested I not blot my copybook by mentioning where the information came from. And Talbot had laughed me out of the building. He'd wanted no part of it. And now I was heading home; heading back to where the Service had first snapped me up. Fine, I'd told Walt he could use the place, but whoever he was bringing with him, my only goal was to find out whether they had any information that could service national security. And that was the job they paid me for, wasn't it?

'You ready?' asked my new friend, at last. He had a little smile peeking out from the corner of his moustache. Something about my body language must have betrayed the fact that I'd reached the end of my train of thought. 'Worked it all out, have you?'

I matched his smile. 'SAS,' I said, giving a little nod at his scarred hands. 'You've got the look of it about you. Got the build too. And the eyes.'

He nodded. 'Aye, I won't contradict you. Was a while ago now though. Different life.'

'Different time?' I asked, finishing the cliché.

He shook his head. 'Nah. World was the same then as now. People hurting one another for a bigger share of shite. I can't see it changing in my lifetime. Not in the bairn's, neither.'

'You have children?' I asked, keeping it light.

'A wee daughter,' he said, and the smile was genuine. 'A boy too but I don't see him. I wasn't good to his mother. He's every right to think the way he does. But I'm getting it right this time.'

I reached out and took another cigarette from the packet. I didn't put it to my lips. Just played with it, keeping my movements and tone as light as falling leaves. 'You're here for me,' I said, closing one eye as if thinking through all the permeations. 'We're not just having a lovely time.'

He shook his head. 'I'd have let you sit staring into space for another three stops if it was up to me. Would let you get where you're going. But that's not going to happen. They've worked it out. If you get off at the next stop there's a direct train back to London ten minutes later. They want you to be on it. Then you can go straight home, have a little lie down and we can debrief properly when you've had your porridge and fresh orange juice.'

I didn't show any emotion. Just stared at him, mulling it over. 'You're with us?'

'Who's the "us"?' he asked, snatching up his cigarettes and pulling a fresh one from the packet. He lit it in a temper, the lights in his eyes growing brighter as he sucked smoke into his lungs. 'Who are you, that's the question. Then maybe I'll get to the who I am.'

'You've already told me about your daughter,' I said.

He shook his head at that. Spread his hands. 'I haven't got a fucking daughter.'

We let it hang there for a while; the absurdity of it all; the great tangled mesh of lies and half lies and truths unspoken between us. We could talk for an age and still never know which one of us was telling the truth or for what purpose.

'I'm Cordelia Hemlock,' I said, letting my vowels lengthen and some serious middle-class pretension bleed into my accent. 'My husband is Cranham Hemlock. You might have heard of him. Department for Foreign Affairs and Commonwealth. I'm an economist with the European Commission. I'm heading to our country house to finalize some repairs before we put it on the market. My children are at school. I'm hoping that if this is all some dreadful pick-up attempt, you're not going to be upset at the inevitable rejection. And if you're a journalist looking for a scoop, I can assure you, nobody is interested in me. I'm a private person and my husband works very hard to keep it that way. So, fascinating as all of this has been, I must ask you to move to a different seat or I'll have no choice but to call for the guard.'

He enjoyed it, I could tell. He started smiling as I found my stride and was outright beaming by the time I reached the end. Only when I started to stand did he look anything other than gleeful. He waved me back into my seat. Patted at the air with his hand. 'Wait,' he grumbled. 'Hang fire.'

He rummaged around inside his coat. I got a whiff of him. He had the smell of petrol about him. Petrol and sweat and cigarettes smoked while wearing damp clothes. Eventually he found what he was looking for. From an inside pocket he withdrew a silver cassette player. Five buttons on the side, a slide for the volume and a fragile looking rectangle of plastic and tape within. We'd been using them as recording devices for the best part of a decade but now they were available to buy on the open market. A wire dribbled out of the back, ending in a plastic halo bookended with two small, orange circles.

'Have a listen,' he said, sliding it across the table. 'It's important.'

I couldn't see the point in objecting to the instruction. I was only just starting to feel afraid and I had the confidence of somebody who's seen a few dangers and come out the other side. Whoever he was he was intent on making me do what he instructed and it was better to play along than to see what he would resort to if I were to object. I picked up the tape recorder and slipped the headphones on. Pressed play.

There was a crackle at first: static, like sausages burning in a pan. Then there was a burst of some unintelligible language; unintelligible words broken up by hard consonants. Finally the line cleared. I heard a familiar voice.

'. . . my goodness, how on earth did you get me here? No, no, that can't just be dumb luck. This is the Pandora line. I'm not even here, it's just I'm the only one who got off my backside. Can I call you back? Is there a number? No, you're still a bit, well they'd call it persona non grata on the top floor but down here we'd just say that you're not exactly Mr Popular. Yes, I'd love to hear all about it. We never even got our farewell drink, did we? Shall we have a catch-up? I'll do the accent for you if you promise not to make fun. OK, sure, I've got it, I'll call you back . . .'

I stopped the recording. Didn't let my features betray me. Of course our department was bugged. The line might not have been tapped but that didn't mean there wasn't a listening device under every second desk and bookshelf.

'So you're a Club,' I said, quietly, making sense.

He nodded, recognizing the description. There were five divisions within MI6 at that time, each with a departmental head. Diamonds, Hearts, Spades, Clubs and Jokers. The Clubs were overseen by a broad-backed, mastiff-jawed monster of a man. Quarrie Cochran-Nab. Scottish, but public school beat the accent and the trade unionism out of him. Distinguished himself with some quietly efficient successes in Poznan, Krakow and Sofia before being called home to take charge of the areas that his opposite numbers found too beastly for their taste. He'd done it well. He'd twice been in the running to take the hot seat: to answer to the name of 'C' and sign his paperwork in green ink. Twice, regrettably, he'd been deemed to be too blunt an object for the role. So he lingered on as an increasingly irascible Ace of Clubs while younger, more diplomatic career politicians joined him at the top table then departed for the House of Commons, the diplomatic corps or private sector consultancy positions. He was feared and adored in equal measure by the rest of the Clubs. His division did the counter-intelligence work; the rooting out of bad apples within our own barrel. When somebody was in trouble, it was the Clubs who did the deep-dive intelligence work and trawled through every last scrap of their life looking for evidence of traitorous leanings. They did the surveillance, the black-bag jobs; snatching up suspected traitors from the streets and seeing what it would take to buy them or break them. They were hard men. Hard women. Ex-soldiers, mostly. They'd been the unit that gave Walt a proper going-over in those unpleasant weeks and months when he was suspected of collaboration.

'Play the next bit,' said my companion.

I did as instructed. After a couple of seconds of silence the recording crackled back into life. I heard myself again. Walt was too far away to be picked up on the recording but I knew at once that it had been made while I stood and shivered in the crypt.

'. . . that's where we are now. I don't even know which side I'm on any more. I swear, if we'd had to insist that every family throw their first-born child in the Thames in order for the Americans to stay on our side, they'd nod it through the House without a second thought. We've lost sight of what we're fighting for. These things . . . these atrocities – you think they're isolated incidents? This is the world we've made. We're lapdogs. We don't know our place in the world so we chum up with a bully so the other tough bugger doesn't shove us around. It's not about ideologies any more. We've picked a side so we have to do whatever is asked of us, even if it's something that makes us sick. We're the sort who'd rather blow up the moon than let the Russians get there first. You think they don't know in Washington what their allies are up to in Guatemala? They showed them how to do it! Every bit of counter-insurgency in their arsenal is either American-made or American-trained and we just look the other way because we need them to be on our side. I can't stand it. Of course I'll do something. I'll have to go through the official channels and you and I both know it will come to nothing but there are some things more important than queen and country – you were the one who taught me that . . .'

The recording stopped. I was left listening to dead air.

'You were talking to Walter Renwick,' said the man, matter-of-factly. 'Our sainted former Ace of Hearts. Quite the legend and still the charmer, it seems. He's been under observation since he arrived back in the country. We knew he had somebody inside the Service but it was a surprise when the recording arrived. Old Poofter Cranham's trouble-and-strife, eh? Who'd have thought. You certainly weren't on anybody's list of likely suspects, though that's what friends in high places will do for you. They'll no doubt make this go away too. Perhaps you've been under pressure. Excess of emotions, that kind of thing. A silly mistake by somebody trying a little too hard. It happens. I've seen it and worse besides.'

I took one of the cigarettes from the packet. It took a monumental effort not to let my hand shake.

'What is it you think I've done?' I asked, and he leant over to light my cigarette with a gentleness that didn't sit with his big hands and scarred features. He didn't reply so I ploughed on with the performance, looking vexed, making big gestures, trying to seem frightfully befuddled by it all. 'Is that meant to be me? And you mentioned Mr Renwick? I think I know the name but, well, he's not the kind of friend you keep if you're after advancement . . .'

He ignored me. He had a look that said he'd heard every kind of excuse, plea and mitigation known to man. He looked dog-tired, suddenly. Looked as if he'd really had enough.

'Where's he got them?' he asked, quietly. 'What is it he even wants?'

'Where's he got who?' I asked, genuine in my confusion. 'I'm just going north for a few days . . .'

I stopped. Thought of Felicity. Thought of the way Walt had sounded so damn sure of himself. He'd already been on his way to Gilsland. He had somebody with him that he wanted me to meet. I experienced a sudden surge of fear. Could I have sent her into danger? Could I have got my friend embroiled in something that I had no way of getting either of us out of?

Damn you, Walt, I thought, grinding my teeth. What have you dragged me into?

'Suspects,' I said, repeating his word. 'What am I suspected of?'

'Of involvement with a known Communist sympathizer,' he said, with a note of apology. 'A politician's wife. Minister for Foreign Affairs at that. Walt must have thought he'd stolen the crown jewels when he brought you into it.'

My patience snapped. 'Into what? Sure, I answered a call and it turned out to be an old friend and I called back to arrange a drink and a chinwag. As for anything else, I've done nothing improper. Ask Mr Talbot – I was in his office today, alerting him to some useful intelligence that I felt it was our duty to follow up. Really, I don't know what you think is happening but I'm completely in the dark.'

The intercom suddenly flared into life above us – the train manager alerting the handful of passengers that we would shortly be arriving in Doncaster. He turned around at the sudden blast of noise from the speaker behind him. As he moved I slipped the recording device into my lap. He span back to me just as I leapt from my seat and lunged for the taut emergency cord that dangled above our seat. He grabbed for my wrist but I managed to wriggle out of his grasp and squirm out of the seat before he could tug me back. I heard him growl my name and then there was a screech and hissing and blaring of metal upon metal as the train screamed to a juddering halt. Suitcases clattered down from overhead and I glanced back to see my pursuer falling over a loose plastic case as I ran for the dividing door, shooting a look back to see him reaching into his inside pocket.

A flash of blue in front of me. The train guard, red-faced, pushing through the dividing door, demanding to know who had pulled the cord, if I was hurt, what was happening . . .

I pushed past him, grabbing his keys from the chain at his waist, unclipping them and slipping them into my pocket along with the tape recorder. I slid the door shut behind me, fumbling with the keys, listening as my pursuer shouted a volley of Glaswegian venom in the face of the guard who was blocking his way. I felt the key turn in the lock. Heard a ferocious hammering on the glass behind me.

The train was completely static. I was standing in the harsh yellow light of the dividing area between the two carriages. The window had been slid open on the exterior door and the darkness beyond looked cold and empty.

I didn't even stop to think. I leaned through the window and opened the train door from the outside. I tottered there for a moment, looking down at the gleaming metal tracks, the damp stones, and then on, to the empty fields and the rain-speckled darkness beyond. I looked back. Heard a crash as my pursuer put his elbow through the toughened glass.

I looked down. It was six or seven feet to the ground. I had the wrong shoes on and I was miles from anything that felt safe.

Felicity, I thought. It was just one word, but it flooded me with panic and energy. I'd sent her to the same place I'd sent Walt. And Walt was clearly a very wanted man.

I jumped.

Landed hard. Rolled right.

Heard the hiss and the roar and saw the terrible white light.

Looked up into the face of an onrushing train.

FELICITY

Transcript 0022, recorded December 1, 2016

'No,' said the little man. 'No, not unless we have to.' I found myself shivering as I asked it; the cold in that dark little kitchen suddenly seeping into my bones. The shock of it all was starting to take effect. I couldn't seem to stop my teeth from chattering and I had an awful feeling that I was going to embarrass myself and lose control of my bladder or bowel right there in front of all those hard-eyed strangers.

'Have to what?' I asked, and it sounded so pathetic that I actually made myself cross. Tears started down my cheeks. 'This isn't right. We haven't done anything wrong. There's a policeman comes past here sometimes, just to check on things. And the next farm over belongs to a young lad who wouldn't back down from a scrap. Please tell me what's happening, look at my husband, he's not well, he's not . . .'

'Give over,' came a familiar voice, weak and gravelly but unmistakably John. 'I'm all right. Just winded. Cup of tea and I'll be back on my feet.'

The two men who'd hurt him turned to look at me. I was half dizzy from the spinning torchlight and the candle flame and they'd taken care not to let their faces be seen, but for a moment I got a better look at the nearest one; the moonlight just managing to throw a little illumination on his features. He was an ugly bugger. Big slab of a face and pockmarks all the way up one cheek. He was all scowl and nasty little piggy eyes.

'Here,' he said, when he saw me looking. 'Read him a lullaby.'

He threw something down onto the floor between us. I picked it up. It was a little leather-bound notebook: a strap of cord wrapped around its front and the letters J.J.H. embossed on the front. It looked expensive. Looked quality. Didn't look like something that would belong to John or me.

'Leave it,' said John again, and reached out a hand. I handed him the book automatically, not sure what I'd picked up. John grabbed it as if it were the Bible.

'John,' I said, kneeling at his side. 'Where does it hurt? Can you breathe? What did they do?'

He screwed up his features. Twenty-odd years together had taught me that whenever he said nothing it was because he really didn't have anything to say. He looked sick. Scared, even. It's a horrible thing, seeing your man scared. I wanted to put my hand on his face but everybody was looking at us and I felt such a silly fool that I just kind of stayed there, half squatting, chattering away about this and that and nothing and asking where it hurt.

I looked up at the sound of the little man shuffling about on the bench. He looked as though something was paining him.

'Suffering?' asked the tall man.

'Only when I breathe,' he replied, with a voice that betrayed real pain. He looked at John and me, giving a little shake of his head. 'This was the only course of action, was it, Pelletier? Couldn't you have just thrown them in an outbuilding or something?'

'Say the word,' shrugged the one called Pelletier. 'I thought you'd want to see if they were familiar faces.'

He leaned forward, angling the candle towards us. His gaze lingered on my face longer than John's. I saw something flash in his eyes, some semblance of familiarity, of recognition. And then he was shaking his head.

'Civilians. Wrong place, wrong time. Inconvenient, but largely irrelevant.'

'My husband's hurting,' I said and I tasted salt as the tears and snot dribbled into my mouth. 'Just let me call an ambulance, please. I don't know what you're doing. I don't care either. I can keep a secret, just ask Cordelia. We did something together, years ago, and I've never said a blasted word – not even to John . . .'

The little man stood up. He wasn't much more than five

foot tall but he had a confidence about him, as if his smallness was just an act and that if he stopped concentrating he would be six foot three and built like an outside lavatory. He slipped the gun into the pocket of his coat. Spoke again to the couple beside him. It was a strange language, like something off one of those documentaries the BBC make about far-flung places. The woman nodded at whatever it was he said. Gave the man beside her a squeeze and stood herself up. She was a tiny thing. Her clothes were far too big for her and there was a nasty lump above her eye. It was hard to tell in the light but her skin had that lovely conker colour to it: a glow like good wood that's been varnished.

'Sera here will help you,' said the little man, and it sounded odd to hear pure BBC vowels coming out of a mouth so mangled. He spoke like an officer, a proper Rupert. It was the kind of voice suited to horseback and cucumber sandwiches and games of croquet on lawns mowed by folk like John and me. 'She has some medical knowledge and a far more kindly bedside manner than any of the rest of our company. Pelletier, tell your two bookends to help the gentleman into the little room back down the corridor there.'

'You heard him,' Pelletier said with a smile to the two men nearby.

Hard hands pushed me to the side and John was hauled upright and dragged across the flags towards the door.

'Do be gentle,' said Pelletier, wincing. 'A little compassion wouldn't do either of you any harm.'

They both shot angry eyes in the direction of the little man. He gave them both a nod, approving the command. I glanced to my left, looking for the figure who had stood in the doorway but whoever had been there a few moments before had made themselves scarce.

'Please, follow me.'

The young woman put her hand out. I reached out without a second thought and she closed her fingers and thumb around my palms as if I were a child that needed help crossing a road. She had hard skin. Callouses on her palm and real coarse whorls on her fingertips. They were working hands, rough as freshly cut timber.

I followed without another word, head down, the fight briefly gone out of me. The foreign-looking man at the table didn't look up as we passed him. The one I was thinking of as 'Rupert' gave a dismissive little smile, then turned away the moment we had passed him. I sensed that we were already forgotten.

'Get off me . . . get off me . . .!'

I hurried down the darkened corridor, my feet slipping on the greasy tiled floor. There was barely any light but the little that flickered out from the torches wielded by the big lads emitted just enough for me to get my bearings. We were heading towards the back stairs, making for the servants' quarters adjacent to what Cordelia always called the 'drawing room'. John was already inside and from the sound of things, he'd recovered his fight.

'Please, gentlemen,' said Sera, that same thick accent echoing off the walls. '*Por favor*, there is no need for violence.' She was trying to get past the man who was standing still in the doorway, pushing at the bulk of his back. 'Please, he is hurt, let me tend him – where can he go, *señor*, please, a little mercy . . . in the name of Our Holy Mother, he does not need to be harmed!'

She managed to wriggle past him and she dragged me after her. John was up against the far wall, holding his side, bleeding from the mouth. The one with the piggy eyes had given him a thump. Temper flashed in me, quick as a flash. I raised my head and glared at him. 'Makes you a tough man, does it? Hitting a man fresh out of hospital when he can't defend himself? I swear, Pike will break your jaw for this.'

He grinned at that, showing teeth stained by strong tobacco. 'Pike? He the local hard case, is he?'

I didn't answer. Just darted to John's side. My heart was thumping and it was all I could do to stop myself from puddling in on myself and giving in to the dead faint that seemed to be nudging at the edges of my vision. Pike? What the hell had I mentioned him for? Pike was a name from the past – a poacher turned gamekeeper who had done his damnedest to keep our lad on the straight and narrow and who had moved away from the area when he realized just how badly he'd failed. I still saw him as a white knight on the hillside, ready to rush in and stop whatever badness was being stirred up in my life. I realized even as I was saying it that Pike wouldn't be coming to our aid. The only person who knew we were here was Cordelia and there was no way she would have sent us here if she'd thought there was a risk to us. So whatever we had stumbled into could very well mean trouble for Cordelia as well. She might be on her way into something very dangerous. These were bad men, I was sure of it. Men with guns and that cocksure bloody arrogance that says they know they'll get away with it even before they pull the trigger.

The two men moved soundlessly out of the room and I heard the door closing and a key turning in the lock. Instinctively I reached up for the cord to switch on the light but nothing happened when I yanked it down. Sera didn't seem to need the light. I watched, mesmerized, as she manoeuvred John into a sitting position, his back straight against the smooth, cold wall. I'd never been in this room before. It was empty save for a medicine cabinet above a little sink. There were no windows. There was a hole in the roof: chunks of plaster and exposed timbers. The wallpaper was peeling and I could smell damp. I could smell John, too: the sickness, the shame.

'Are you a nurse?' I asked Sera, when I could get my tongue working. 'Is he all right? Can you stop him hurting?'

Sera's hands moved deftly over the yellow-stained bandages. She touched the adhesive strips and her rough fingertips probed the edges of the surgical scar. I got a whiff of something bad.

'The stitches have torn,' she said, apologetically, and crossed herself, lips moving in a prayer I couldn't hear. 'Only three or four sutures gone and the bleeding is not so terrible, but he is at risk of infection. He will need antibiotics. For now all I can do is bandage him up again and provide fluids. He will need a doctor. The sooner the better.'

I heard myself giving little ragged breaths, all scared and pathetic. 'Will you tell your friends that?' I asked, looking at John. His head was lolling a bit, eyes all glassy. 'Will you make them understand we're not a bother. We're not a problem.'

'My friends?' she asked, looking back at me.

'The other people? Pelletier, was that his name? The little

goblin man as well. The other fellow – is he your husband? I don't understand.'

She readjusted her position, squatting between John and me and taking one of my hands and one of John's, making us into a silly little trio of paper dolls. I didn't know how to react. I've known people nigh-on half a century who wouldn't take my hand without permission and here was this dark-eyed stranger with the foreign accent clutching at my fist like we were sisters.

'They aren't my friends,' she said, gravely, her eyes wide as teacups and looking right into mine. 'This is a . . . how do you say it – a marriage of convenience, *si*? Is that the expression?'

'Not in Brampton,' I said, not having a clue what she was talking about. I threw my hands in the air, fear giving in to frustration. 'Look, do they think we're somebody else? They don't think I'm Cordelia, do they? Do they think that I'm having everybody on? Look, I'm not anybody really. I only live a few miles away. I used to live near here . . . the village by the old church. It's all farms and fields and Roman wall and I know Cordelia well enough to promise that if they just go away now, there'll be no bother. Even if you're burglars, she'll say nowt. She only keeps the house on out of sentimentality. Her boy died here, you see. Little Stefan. Happy bouncing little lad he was. Must be fifteen years since he passed on, but she can't stand to let this place go and her Cranham, he's got money to burn so doesn't make a fuss. So whatever's been done, it can be undone, that's what I'm saying . . .'

I saw her lip tremble. Her eyes filled for a moment with tears, like rose petals in the rain, but she managed to get herself together before she fell to weeping.

'The less I tell you, the safer you will be,' she said, and there was a tremble in her voice. 'Please, let us tend to his injuries. I have only basic training – field dressings, tourniquets, checking for concussions, stemming bleeding. I can stitch, but I would need a cleaner place than this if I were to not do more harm than good.' She let go of John's hand and unfastened her coat to access the inside pocket. She was plumper than I expected her to be, her frame all curves and softness. She wore a stained shirt beneath the jacket and I could make out three or four different beaded necklaces dangling at her neck. From inside her jacket she retrieved a little purse, its front decorated with beads. She crossed herself and retrieved a rosary from inside the purse, crossing herself again and slipping it over her neck. I didn't know what to do or say so I just sat there until my legs got sore and I had to pull myself up or fall down.

'Water. Iodine. Bandages and clips.' Sera didn't raise her voice very much but whoever was listening beyond the door had clearly heard as a moment later we made out the thud of footsteps moving away.

I leaned back against the wall. I didn't know how to stop shivering. I was wet through and could feel the chill all the way to the meat inside my bones. I put my hands in my pockets just to keep them warm.

I watched as Sera lowered John down to the floor. Saw her put her hand on his brow and whisper something in a foreign language followed by a soft 'Amen'.

I hadn't said a word to God since he'd taken our James. But suddenly it felt as if there was something in that room that might look softly upon me if I could swallow my pride and ask for help.

I didn't have the tongue for prayer. Not properly. Couldn't remember psalms or sermons. But if God was anywhere, it seemed he was in that strange young woman with the soft eyes and rough hands. So I directed my prayers to her.

'Please,' I whispered. 'He's good, I swear. He's a good man. He doesn't deserve this; he's never hurt anyone.'

By the morning, he would have made a liar of me.

CORDELIA

For a moment there was just the thunder of locomotion: the dreadful otherworldly screech of metal on metal and the rumble of the shaking earth. There was the harsh yellow light and the massive solidity of the train filling my entire world. I was on my knees, a sharp pain jabbing at my ankle, one hand up to shield my face, already seeing myself smeared into mush and meat upon the gleaming tracks. And then I was throwing myself bodily to my left, rolling over sharp stones and discarded sleepers; the noise of the train shaking my senses with such fury that for a moment it seemed as if the whole world was tearing itself into strips.

Then I was tumbling down a little slope, all mud and grimy water, spilled oil and mounded-up rubbish. Dizzy, my world spinning, both hands pressed to my temples, I lay there for a couple of precious seconds, my chest heaving, tucking myself down into the darkness at the edge of the railway track. The train that had almost ploughed through me was still rumbling by so I knew I wasn't yet being pursued. I put my hands down and felt a sharp pain in my palm as a shard of broken glass punctured my skin. Gingerly, moving as if on autopilot, I dragged myself upright and glanced around. To my left a grassy slope led up to the edge of a shabby field. Up ahead, perhaps a mile or so in the distance, the lights of the next town gave off a little haze of gold and yellow illumination, like the last ashes in a dying hearth. I could see the rear of the train rattling and clunking past me and knew that if I didn't move I was going to find myself completely exposed. Ignoring the protests in my ankle, the taste of blood at the back of my mouth, I hauled myself upright and scrambled over the tracks and the piles of rubbish to the little muddy rise, desperately trying to keep my feet as I slithered and crawled my way up and over the slick, sodden grass. I made it to the top of the hill just as the rear car chuntered past, hurling myself over a patchy little line of hedge and sprawling down in the soft wet earth of the field. As the echo of the passing train drifted away into the silence of the night, I made out the sound of raised voices coming from the static train at the far side of the tracks. Every light was on and from where I lay, my head inches above the ground, I could see two train guards having an angry confrontation with half a dozen passengers in the nearest carriage. I scanned the length of the train, looking for my companion. I couldn't see him. Nor could I make out anybody on the track at the bottom of the slope.

I moved away from the edge of the slope and crawled deeper into the darkness of the field. Beneath the top layer of damp earth the soil was hard as iron and my elbows and knees were soon burning with agony as I wriggled further and further away from the tracks. When I was sure that I couldn't be seen over the rise of the hill, I pulled myself up and started to run, my only goal to get far away from the man with the Guatemalan cigarettes.

I cursed myself as I stumbled through the darkness. I wasn't panicking, not yet, but I was scared. There was no doubt that the man from the train had been MI6. He'd known too much to be anything other than a senior figure from the Service. I started trying to make sense of it all as I plunged deeper into the field, senses alert for any sounds of pursuit. Could meeting with Walt really be the kind of infraction that would see me followed, interrogated and hauled back to London? I knew his name was far from popular in the corridors at Whitehall and Millbank, but all that I had done was meet an old colleague. I cursed myself for my own naiveté as I tried to make my mitigation sound less feeble. Was that really all I had done? I'd met him at the crypt. I'd used a covert location for a clandestine meeting with a disgraced former member of the intelligence community. I'd rambled on, unguardedly, about my frustrations with the Service, with the West, with Great Britain's place in the world. My God, I'd made myself sound like somebody on the very cusp of defection. And I'd been recorded saying it. That recording had somehow made its way into the hands of my employers. And then I'd gone to see Talbot, all guns blazing, telling the silly sod some cock-and-bull story about a secret source offering information that flew in the face of current policy. Not content with that, I'd given Walt use of my old country house and set off for the cold and distant north without so much as a cover story in place.

'Felicity,' I muttered, as I ran. 'Flick, please, tell me you're home safe. Tell me you didn't even go to the house. Tell me you're sitting there feeling guilty that the roads were too dark or the rain was too hard and you never made it out to Gilsland.'

I looked up and saw a haze of soft light rising up out of the darkness. I was nearing the brow of a hill and could tell from the intermittent swish of tyres on damp road that I was only a couple of minutes away from the motorway. I slowed my pace, controlling my breathing. I was fit and strong and had always pushed myself to the limit on the training courses and physical fitness sessions that were mandatory for intelligence analysts and field agents alike. I could keep going long past the point when my muscles screamed and my heart felt like it was going to explode inside my chest. But now I needed to conserve some energy and at least take stock of my situation. I stopped just before the brow of the hill, checking myself over for any cuts or fractures that had not yet made themselves known. My hand was bleeding and there was a tender place behind my left ear but it was mostly just grazes and bruises. I was soaked through. My coat was filthy with mud and dirty water. By some miracle the wig was still in place so I snatched it off and tucked it into the sleeve of my coat, unsure whether the man from the train knew me better by one appearance than the other.

I rummaged in my pockets. Felt the lighter, cold in my palm. It had been pure instinct to snatch it up. I'd left my bag on the train but it contained nothing much of any worth. My purse was in my pocket so I knew I had a little cash. I found a couple of boiled sweets in an inside pocket and sucked on the sticky flavour gratefully, making my way towards the lip of the hill. It was a dual carriageway, busy even at this hour. A few hundred yards down the road were the lights of a service station, the forecourt empty and a phone box standing sentry at the side of a brick outbuilding.

I stayed still for a moment, my hand closing on the recording device I had snatched on my retreat from the train. Who had bugged the crypt? And why send it to my employers unless it was part of some unfathomable conspiracy to make the Ace of Clubs and his team start raking through my life. Were they heading to Gilsland even now: a snatch-and-grab team briefed to bundle up old Walt and deal with any other civilians who might happen to get caught up in the crossfire. I felt sick at the thought of it. Flick was capable of so much more than she thought she was but she didn't know much about the world beyond her own little perimeter. She'd witnessed me do unspeakable things but still thought I was a thoroughly good person. She didn't doubt my cover story about working for the United Nations. She didn't question anything. She'd come apart like damp paper if she found herself being interrogated by the Clubs about her involvement in some botched conspiracy.

I slid down the bank, waiting for gaps in the traffic so I could make my way up to the service station without being observed. I caught a glimpse of myself in the darkened glass of the phone box and didn't recognize the gaunt, pale-faced woman with the short hair and sodden clothes who yanked open the door and slipped inside. I got the familiar whiff of it: the cigarettes and ammonia; the petrol and smoke. It was almost comforting.

I fed coins into the payphone, forcing myself to relax. It took a moment to remember the number but I could see it written down on a scrap of paper and could read it from memory as if looking at a photograph. There was no answer at first and then a sleepy, snappy voice answered with a curt 'Hello'.

'Gwen? Hello, I'm so very sorry about the hour but I really need to speak to Felicity if you could stand to give a knock on the wall. It's Mrs Hemlock.'

She took a moment to get herself together. I think I heard her take a sip of water and light a fag. 'She's not back, Mrs Hemlock. She and John went out in the car not long after you called this evening. It was good to see him out and about. I've been keeping an eye out for the car but no sign yet. No doubt there's a tree come down on the road or John's started to feel poorly. I wouldn't worry just yet. Can I take a message?'

I managed to keep the panic out of my voice. Thanked her for her time and hung up. I leaned forward, my head against the telephone. I didn't know what to do. I didn't have a friendly face back at HQ who might be able to tell me something useful without betraying me. I couldn't help but think that the sensible thing to do would be to call Cranham, but my stomach lurched at the very thought of asking my husband for help. Our arrangement just about worked. We'd always been admirably civil to one another and each were more than aware of what we owed the other, but whatever I had tripped into could have consequences for him if I brought it to his door. He wasn't the father of our children but they called him Dad whenever they saw him or spent the occasional night at what we jokingly referred to as the 'family home'. They were at school most of the time. I called most days and we wrote constantly and I did my best to be all I could be, even as I tried to climb the career ladder. Cranham could have made it all much easier for me if I had only asked. He was decent enough and knew me well enough not to proffer advancement without me first asking him for help. If anything, my marriage to one of our most senior civil servants had hampered my ascent. To now come running to him and demand answers over who was chasing me – it felt repugnant.

I stayed where I was for a full minute, just breathing and thinking, listening to the sounds of the cars race by.

With a weary sense of inevitability, I retrieved the recording device from my pocket and held the little earphones up to my throbbing ear. I listened to myself again. Felt nauseous as I heard myself eviscerate the direction of MI6 and our increasingly inhuman, self-serving approach to international affairs. Good God, the recording alone was enough to have me thrown out.

I was about to click off the recording when I realized that the tape was only halfway through. I let it run. Heard the crackle of a wiretap and the distinct ker-klunk of one recording stitched over another.

'. . . can't say I'm surprised. Hero-worshipped him, from the little I know. Always was the bleeding heart. One may as well try and explain the concept of pragmatism to one's horse.

Of course, one can invest one's time and money and one's patience but sometimes the bad blood will overcome the attentions of even the most patient handler. I'd tell you about her father but her mother was too free with her affections to be able to keep the list of possible suspects under the thickness of the telephone book. Good God but she's put me in a dashed awkward situation. I won't go, that's the long and the short of it. They can bark all they want but I need to steer well clear or the minister will have lied to the Commons and we might struggle to survive the fallout. It should never have come to this. Did you see the operational notes from the Greenham Common operation? Good God but she was more protester than a member of the intelligence services. She stuck photographs of our children to the fence. Our actual children! A show of solidarity, part of maintaining her cover – that's how she explained it when her superiors dared to question it. But our actual children? Even poor Stefan, God rest him. And now, this dalliance with that bloody nuisance of a man. I won't be giving him what he wants and damn the consequences, for him, for me and especially for Cordelia. Have I not tried? To suddenly turn her back on queen and country, on her own family – I know that we can make all of this irksome business go away but it's going to have a terrible knock-on effect and the Americans are going to feel dangerously over-exposed. I'll keep trying to get Pelletier on the phone. Really, there's the most frightful flap going on in Washington about all this and it's most embarrassing to have to tell them that it's my own bloody wife who's right at the centre of an international incident. Clean it up, softly-softly if you could. Best if she doesn't ever know I gave the nod, if it can be avoided. Keep things between the gentlemen, as it were . . .'

It was my husband. It was Cranham Hemlock, Assistant Private Secretary to the Foreign and Commonwealth Office and one of the senior civil servants sitting on the Joint Intelligence Committee. He'd been bugged. And he'd given me up without a second thought.

I felt cold. Felt goosebumps rise all over my body. Felt a desperate desire to walk out into traffic and end the screaming in my head.

I thought of Stefan. Thought of Louis and Tamara. Thought of Flick. Looked away from the road, and back towards the light.

In the forecourt of the petrol station, a tall, harried-looking man was filling up a maroon Austin Allegro. I watched as he knocked the drops off the petrol pump. Watched him walk away to make payment. The lights of the car were still on. The keys were in the ignition.

I was across the damp tarmac and into the driving seat without a sound. I didn't drive away fast – just pulled out as gently as you like and didn't hit the accelerator until I was beyond the line of sight of the cashier.

By the time the tall man came outside I was half a mile away, doing seventy miles per hour, heading north as if fleeing a fire.

FELICITY

Transcript 0023, recorded December 1, 2016

The men outside the door did what Sera asked them to do. The door opened and they tossed her a little canvas bag full of medical supplies. The taller of the pair handed Sera a torch, one of those proper lantern types with the handle on top. He didn't say a word but I could tell from the slightly sheepish way he was lowering his eyes and hunching his shoulders that he'd had a telling off. My eldest used to look like that when he'd been caught taking food from the pantry.

I didn't speak until he was gone. I stood up, stretching my back, feeling the beginnings of some nasty bruises all down one side. I stretched as if I'd been picking vegetables, trying to work the knots out of my back. Crossed to the sink and turned the tap on, splashing some water on my dry lips and giving my face a bit of a scrub. The water was icy cold and made me shiver twice as much but it felt good to get the mud off my face. I stood with my back to the sink, the room changing colour as Sera switched on the lamp. She and John were suddenly enveloped in a perfect circle of gaudy yellow light. I had to look away when I saw her unwrapping the bandages. Felt my sickness coming on and had to fight the urge to put my hands over my ears as John made a sad, sore, mewling sound.

'It is OK, hush, be brave, be brave . . .'

There was something of the lullaby about the way she talked. She was so gentle in her manner, so tender in the way she touched him, I swear it made me feel like a right battleaxe of a wife. I'd never spoken to him like that. Never put my palm on his forehead and looked in his eyes and told him that it was all going to be OK. He'd never done it to me either. We'd

have felt too bloody embarrassed. But it came to her easy as
breathing.

'Who are you?' I asked, a little catch in my voice. The
question surprised both of us. I just blurted it out. I don't
like to put myself forward. Don't like to pry. But things were
so far from normal that I thought I might as well just start
being Flick rather than Felicity. And Flick would damn well
ask.

'Sera Avendano,' she said, in the same soft voice. John
hissed as she started sitting him up, gauze and a cotton wool
pad pressed against the open wound. 'My brother is Kaapo.
And you?'

'Felicity Goose,' I said, automatically. 'I was Felicity Eagles
before I was married. This is John.'

'A pleasure to meet you both,' she said, as if we were guests
at a tea party and all on best behaviour. She gave me a warm
smile. Her eyes were really lovely. Skin too. 'This place – we
are in Scotland, *si*?'

I shook my head, concentrating on the question so as not
to be scared by the pain on John's face. 'Scotland's up the
road. We're halfway between Newcastle and Carlisle. It's on
the edge of everywhere. Gilsland.'

'Gilsland?' She tried the word out in her mouth. Said
it again. 'I saw a lot of green. The fields are very bright. It
looked like a tapestry – no, a, quilt, *si* – a patchwork quilt
thrown over a table that is still covered in dirty plates.'

I liked that. Liked the way she spoke. I tried the image out
in my mind and realized that she must have seen it from the
air to think of it in such terms. It all felt too big, suddenly.
I've never flown. Never been anywhere really. The idea that
she'd arrived here by plane and that she was better equipped
to look after my husband than I was made me feel almost
resentful. Here was another bugger better than me. There were
plenty of those already in my life and now we were flying
them in from overseas!

'When did you get here? Where are you from?' I felt a tear
threaten to come down my cheek and my lip gave a real little-
girl wobble. I felt bad at once for thinking such things about
this lovely kind lady. She must feel awful, far from wherever

home was. It all got too much in that second and it came out in a silly little screech of frustration. 'I don't know what's happening,' I said when I was done. Then I whispered it again, feeling like a daft old woman, and it was hard not to just slide down the wall and start wailing.

'I am from Guatemala,' she said, working on John all the while and not showing the slightest reaction to my tantrum. 'La Libertad. El Petén. Perhaps sixty kilometres from San Benito.'

I don't think I made out any of it when she said it the first time. It was good of her to go on repeating it until the words went in. It was double Dutch, and Spanish and sounded like she was playing castanets in her mouth.

'Guatemala,' I said at last, the word unfamiliar in my mouth. 'Is that Spain?'

She gave me a funny little look. 'Central America.'

I pulled a face. I can't read a map and I only know that on a picture of the world, Britain's in the middle. I can't even watch the weather forecast without finding the thin bit of the island and moving halfway across to find out where I live. 'America? I know New York's on one side and Hollywood's on the other,' I said. 'We watched a programme.'

She stopped what she was doing. Looked at me as if I were a little bit soft between the ears. 'Latin America,' she said, and lifted a hand to draw a picture in the air. 'Mexico is here, yes. Beneath America. Then look, here you have Honduras and El Salvador. Belize is up at the top here. And in the middle – Guatemala.'

I said it again, just to show willing, but she'd have had as much luck telling me she lived at the bottom of the sea or on the far side of the moon. I felt a right wally for not knowing where places were, but then, she didn't know she wasn't in Scotland, did she? And hadn't given so much as a flicker of recognition when I'd mentioned Carlisle. We were proper strangers in one another's worlds.

'So what are you doing here then?' I asked, surprising myself by suddenly changing my voice and starting to whisper, as if the answer was probably secret.

She stopped what she was doing again. Shifted position and looked at me for longer than felt comfortable. She looked a bit exasperated, like she didn't even know where to start. 'My country is at war,' she said, at last. 'It has been at war for many years. Perhaps it is a civil war – perhaps it is an uprising. It is several revolutions happening at once. Those who ascend . . . they promise much and deliver nothing more than disappearances and bloodshed. I am . . .' She swirled a hand in the air as if looking for the right selection of words. 'I am trying to make things better, somehow. So too my brother. We have truths to speak that some important people need to hear. There are many lies in my country. I dislike lies. I have had to speak many lies in the name of a greater truth. Now we are come to a place where the lying can stop.'

I must have let my face betray my feelings. 'I'm sorry, I don't really understand any of that. I mean, well . . . look . . . I don't know what I mean, if I'm honest with you, but what has that got to do with Cordelia and why her house and why here and why now? And what did John and me do? What's happening that's so secret it's worth sticking us in here and hurting him and flashing guns? Who brought you here?'

'The man Pelletier,' she said, her tongue flicking over her dry lips as she started re-fastening John's cardigan. She put the back of her hand to his forehead. Held a canteen to his lips and rubbed at his throat with her finger and thumb. He dribbled a bit but she didn't wipe her hand. Just held the canteen and told him he was doing well as he swallowed down a few slurps of water. 'Pelletier has been helping us,' she said, not losing her train of thought. 'Pelletier can be trusted, even if he can only be trusted to continue to act as Pelletier. We came by aeroplane, a cold and noisy journey, bones rattling and bitter . . . squashed up against some wooden crates and almost deafened by the thunder of the engines. Pelletier, you see . . . he has proven himself, in his way. And what choice do we have? He told us that all will be well. That here there are people waiting for us who will help us change the story to the way it should have been told.'

I didn't follow her. Didn't understand. But by then she was more talking to herself than to me.

'I glimpsed the ground beneath us only for a few precious moments – the sun rising like a perfect crimson ball, spilling its light through the little windows. I sat and prayed, held my brother, felt the world right itself as the wheels bounced down on the precious ground. And then Pelletier was shouting at us to follow him and the rear of the plane was slowly opening and there were soldiers waiting for us: men in black, hats down low, as terrifying as those who come in the night to do the slaughter that their leader demands. I feared Pelletier betrayed us – that these men were Kaibiles and we were to be handed over to those who would butcher us for their own amusement. Instead we met the little man you saw. He promised us that we were safe, that we were here for our own protection. I saw only some brick buildings and the morning mist and then we were being hurried in to a building with an oval roof where we were given coffee and bread and permitted to curl up on a low bed with green blankets and I slept. Woke to find myself being photographed. Woke again to hear my brother demanding to see Pelletier, telling them he knew that they had lied. And finally we were hurried to a big black car and told to sit in the back beside the little man who spoke to us in Spanish and in *Q'eqchi'*. I saw little except for these great walls of trees – trees like those from the Christmas cards we used to receive from the father churches in Europe and America – and then we were told to put our heads down. We had not travelled for very long. Nine miles, perhaps less. The house looked like something from a ghost story. Pelletier was waiting here. He and the little man exchanged a few words. They spoke of our "other guests". And then we were brought inside. We drank water. Prayed, my brother and I. Waited to be told who else was lingering in the other rooms; who we were to tell our truths to. We had not been here very long when we saw the car. Your car. The little man was expecting you to be somebody else.'

I realized I'd been holding my arms in tightly at my sides, corsets of skin and bone squeezing me tight. I barely dared breathe in case she stopped talking. I didn't always mind not understanding what was happening but suddenly I wanted to tip her upside down and shake every last scrap of information from her. My mind felt like it was dribbling out my ears. None of it made sense. Why here? Why Cordelia's place? She knew people were coming, that's why she'd asked me and John to come retrieve the things that mattered. But she'd never have sent us into this.

John started coughing. Grimaced and heaved himself into a more comfortable position. As he did so the book he'd taken off me slipped out of his pocket and landed on the floor. John barely glanced down at it. Sera picked it up. Handed it to me. I took it from her. John hadn't wanted me to see it but I needed something to do with my hands, with my eyes, so I started flicking through those lovely creamy pages without even really knowing what I was doing.

It was all in John's handwriting. Blue ink, sloping backwards, hard to read but pretty in its way; the capital letters just little letters done big. It was all laid out neatly. Four lines, then a space, then four lines, and a space, page after page, each with a heading and a date.

It was a poetry book. John had been writing out some poems in his best hand.

When had he been doing that? What for? I peered at a page at random. Saw our James's name. Saw mine, too. Peter's. The name of the church where we'd wed. These weren't somebody else's poems. They were his.

He'd been writing poems. Our John. Proper rhymes. About our lads. His mam. About me. He'd written one to the grandson who he was going to play Cowboys and Indians with some day. He'd written about the white horse out the back field – 'a summer cloud, swift and proud' – and the smell of the sawmill behind our house. He'd written about the kingfisher on the River Irthing and the big purple dragonflies 'darting like spitfires, crumpled tinfoil wings' out at Talkin Tarn. He'd written about me. My eyes. The 'honey and hay and edelweiss' of my hair, which sounded to me like a fancy way of saying that the white was overtaking the mousy brown. The curve of my back just above my bum. I snapped the book shut like I was trying to kill a bee between the pages. It took all my effort not to throw the thing across the room and duck before it exploded. When had he done this? What was I supposed to think?

'He has a little more colour,' said Sera, looking up. 'I know Pelletier and he does not cause suffering or permit it if it can be avoided. He will speak for you. I will speak for you. It would be best if . . .'

I stopped listening then. I'd flicked to the front of the book and read the dedication. It was Cordelia's handwriting, every bit as pretty as she was.

To a true poet. Don't be afraid of asking for what you want. You have a voice that people deserve to hear. I'm glad to know you. Sincerely, CH.

I felt like I'd been kicked in the side of the head. Everything just went dizzy and dark. I think Sera must have seen the change in me because she leapt up quick as a hiccup and grabbed me by the arm, one hand on my cheek, trying to get me to look at her.

The door swung gently open. Pelletier leant against the doorframe, hands in his pockets. He looked relaxed but the open door permitted me to hear the angry voices drifting from down the hall. He looked to John. Gave a little nod, satisfied.

'Sera,' he said. 'Your brother is making too much noise. I've told him there are several ways in which my colleagues will secure his silence. I trust you see the sense in helping him choose the route that does not involve his suffering.'

Sera nodded, her head jerking up and down. She rushed to Pelletier without a backwards glance and ducked under his outstretched arm. Pelletier gave me a rueful look. 'I'm sorry about before. I'm sorry about all of this. I wish it were different. There's much at stake. I can't stomach another noble sacrifice but if it's required in the name of our goal, I will have no hesitation in doing what must be done. Look after your husband. Stay quiet. I will try and make the next few hours no more uncomfortable for you than they must be.'

I didn't get a chance to speak. He closed the door and turned the key.

And then it was just me, and the silent mess of my husband, and his posh little book full of fancy four-line lies.

CORDELIA

The rain started once I got past Leeds. It went from a few little splashes to monsoon season inside a few seconds. It was already black as ink beyond the glass and with the sheets of water cascading down it felt like I was driving through the middle of a broken TV. It was all static and flashing lights, my foot hard to the floor and only glimpsing the rear of the cars in front at the very last moment. I had my window down to relieve some of the steam on the inside of the glass so the car was filled with gusts of cold wind and little flurries of tooth-sharp rain. I kept going. Kept yanking at the wheel and sticking my head out of the side window, wincing into the distance to try and glimpse any obstacle before it was too late to avoid.

I'd picked the right vehicle, that was clear. Nobody was going to go to much trouble to get a maroon-coloured Allegro back so I was unlikely to be seeing any police roadblocks any time soon. It was as dispiriting a vehicle inside as out: patchy grey seats and a dashboard held on with sticky tape. Whether it had left the British Leyland factory in that condition or if the owner had done it himself was anybody's guess.

I'd calmed down a little after the initial adrenaline rush. It was well short of serenity but there was a certain kind of pragmatic numbness sloshing about in my head. It all felt a little too big to take in and I was absolutely conscious of the gaps in my knowledge. As such, I couldn't expect to think my way to a conclusion. I simply didn't know enough. All I could do was run through the little that I did know and try looking at it from different angles. I'd always been good at puzzles and I've lost count of the people who've told me that I'm too clever for my own good, so I took comfort in the knowledge that I was well suited to the task of working out what was going on and then what to do about it.

I broke it down into a few key pieces, writing down names

on a little white pad inside my mind and then taking a virtual photograph of the page. I put the heading 'Walt' and underlined it with a black fountain pen in my imagination. Then I started writing.

> Walter Renwick. Recruited at Cambridge, '47. Key postings at Moscow Centre, Middle East. Damascus station chief. Time at GCHQ then back to the Service. Indiscreet critic of colonialism and capitalism. Seen as a Red sympathizer by many. Questioned hard in the wake of Philby et al. Cleared but moved sideways. Reduced interaction with Control. Given responsibility for South and Central Americas. Operation Prickly Heat, information sharing with US. Parts ways with Service in '76. Teaching, travelling, possible private contracting work. Dec '82, contacts former protégée, CH, offering information on war crimes taking place in Guatemala. CH instructed to take snippet of info to department head. No sale. Anonymous recording sent to Service. CH complicity, fraternizing with a subversive, making dangerous comments on direction of the West. CH permits use of country house and travels north. Intercepted by picture card from the Deck of Clubs. Told to return home ahead of debrief . . .

I yanked the car to the right, the windscreen filling with the big yellow back of a goods wagon. I shot a glance at the clock on the dashboard. It was pushing midnight and I was still ninety miles from Felicity and from whatever else was waiting for me back in the place where Stefan and I experienced the only gentle happiness of my whole bloody life.

I screwed up my eyes for a second, trying to regain control of myself. Skimmed my mental notes and looked for something that might make sense. Nothing came. It was clear to me that somebody was trying to make it seem that I was, if not actively betraying queen and country, at least in the market for it. So who might have that level of venom towards me? Nobody sprung instantly to mind. I'd made my share of enemies over the years but they were more petty rivalries or the consequence of rejected advances and not worth staging anything so elaborate over. I'd been involved in operations that had severe repercussions for those who were caught out in their lies, but I was only ever a part of a larger team and nobody had ever vowed to make sure that I spend my days in the misery of a jail cell with my reputation in tatters. Try as I might I couldn't work out why anybody would want to make it look like I was on the verge of defecting, or at the very least open to some light subversion. I thought again of Cranham's voice on the recording. He'd sounded so withering, so utterly bereft of affection, compassion, for the woman who had been his wife for twenty years. Of course the marriage was a sham and had served as nothing more than a camouflage jacket that permitted us both to live the lives that suited us best, but I had kept his secrets and he'd kept mine. Was that it? Was it Cranham? Did I know something about my husband that meant I had to be discredited? Surely the de facto father of my children wouldn't do something so vulgar as to set the security services on his wife. For all his faults, there was a strange form of old-fashioned decency running through him.

I chewed at my lip. Twisted the steering wheel with my damp palms. Could it be that somebody was trying to discredit Cranham? He was a very senior figure, cheek-by-jowl with all the serious power brokers and able to wield significant resources and make the kind of decisions that give power-mad public schoolboys funny feelings under their pyjamas. Had he made an enemy who wanted to inconvenience him through the implication that his wife was ripe for defection, or worse, actively working counter to the interests of the Crown. A chap would need to resign over such a scandal, that much was clear. But any Fleet Street hack could ruin Cranham with a little light digging. He'd been involved in a succession of gay relationships throughout our marriage and none of his partners would be above selling their story for the right price. But there was something ungentlemanly, something inelegant, about that kind of scandal. This felt as though it had someone more sophisticated pulling the strings.

I worked through the other scraps of information. Thought upon Guatemala. I knew nothing about the place save for the

occasional overheard headline or glimpsed telegraph communication. I knew that the Americans had picked the side most
likely to help them hold back the threat of communism but in
so doing they had got into bed with a genocidal regime. I had
no insider knowledge. I'd assisted with some meat-and-veg
stuff in Central America shortly before Walt got the boot and
I'd only just started getting to grips with the brief. I hadn't
looked back since. It wasn't my area. Within forty-eight hours
of Operation Prickly Heat being rolled up they'd stuck me in
an import/export business in Turkey with a view to bringing
a couple of disaffected KGB over to our side. And once I got
home I'd barely looked west. I'd been involved in more
domestic dramas for the past few months – gathering intelligence on pleasant housewives and lentil-scented hippies at a
peaceful protest at Greenham Common.

I gripped the steering wheel tighter. I could feel pain blos-
soming across my back and shoulder and had to make a
conscious effort to unclench my jaw. I leaned over to the glove
box and rummaged through the contents. Boiled sweets, a
couple of maps, an owner's manual. Cigarettes in a gold packet.
I managed to find the purloined lighter in my pocket and lit
up, sucking the smoke into my lungs. It wasn't my brand;
it tasted foul but it offered some kind of comfort and even a
little sense of imagined warmth. I played with the lighter for
a moment, flicking it open and closed and running through it
all again and again in my mind. Why me? Who would want
to set me up? Why had Walt come back into my life?

I replayed the conversation. Who was it who had suggested
that he take himself to my place in Gilsland? He'd already
been on the way when I'd made contact with him from the
phone box. But the previous night, shortly after I told him I
was going to take his information to Talbot, he'd asked whether
or not there were any serviceable safe houses where he could
keep his source out of harm's way. He'd asked that it be outside
of London – the further north the better. I'd made the offer of
the Gilsland house almost without thinking. Had he planted
that seed? He'd already known about the property, that much
was clear. But if he just wanted a place to lie low he could
have broken in without me ever being involved. Clearly, he

wanted me to be a part of whatever it was he was trying to pull off.

I slammed my hand on the wheel, scattering ash. All I wanted was to sit the slippery sod down and growl at him until he told me what he'd got me caught up in. I felt my temper rising: a warm blush on my cheeks and chest. The rain slowed just long enough for me to glimpse a sign pointing left towards Preston. Still bloody miles away. Still no idea what I'd do when I got there.

I realized I was still playing with the lighter. I felt its sleek coldness against my fingertips. Turned it this way and that, wondering whether the man from the train would be cursing me for its theft. Wondering whether it was something dear to him, a gift from a loved one; an object of sentimental attachment.

The lights of the motorway glared through the rain-soaked glass. For the merest fraction of a second, I could make out the inscription on the outside of the lighter. It was barely there, almost worn away by the ministrations of a rough thumb. But holding it up and angling it towards the open window I was able to make out the ghost of the original wording.

Big T, Belize City
Veni, Veni, Veni!

And my memory filled with the scents of still-wet blood, and the screams of the man we sent to his death.

PART TWO

FELICITY

Transcript 0024, recorded December 1, 2016

He started waking up not long after. I don't know if he were ever really unconscious but once his nursemaid had headed for the door he obviously couldn't see any reason to keep milking it. He groaned a little bit. Sucked his lips like a baby with a bottle. Put both of his hands to his temples, like he was waking up from one of the drinking sessions that he'd thrown himself into for a while after our lad's death. When he opened his eyes he had a scared look about him. It took him a moment to get his bearings. I could see confusion all over his pained, bloodied face. I just stayed where I was, still as a statue in the murk of the room, seeing how long it would take him to remember what had been done to us and where the hell we were.

'There was a lass,' he said, a slur in his words, looking up at me with heavy, glassy eyes. 'Warm hands.'

'Sera,' I said. 'She's Guatemalan.'

He pulled a face, not sure he'd heard. 'She's what?'

'Guatemalan. It's in Central America, under Mexico. She's been looking after you. She's very nice.'

He looked down at the fresh bandages. Pushed a finger into his mouth and probed at his lower denture. 'Bit my bloody tongue,' he grumbled, as if it was just one injustice too many. He gave me a quick glance up and down. 'You all right? You look cold.'

'Don't fret,' I muttered, rubbing at my arms. 'And don't ask me what's going on because I've no blasted idea.'

He got himself to his knees. Readjusted himself then hauled himself upright. He cleared the space between us and put his hand out, squeezing my arm. 'You've been crying,' he said, accusingly. 'Are you hurting?'

'Bumps and bruises,' I muttered, being as cold with him as I knew how to be. 'I went a right clatter down the back stairs.'

He winced again, memories seeming to pop behind his eyes. 'Cordelia's,' he said, at last. 'Two big blokes. Punch like a kick from a donkey on one of them.'

I nodded. 'Sera and her brother have got some information for some important people. They've come a long way to tell them about the bad things happening in their country. I think we just got in the way, so as long as we don't upset anybody we'll probably be grand.'

He didn't look convinced. Looked around him, getting a feel for our surroundings. 'Maid's quarters, is it?' he asked, curtly. 'By the back stairs?'

'You'll know it, I shouldn't wonder,' I said nastily. 'No doubt there isn't a room here at her majesty's that you don't know like the back of your hand.'

He was gazing up at the hole in the roof. Reached past me and looked inside the medicine cupboard. There was a dirty mug and an empty bottle of talcum powder. He squatted down, grimacing, and ran his hand up and down the porcelain under the sink.

'Did you hear me?' I asked, huddling into my coat. 'Want me to make it rhyme for you, is that how to get your attention?'

He stopped what he was doing. Straightened up. There was sweat running down his face and the whites of his eyes were the yellow of a smoker's teeth. But he gave me his full attention.

'You saw the poems,' he said, without emotion. He shook his head. 'I asked you not to look.'

'Aye well, I did look. Very lovely, I'm sure, though of course I'm not one to judge. That's probably something for you and Cordelia to chat about, once you've finished doing whatever else you do.'

He jerked his head back like I'd hit him. 'What else we've been doing? What does that mean?'

'I saw the inscription,' I hissed. 'God, I knew she had an eye for a bit of rough but I thought she had some bloody standards. Thought she cared more about me than this! John

Goose, I swear, this is going to kill me. I can feel it, right now, getting bigger – I can feel my heart ready to bloody pop!'

He stepped towards me, his eyes on mine. It was odd and intense and not completely uncomfortable. He shook his head, keeping his eyes on mine. 'It's not that, you silly sod. God almighty, you think we'd be carrying on with one another? Felicity Eagles, you will be the bloody death of me.' He put his hand on his injury. Gave a little chuckle as if he were imagining it. 'Me and Cordelia? Bloody hell, I don't think I'd be able to! She scares the living daylights out of me, that one. It was a present – a thank you for something. Don't be bothering your head about it.'

I wasn't going to leave it. My dander was up and too many people had been unkind to me. I wanted an explanation.

'You don't write poetry, John Goose. You're a plumber.'

He looked a little hurt at that. 'I wrote you poems when I was at sea,' he said. 'When we were courting I put nice words in our letters. You said you liked it. And I did those limericks for James and Peter when they were little. It's just a silly thing, something I play at. It's embarrassing. I didn't mention it to you because there was nowt to mention and they're just rubbish really. Just doodles but with words.'

'But you showed Cordelia?' I demanded.

He gave a shrug that almost got him a slap across the chops. 'I said something about a tree looking like something-or-other,' he mumbled. 'Some nice little phrase that she was taken with. She was up visiting you and you'd gone to get something and we were chatting in the kitchen. She said I had a poet's soul. Nobody's ever said owt like that to me. So I told her that I scribbled down bits and bobs now and then. She asked to see. I thought she were just being polite, like. But she read the few I gave her and gave me some notes and, well, I've got OK at it. And then she gave me a nice book to put them in. She thinks I should show them to you but I've never felt like you'd want to see them. They're not all jolly, Felicity. There's sad stuff about Peter. Some of it's just plain rubbish.'

I shook my head at him, not yet ready to forgive him. I'd imagined all sorts and I wasn't about to be so easily persuaded down from my high horse. 'You wrote some things about me,' I said. 'Rude stuff.'

He looked past me, embarrassed. 'You weren't meant to look.'

I held the book out for him. 'Go on then,' I said. 'Take it back. It's obviously special if you carry it everywhere with you.'

He took it from me. Put it in the pocket of his cardigan. 'Did you like what you read?'

I made myself meet his eyes. 'Aye. It were all right.'

'Good, then,' he mumbled. 'That's good.'

We stood there for a bit, feeling daft. Then he nodded like it was all dealt with and he turned around and started fiddling behind the sink again.

'What is it you think you're doing?' I asked, leaning over and trying to see what he was up to. 'Are you looking for a key or a rounders bat or something?'

He didn't turn back to me. Spoke as he carried on fiddling with the workings of the sink. 'She's not here, then.'

'Who? Cordelia? No. I don't even know if they know her.'

'So who is here?'

'Sera and her brother. He's Guatemalan too. Then there are two big blokes and a skinny little goblin man. He's got a gun. The tall one is Pelletier. I think that's right. And I think I saw somebody else in the doorway but my eyes might have been having me on, and . . .'

I stopped talking. From outside came the sounds of raised voices and clattering furniture. I couldn't make out what was being said but it was clear that somebody was ranting and raging and the other voices were trying to calm them down.

'What is it you're doing down there,' I said, shivering again and trying to take my mind off the fright by snapping at John while he touched up the sink.

'You never bloody listened, did you?' he said, ignoring me. I watched as he shuffled sideways, sliding his finger under the edge of the carpet and gripping the edges, softly tugging it free of the flagstones. 'All those times I told you what she did and you just laughed it off. I was bloody serious.'

'What who did?'

'Cordelia. Five years? Six? How many hints do you need before you cotton on?'

'Cotton on to what, John?'

'She's a bloody spy! This is a safe house – like from the films. Why do you think I've been calling her Jane Bond all these years?'

'Don't talk soft, she works for the United Nations . . .'

'Aye. As a spy.'

'Well, who does she spy on?' I asked, getting all hot and stroppy.

'Andrea Domney,' he muttered, still tugging at the carpet. 'That's what the name badge said. She saw me and I saw her and there were no doubting who she was, even with the wig and the glasses. It was Cordelia, and she was pretending to be some bugger else. And it weren't long after that they tapped me up and reminded me of what I'd signed.'

I was getting upset. I wanted him to stop tearing at the carpet and just tell me what he was prattling on about. 'Official Secrets Act. You remember, I signed it when I got the job at the airbase, solemnly swearing not to talk about anything I saw or heard or was involved with as part of the rocket programme, on pain of prosecution and jail. They were nice enough about it but they made it clear that I wasn't to breathe a word or I'd be for the high jump.'

'Breathe a word about what?' I shouted, my voice suddenly shrill and full of spite.

'When they sent us over to Woomera. That trip in '76. Far end of the bloody earth and hot as the inside of a bread oven. Learning how to clear the liquid oxygen tanks. Longest I've ever been away from home. Cordelia was there. And she were called Andrea Domney. I swear I even said her name out loud and she gave me a look that would tear the skin off a person. And it wasn't long after I got back that they came and made their reminder. And then they offered me a chance to make some easy cash-in-hand.'

'You're scaring me, John,' I said, my head in my hands.

'It was just a case of picking up the occasional parcel from one place and taking it to another. Sometimes I had to pop a letter in the post. Once or twice I had to come here and give the place a once-over . . .'

'Cleaning?' I asked, affronted. 'That's my job! And you don't even lift a duster at home!'

'Cordelia never said a word about it when we were with you, but those couple of times when we had five minutes, she'd ask if the money was coming in as agreed and said that I was doing the job right. It wasn't a bother, and the little bit of extra money was a help.'

'Cordelia had you doing this?' I asked, angry and confused. 'But why's she been paying me to look after the place, then? You don't think . . . aye, I know that devious madam, this'll be her fancy way of giving us charity and making us feel like we've earned it. I've told her, that's not why we're friends, I don't need her handouts, we're doing fine, thank you very much . . .'

He gave a grunt as he stuck his fingers inside a knothole in the wooden boards that filled in the spaces between the flagstones. It came up without much effort. He reached inside and started twisting at something in the darkness. I heard the sound of rushing water and then the gurgle as it slowed. He grunted again as he pushed himself back and I offered my hand to help him up. He took it and as I got him to his feet he sort of fell into me. His clothes were stinking and there was muddy water all over his front but it felt nice to hold him for a moment, to feel the sturdiness of him against me. It made the things I'd been thinking seem silly. He was my John. He was a decent lump of a chap: dependable and a bit of a grump. Writing poetry? Picking up parcels for a government spy? All that stuff was the work of a stranger. This man, this man in my arms, this was the real John and I could have kissed him for just briefly being himself.

'Here,' he said, and handed me a length of ceramic pipe. He wielded one himself too, a hefty great truncheon with an unscrewed brass cog at the end. 'If anybody touches you again, wallop them with the hard end.'

I looked at the length of piping. Turned it over. 'I think they're both hard ends,' I muttered, feeling lost. 'John, I said . . . they're both hard ends . . . don't go sniggering, you . . .'

When I looked up, John had one foot in the sink and was pulling himself upwards with a hiss of pain. He stood on his tiptoes and without so much as a look back, he rammed the length of pipe into the hole in the ceiling. Plaster and timber and horse-hair rained down.

Then he was reaching both hands into the gap. Bracing himself, he hauled himself up like he was a gymnast – albeit a gymnast in pyjama trousers and a nasty gash in their belly.

'John Goose, come down, you silly beggar, you're going to tear yourself open!'

He tumbled back into the sink, his knee jarring as he slipped sideways and half cartwheeled down onto the floor, the air coming out of him in a great, painful thump.

'What the blazes did you do that for?'

He held his hand in front of his face. Opened his fist as if he held a jewel on his palm. The device was a couple of inches by a couple of inches: a little black square with a thick wire protruding an inch or two from the top. I'd watched enough spy movies to know what it was.

'John?' I asked. 'John, how did you know . . .?'

Even through the pain I could detect the faintest whiff of pride; a little smile at having a secret and of having kept it well.

He looked at the roll of carpet, and then back to his hand.

'Snug as a bug in a rug.'

CORDELIA

held the lighter in my hand as if it were a damp sponge. I wanted to wring the truth out of it, juice the damn thing of all its secrets and concealments. Glancing at myself in the rear-view mirror, I caught my own eye. I wanted to do the same to the sly, deceitful woman looking back at me.

In my head I was treading water at the edge of a widening whirlpool. I didn't want to get sucked down into memory. And yet even as I kicked away from the darkness and the tragedies of the past, I could feel my resolve weakening and the undertow grabbed me, hauling me back into that little room at HQ. It was November 1976 and I'd been part of Walt's unit for six weeks. Already the excitement of the posting was beginning to wane. I'd been honoured to have been personally selected for the specialist unit reporting directly to the Ace of Diamonds but it didn't take long to realize that Walt's star had long since lost its shine and that anybody hoping to ride his coat-tails had better get used to being dragged through the dirt. I'd only actually seen him once since the approach was made. I'd served my time out in Tel Aviv and although the kids were in a nice boarding school at home, I was missing them terribly. More, Cranham was starting to feel that he wasn't getting what he paid for. He'd made serious progress up the greasy pole in the preceding years and needed to be seen as the quintessential family man if his next promotion was to be formally approved, which meant that he needed me on his arm for the occasional photo opportunity, or at the very least, to ring the office once in a while and arrange a lunch that we wouldn't actually take. My dissatisfaction must have reached Walt's ears. He offered me a position within Operation Aletheia, the clandestine unit looking into matters that might jeopardize relations with our colonial cousins and keeping abreast of anything we needed to know in Central and South America. On the first day in the new post I was given a stack of newspapers and told to cut out anything that offered a hint of discord between Westminster and Washington. There was plenty to find. It was a little menial for somebody with a decade of experience, but I made it home at a sensible time and nobody seemed to wish me ill. Gradually I was given meatier jobs, scanning transcripts of clandestine recordings and wire taps made by GCHQ, or deep-diving into fiscal accounts of key personnel: friendlies, enemies and those who had yet to make up their mind. I spent my days in a little boxy office with a dead pot plant and a swivel chair with a missing wheel, but when Walt finally did make his presence felt, he made it clear that I'd been doing my job well and was ready to be involved in an operation that was, he claimed, a little bit more clandestine than I was used to. I didn't have a moment's misgiving. I'd known him since recruitment. He was one of the good ones; a decent person trying to keep on the right side of his conscience in an increasingly complex world. Chain of command dictated I do whatever he asked so I made it clear that I was at his disposal.

He never really explained what part I played in the bigger picture. That was Walt's way. He was the only person who could ever see the whole playing field at once. All he asked was that when a certain call came, I be there to listen.

'No need to bother those worry-waters at GCHQ,' he said, sitting on the edge of my desk in a shabby blue suit and with a drop of moisture threatening to fall from the end of his nose. He was tanned and there was some nasty rash beneath the thinning strands of hair across his pate. He looked older and sicker than when we had last worked together. His ebullience had gone. He wasn't trying to make me laugh. He stank of drink and American cigarettes. But he was a legend in the Service and he rated me highly. So I did as I was bid.

'A useful source will be making a transmission at a pre-appointed time on a pre-appointed frequency. The frequency in question will be provided for you when required. So too the radio receiver. It might be in the next week, it might be a month from now. I'm sorry it's so vague. You are to listen in, make the recording and provide the transcript. You are to give it to me in person, or nobody at all. You place the recording where I tell you. If I never ask you for the transcript, you destroy it. If anybody else asks you for it, you destroy it. Only if I ask, and reference a Mrs Tenebrae when so doing, do you provide it for me. Do you understand?'

It wasn't that outlandish a request. I'd been tasked with doing stranger and more dangerous things. It felt good to be trusted with something that was clearly important to him, even if it bent some of the very protocols that Walt had first established. I remained on high alert. Eight days later, I came back from a brief leg-stretch to find a copy of *Tenebrae* by Ernest G Henham on my desk. It had a library ticket in the title page. It was due back the following day. Recognizing Walt's favoured technique, I took the book back to the little library in Wandsworth. The librarian looked as though she was trying to chew a lemon with her buttocks: all sour and pinched and puckered up. But when she stamped the book she handed me another and told me there was a reference section where I might like to go and read. Out of sight, I ran my finger down the binding and found the little scrap of paper that one of Walt's men had left for me. It gave me the time, date and radio frequency. The little collection of line drawings on the flip side weren't hard to work out. They marked out the O'Farrell mausoleum. Highgate Cemetery.

I can see myself there. See me in my prime. Dark jacket, black jeans, thick woollen hat and leather gloves. Can see myself moving through the headstones and the footpaths without a word. Can see myself sidling in between the big iron gates and ghosting inside the cold, damp tomb.

The radio was waiting for me. So too the reel-to-reel recorder and a little headset. Whoever had left them for me had also gone to the trouble of leaving a tartan blanket and a corned beef sandwich. Walt clearly wanted me to know he appreciated what I was doing.

I drank rum from a hip flask. I ate my sandwich. I read by the light of a torch. I smoked. I checked my watch over and over. A full hour and twenty minutes after the agreed time, the radio crackled into life. I did only as I was instructed. I recorded the communication. But I remember what was said as if it were embossed on the grey matter of my brain.

The voice was American. Texan, if I was any judge. There was appalling static on the line and I fancied I could hear the thrum of a light aircraft's engines, but if I pressed the headphones against the sides of my skull I could make out most of what was being said.

'. . . only a matter of time until they make good on their threats. The numbers don't matter. They could disappear half the population and still be able to deny it. There's so much damn jungle that finding evidence is like looking for a grain of salt in the sugar bowl. They think they're going to scare us away but they don't know the level of our resolution or what a shepherd owes to his flock . . .'

Another voice cut in. This one was British. Refined. Officer class.

'You've done enough. Nobody could ask for more. Not even God wants you to give your life, Father.'

'Don't tell me what God wants of me,' came the reply. 'I never expected God would want me out here. I didn't grow up believing I could serve Him out in this lawless wilderness. But He has guided me. Pride is sinful, my friend, but I look upon what we've achieved these past years and I feel no shame in admitting that I am proud of what we have done. And for these bullying sons of bitches to undo it? To expect my flock to turn their back on their years of hard work and slip away without a backwards glance? To ask me to turn tail and run just because they've got the guns and the ugliness of spirit to threaten my life? Hell no.'

There was a pause for a time. I heard the sounds of muffled conversation. Another voice cut in, barely audible but unmistakably female. Then the Englishman spoke again.

'Belize City,' he said, raising his voice above the drone of the engines. 'Father Seneca. He made it all the way to the rendezvous. Big D's. I think some of what he saw made his nose bleed a little. I was sorry to hear he didn't make it back. What you're providing, what you claim – you realize it flies in the face of all official explanations for what happened, you understand that, yes? You're asking the Crown to make a decision that flies in the face of all national interests and jeopardizes our relationship with our closest allies.'

'I must be naïve,' said the Texan. 'I was brought up believing that America was a force for good. Damn the cost. Damn oil and politics and keeping your enemies close. People are dying. People are being forced off their land. Every decent citizen is finding their name on the lists of the death squads and disappearing without so much as a whisper of outrage from the international community. Britain has a chance to stand up for what's right. I was told that your patron understood these things – that he was somebody my people could trust. I don't fear for my own life but those who work with me, who risk their lives, who've seen their . . .'

And then he stopped. I'd like to tell you that he said something that explained the sudden, jolting silence. But one moment he was talking and the next all I could hear was the sudden, terrible silence. Then the Englishman shouted, something indecipherable and filled with a terrible rising panic. I heard a woman shriek. Then there was just the dreadful rush and screech and crunch of metal upon metal. Then silence.

I knew what I'd heard. I'd been mute witness to a catastrophe. In my mind I think I probably pictured a meeting in the rear of a wagon: the sudden squeal of tyres and then the carnage of a fatal plunge into some deep ravine. But I couldn't be sure. Nor did I have anybody to ask.

I sat in the dark, heart thudding, and took comfort in procedure. I did as I was instructed. I transcribed every word of it, fountain pen moving over page after page of plain paper. It took up half the book and my arm was aching when I was finished but I'd got every word down. Then, as bid, I removed the recording from the device. I wrapped it in the tartan blanket and placed it, as instructed, in the little crevice beneath the big marble tomb. I dismantled the wireless. Placed the transcript in the pocket of my coat. And I went home.

In the days that followed, I monitored the newswires for anything that might indicate whose death I had been witness to. I waited for Walt to get in touch. I even made discreet enquiries about Big D's in Belize City. It was a brothel, army approved, and favoured by the British soldiers stationed at various posts along the border. It was a place where a person could keep their secrets, and where anything could be bought or sold. It wasn't mentioned in connection with any accidents on the international news pages. And nothing on the radio broadcasts spoke of a crash involving an American, a Brit and a Spanish-speaking woman.

Walt never asked for the recording. He didn't even say goodbye. A fortnight after that night in the crypt, word reached me that his unit was being wound up and that Walt had either quit or been given his marching orders. Nobody really understood what he'd done wrong but the presumption was that he'd simply pissed off the wrong people one too many times. I was transferred to a new posting almost immediately. It was weeks later that one of the Deck of Clubs tracked me down and gently enquired whether I knew what Walt had been up to in his last few days in his post. Had he, by any chance, asked me to listen in to a recording? I denied it, of course. Then I went home to destroy the transcript. I don't think I could tell you why I decided not to burn it. Perhaps it was the use of the word 'Father'. It represented the last words of three people in their last moments of life. Who was I to put a flame to it? So I put it inside one of my battered old textbooks from university and shipped it up, along with two other crates of dog-eared paperbacks, to the increasingly dilapidated Gilsland house. It was the sort of place that welcomed secrets.

Walt didn't ask about the recording when we met in the cemetery. I don't know who took the recording from beneath the tomb in the intervening years. It wasn't there last night, I know that. I popped back after Walt had vacated the place and rummaged around in the dark. The blanket was still there, soggy and almost rotten away. But the recording was long since gone.

I gripped the lighter. Thought again about the man on the train and those scars on his neck. He'd served in Belize. Walt's network utilized a brothel in Belize City. And now Walt was back in my life and I was being set up as a potential subversive. There had to be a link but I couldn't make the pieces fit.

And then I was half an hour from home. I was turning off the motorway and heading down the glittering black road that cut deep into the countryside: sheep-speckled grass and walls of rugged fell and brooding sky.

I felt my fear like a fist, a hand gripping at my heart and squeezing it like ripe fruit. I'd sent Felicity into this. Felicity and John.

Christ, *John*! At the house. The house where he'd betrayed his vows.

All I could do was trust that he could keep his mouth shut.

If Felicity knew the truth about what we'd done, she'd damn well die on the spot.

FELICITY

It's a strange feeling, finding out that your husband isn't who you think he is. I'd imagine some people find it quite exciting – a real shot in the arm for the relationship and a chance to spice things up a bit. I don't like spice. Never have. My favourite meal is stew and dumplings with apple cake for afters. I don't even like the parsley bits in frozen fishcakes. I didn't want John to be anybody other than the man I'd married. He was solid. Dependable. A bit of a grump. He had a silly side to him and a kind heart and he loved me, in that quiet way of his, putting up with the nagging and the fretting and the never wanting to go further than the horizon. We understood one another. He'd seen the world during the war. Rode giant turtles on the beach in Singapore and watched Japanese torpedoes sink the ship he'd have been on if he hadn't caught some nasty tropical illness. He even got to go to an airbase in Australia, all bought and paid for by those fine people at Rolls-Royce. Came back with a suntan and plenty of stories. Told me about the weather and the food and the silly sod who'd fallen into one of the big industrial drums and had to be hauled out by his ankles. But he never told me he'd seen my best friend over there, or that she recruited him to work as an asset for the Secret Intelligence Service.

I can see him clear as anything, laid out on the floor, holding that little recording device in his hand and laughing at something that didn't strike me as the least bit funny. It felt like somebody else had taken over John's skin. He was a stranger to me.

'Help me up,' he grunted, when the amusement had worn off. 'I'll need a boost if I'm going to get up there without ripping open.'

I followed his gaze. 'Get up there? Why would you need to get up there?'

'Well, we can't get out under the floorboards,' he said, as

if explaining to somebody half-daft. 'Concrete partition wall. There's a gap between the ceiling of this room and the floor of the guest bedroom that I can just about wriggle through.'

I looked at him as if he were mad. 'And why would you go and do that, John Goose?'

He waved at the room in general. Pointed at his injured guts and then at me, all wet and shaking and sore. 'We're locked in, Felicity. And the people out there have already hurt you and hurt me and whatever they're up to, I don't think they're going to suddenly wave us goodbye and head for the hills when they're done. We need to get ourselves far away.'

I shook my head. 'You're expecting me to go up there too? I'm fifty-five next birthday! I've got gallstones! There could be all sorts up there!'

He took the tail of his cardigan and wiped the sweat from his face. 'This little thing,' he said, holding up the black cube. When he spoke it was like he was reciting something he'd learned off by heart. 'It's a listening device. You've seen them in the films. It switches on when the electrical vibrations nearby undergo a significant alteration. It switches itself off after a certain amount of time without a frequency change. Basically, if you're in the room above and switch on a lamp or the wireless, it starts transmitting.'

He sounded like he was speaking a foreign language. I started slapping the length of copper pipe against my palm, jittery and frozen through. 'And how do you know that?'

'I put it in,' he said, with a shrug that didn't suit him. 'Cordelia – she set it up. I never had to do anything dangerous, I swear. Just once in a while a package would appear in the glove compartment of the car and I'd have to pop along to the house and retrieve one gadget or put another one in. She explained it all. I didn't give it a second thought. I stopped when . . .'

I stared through him, unsure why he stopped. He met my gaze, a sheen to his eyes, and I knew what had happened. It was our boy's death that changed him, and us, and the whole of our world.

I gave a little nod. It wasn't the hug that some people would have offered, but in the language of our marriage it stood for pretty much the same thing.

'I'll give her merry hell for this,' I muttered, as John started fiddling with the gadget, gripping the pipe between his knees.

'Cordelia? Aye, when she warned me about breaking the Official Secrets Act she said that it was your temper that we should both be afraid of. Does she know about the time you stuck the fork in the wall?'

I couldn't help but laugh at the memory of it – at the ridiculousness of our situation and the secrets that were leaking out. 'She does, aye,' I said. 'She's seen me with my dander up. But she gives as good as she gets. That business with the body in the blue suit, with Loveday – the farm next door.'

'Don't think on it – you'll only get upset.'

He bent down and picked up the little lamp. Looked at the sink as if he was about to leap up and then spring into the rafters. He looked too shaky on his feet for it to even seem vaguely possible. He tottered a bit and reached out for me. I grabbed his arm and he half fell against me. The heat coming off him was intense, like I'd opened the oven door. He was slick with sweat and there was a new smell coming off him, like food left out in summer.

I didn't get a chance to ask him what was happening inside him. The next thing the door handle was rattling and then a key was turning in the lock and the sound of raised voices was flooding in from outside.

'. . . one bloody thing! One piece out of place and it all goes wrong!'

'. . . more to lose than you. These aren't names on a printout, they're real people, real lives . . .'

'. . . how long I've been planning this! We need to put on a united front, if he gets any sense of what's coming he'll pull the plug and then we're all in shit so deep you'd never come up for air . . .'

Pelletier was in the doorway. He spread his hands wide. Gave us a rueful smile as if he were a dad whose kids were making a fuss at a birthday party. He placed a flask and two metal cups down by the door. 'Sera said you might need something to warm you up. She's a kindly soul, don't you think? It's no hardship to make her happy.'

John gave a little groan and then slithered down to the floor, knocking the lantern over. The angle of illumination changed completely and the hole in the ceiling above the sink was suddenly in complete darkness. I felt him grip my arm. He was putting it on.

'Jesus, you look awful,' said Pelletier, wincing. 'Here, let me help you . . .'

He came towards us and John waited until the last minute before nudging me out of the way and swinging with the pipe. He swung it hard but Pelletier moved as if the blow was delivered in slow motion. His feet stayed where they were but he swayed back like a ballet dancer. He shot out his arm and caught John a crack on the elbow and the pipe clattered away to the ground. Pelletier kicked John's legs out from under him, catching him before he fell and lowering him to the ground like they were dancing. I just stood there, too shocked to move, holding my own pipe out in front of me like it was a church candle. When Pelletier turned he put out his hand and I handed over the makeshift weapon without a word. He shook his head at the pair of us and then walked past me and out of the room. I heard the key turn.

'John,' I said, my hand on his cheek. 'John, what were you thinking, you daft . . .'

He grinned. It showed the blood on his teeth and I could see that every bit of him was hurting. But he looked like something had just gone right.

He held up his hands. Spread his fingers and showed his empty palms. 'In his pocket,' he said, and started coughing. 'I reckon that'll be just about close enough to start transmitting. Just sit tight now. Somebody will pick it up.'

I didn't know how to respond. Didn't know what to do. So I took the flask and unscrewed the lid and hoped to God that a cup of tea really did have magical properties.

I could have burst into tears when I poured myself a cupful and realized he'd brought coffee.

CORDELIA

I was ten miles from home when I knew for sure I was being followed. Whoever was behind me had picked the wrong car for the job. They had big white lights that stood out like pearls against a black velvet dress. It was too loud for the stillness of the landscape too: a throaty rumble that betrayed the power beneath the bonnet. It was a big car with an engine far grander than mine but the driver kept hanging back, staying in the shadows or lingering just behind the curve in the road, deliberately refusing to catch up or overtake. I'd been on the vehicular surveillance courses and recognized the techniques. I'd utilized them myself plenty of times, though the dark country roads between Carlisle and Gilsland were a true nightmare for any agent trying not to be spotted. I'd turned off to take the country roads that snaked through the fields beside the railway line and the darkness was absolute.

I tried to make sense of it. I was in a stolen vehicle. I'd been driving for two hours and hadn't betrayed my position or stopped to make a phone call. If somebody knew that I was driving the little Allegro, it was because a police report had been filed and somebody with a decent IQ had recognized the description of the woman wanted in connection with the vehicular theft. That could only be somebody within the intelligence community. My destination couldn't be hard to fathom. A quick glance through my personnel file would show where I was living when I was first recruited, and no doubt Cranham had given my pursuers a heads-up about where best to get their hands upon his errant wife. That meant I had somebody behind me and no doubt somebody coming in from the opposite direction and headed for the house. I gripped the wheel, palms oozing sweat, feeling the perspiration on my brow turn to ice as the cold air blew in through the open window. I breathed in deep, trying to centre myself. Despite the panic in my gut there was something almost comforting about breathing in that rich, complex, rural smell. I inhaled the scents of damp earth and fresh rain, churned-up fields and the great empty nothingness of this rugged, barren land on the edge of England. Memories flooded back. Tears prickled at my eyes as I thought upon Stefan, his weight upon my tummy as I lay on the dew-damp grass and read him his stories; the gritty sand of his ashes upon my rain-soaked palms as I scattered his remains among the bluebells and cow parsley at the little church where Felicity and I first became friends. I heard myself give a great rasping sob and had to squeeze my eyes tight shut before the tears betrayed me and started to fall.

I glanced again in the mirror. There was no doubting it now. I was five or six miles from Gilsland, adjacent to the little hamlet I knew as Low Row. I could pull in at one of the farms and kill the headlights, but even if they drove on by, what next? I'd still have to work out whether Felicity was best served by my presence or by my absence and if the person behind me was the piggy-eyed bruiser from the train, I didn't want him getting to the house before me. He wasn't somebody I ever wanted Felicity to meet.

I kept driving; an ache across my shoulders and up my neck into my skull. There were no other cars on the road. It felt like my pursuer and I were the only people in the world. The windscreen was all streaky rain and dead flies and the headlights barely managed to cast light further than a couple of car-lengths. I glimpsed a couple of rabbits in the road, scurrying into the little hedgerows; saw a great oak at a bend in the road, turning left towards the slope beneath the railway bridge. For a moment I thought about slowing down and exiting the car, throwing myself onto the grass verge and permitting the vehicle to continue without me for a few hundred yards, but once the ruse was discovered I'd be no better off. I had no weapon, no way of contacting anyone, and would have done nothing but slowed myself down. I thought upon the airbase, two miles above Gilsland, out past the great empty vastness of the peat bogs. There would be airmen there. A phone. People who could be counted upon to ask the right questions and not spot the wrong answers. I was an MP's wife. A senior intelligence officer. I could bluster my way in – use the upper-crust voice and give off the air of innate superiority – insist upon the despatching of military police to the house under instructions to pick up whoever they found. It would be reckless, riddled with potential disasters, but I couldn't think what else to do. All I had to do was lose the tail, and I knew the roads well enough to fancy my chances once I got past the railway bridge and into the stygian black of the farmlands beyond.

My pursuer made the decision for me. I heard the unmistakable rumble of a big engine brought to life. I glanced in the mirror and saw that the vehicle was surging towards me, the headlights suddenly flicking to full beam and dazzling me with their sheer brilliant whiteness.

The big car didn't crunch into me. It was more of a caress: a perfectly placed little shunt that pushed me sideways as if we were moving on ice.

I felt the tyres bounce over divots and gravel then the bonnet screech against stone. My front headlight exploded and I was thrown forward in my seat before I yanked the wheel to the left and prayed for the tyres to find purchase. I glanced out of the passenger window and saw the man from the train. We were parallel, locked together like chariots racing at the coliseum. A cold fury flooded through me and I pushed the accelerator all the way, turning the wheel as far as it would go and slamming the side of the car against his, nudging him out into the centre of the narrow, pitch-dark road as I surged down the grass verge beside him, metal grinding against stone in a shower of sparks.

We saw the tractor at the same moment. It was backing out of a farm gate just beyond the railway bridge, solid and huge and encircled in a cone of soft yellow light.

I slammed on the brakes. Put every ounce of willpower into stopping the Allegro before it crunched into the high stone arch of the bridge.

I heard the dreadful wail of tyres screeching against the damp road, heard the brakes lock up and the suddenly static tyres lose purchase on the slick surface.

The driver threw up his arms to shield his face and then he was out of my line of sight. I heard the horrifying impact: a cacophony of crunching metal and smashing glass.

I sat there, the bonnet of the car inches from the railway arch, blood rushing in my ears, my arms aching, gasping for air.

I had to climb into the passenger seat to get out of the car. The driver's side was pushed up against the stone wall. I stepped out onto the road with legs that shook like a newborn foal's. Half a dozen tottering steps and then I was staring at the carnage of the scene beyond the bridge.

The vehicle had gone into the tractor at speed. The whole of the bonnet had crumpled in on itself. The impact had shattered the glass of the rear windscreen and through its jagged edges I could see the hole that the driver had left as he catapulted from the seat and through the front windscreen.

I staggered forward. I could hear a man's voice, shouting for help. Beyond the tractor, a man in overalls was standing in the road with his hands on his head. He snapped his head towards me as he heard me approach. There were tears on his face and all the blood seemed to have leached out of his features.

'Don't, love, don't look, it's . . . he came out of nowhere, you don't want to see . . . my wife's calling for help . . .'

I squeezed past the colossal back wheel of the tractor. Looked down at the man from the train, laid on his side in the middle of the road, blood leaking like jam from the crater in the side of his head. One of his legs was stuck out at a gory angle. His lips were moving but no sound was coming out.

'He must have been doing seventy!' sobbed the man from the tractor. 'I didn't see him. Christ, he's going to die, I know he's going to die.'

I put a hand on his arm. Made him look at me. 'You have a phone?'

He nodded. 'I shouted for the wife to ring.'

'Go and make sure. I'll stay with him. Sometimes these things aren't as bad as they look.'

He looked at me with eyes so grateful that I nearly wept for him. 'Will I get in trouble?' he asked, investing me with a level of authority. He didn't ask who I was and where I'd been going but he wanted to know if everything would be OK.

'It wasn't your fault,' I said. 'I saw what happened. You couldn't have done anything.'

He gave a grateful nod and then hurried away towards the open gates of the farmhouse. A moment later I was alone, squatting down beside the man from the train. I put my face in his line of sight but he didn't respond, just kept moving his lips and making horrible little fluttering noises. I went through his pockets. He had a Heckler and Koch P7 9 mm handgun in a soft leather shoulder holster. I took it. His wallet contained nearly forty pounds and a driving licence in the name of Alexander Ross. His inside pocket bulged a little. Inside I found a radio. It was service-issue, switched on, red light blinking away.

I didn't know what to think so I didn't think anything at all. Just left him there and walked back to the mangled remains of his car. It was a Mercedes W123 200 and still smelled new. The inside was a mess of loose documents and shards of glass. I opened the back door and scooped up handfuls of shiny white paper. There wasn't much light but I could make out enough. This was my personnel file.

I took everything. Took the key from the mangled ignition and opened the boot. Two cases, service-issue. A long black case and a larger, boxy unit. I unclipped the latches. The camera was state-of-the-art, with a night-vision scope and built-in microphone that could pick up a conversation at 300 yards. The rectangular box contained a Walther WA 2000 sniper rifle and scope. I took both cases. Hefted them back to the car and climbed back into the passenger seat, shuffling across to the driving position and leaving both boxes on the seat beside me.

I took a breath. Closed my eyes and let my breathing settle. Then, with some reluctant hissing of tyres and the kind of clunking noise that made me glad I wasn't the owner, I managed to pull the Allegro back onto the road and effect a painful seven-point turn.

I nursed the car back up the road and out of sight. Only when I'd put a couple of miles between myself and the crash scene did I pull in through an open farm gate and switch off the engine, killing the lights. I smoked a cigarette, fingers trembling. I checked the handgun. Two bullets were missing from the clip. I couldn't help but think of Felicity and John, but my rational mind told me it was impossible. He'd been following me – there was no way he could have got to the house.

Finally, by the flickering flame of the dying man's lighter, I looked through my file. Read about my successes and failures, my every assessment, my potential usefulness to the enemy. I was marked as 'high risk' and my political affiliations were classified as 'potentially subversive'. Somebody had circled a line buried in the conclusions. It read: '. . . briefly considered for role within Joint Intelligence Division's classified Angels programme'. Had I? What the hell was the Angels programme?

Then the radio crackled into life.

'Munkar, this is Samael. Is the package secure? Over.'

I stopped breathing. Closed my eyes. There was no doubting the voice that hissed from the radio on the passenger seat.

I couldn't help myself. I picked up the radio and spoke through gritted teeth.

'Hello, Walt.'

CORDELIA

He recovered himself quickly. There was only the slightest pause before the radio crackled back to life and his voice bled into the dark stillness of the creaking car.

'Mrs Hemlock,' he said, softly. 'Mrs Cordelia Hemlock. This is a surprise.'

I didn't give him the satisfaction of a reply. I didn't know what the hell was happening so I couldn't think of anything smart to say. He wanted to make sure that anybody listening in knew exactly who I was, but as to who that listener might be, or why I was at all relevant, remained a mystery.

'Can I presume that some mishap has befallen our mutual friend?'

I swallowed hard. Lit another cigarette with the lighter and looked again at the faint writing on its side. 'Big D's,' I read, coldly. 'Belize City. Our mutual friend got himself a souvenir.'

'He mentioned that you'd taken it,' said Walt, matter-of-factly, in a burst of static. I could almost hear him thinking, moving the pieces around in his head. 'He got himself in quite the state after you left him on the train. I fear he may have one or two speeding tickets as a result of making up for lost time.'

'They're the least of his problems now,' I said. 'Nasty accident. Tried to run me off the road and it didn't end well for him. Last I saw, he was leaking from places you shouldn't leak from.'

There was silence for a moment. I stared out through the dirty glass. In the distance was the little hill that dipped down to the valley where Gilsland lay. Across the road was the big old castle and the remains of the old prisoner-of-war camp. I hadn't realized until that moment just how much this little pocket of desolate land felt like home.

'He's dead?' asked Walt, and there was a note in his voice that sounded a lot like sorrow.

'Not yet,' I said. 'Went into a tractor at sixty. Went through the window. I don't think he'll be getting up.'

Walt fell silent again. 'I'm sure you feel like you've scored a point, Cordelia. I have no doubt you believe yourself to be the victim of persecution and that you have defended yourself from unimaginable horrors. Would it matter to you if I told you that he was not your enemy?'

I finished the cigarette. Threw the butt out of the window, pissed off at everybody and everything. 'He tried to kill me.'

'He tried to stop you.'

'He threatened my life. Told me I had to go back to London to face the inquisition.'

'He tried to keep you out of harm's way.'

'I've played the recording,' I said, refusing to believe him. 'They've got you and me talking in the crypt. They've got Cranham giving the go-ahead to do what needs to be done.'

He gave a noise somewhere between a laugh and a sigh. 'I recorded us, Cordelia. Do try and use that marvellous mind of yours. I recorded Cranham. I sent the recording to your superiors as a courtesy to our friendship and the fact that I remain fond of you. It was clearly a mistake for which I will pay heavily. You are bringing nothing to this operation but difficulty and nuisance.'

'Nuisance?' I shouted, furious at the word. 'You approached me! You're the one using my bloody house! You're the one who told me to take it to Talbot . . .'

I stopped, bitterly conscious of how skilfully I'd been manipulated. Everything that had happened in the past twenty-four hours had occurred exactly as Walt wanted it to. He was playing a game and I was a piece to be moved around the board. But how to win? Who was the enemy?

'I'd imagine you're giving yourself a headache right about now,' said Walt, chattily. 'I should imagine that excellent mind of yours is fizzing with questions. Give me your location and we can finish this conversation in person.'

I stayed silent. I became aware of the perfect quiet of the night. There would be sirens soon, I was sure, but for now the darkness was a velvet curtain swallowing up every tiny sound. I stared out through the open window, my senses on high alert. I needed to get to the house. Needed to get Felicity and John somewhere safe. Only then could I try and put it all together and work out what kind of danger I was in.

'Your friends are comfortable,' said Walt, flatly. 'Comfortable enough, at least. I fear that the gentleman took quite a beating but the lady seems to be without injury.'

I froze, the blood in my body suddenly feeling ice-cold. 'He's ill. He's been in hospital . . .'

'And yet you sent him to the house.'

'You said you were bringing people. There were personal items I didn't want you to see.'

'Pictures of your son, yes? How sweet. A lie, of course, but a sweet one.'

I chewed my lip, cursing myself for ever involving my friends. 'Whatever it is that's happening, they're no part of it.'

'You're right,' he said. 'They're flies in the ointment and you put them there. You've put yourself there too, despite my best attempts to keep you from becoming involved. Why won't you listen to those who care about you?'

I didn't reply. He sounded just like my old tutor at Oxford, puce with rage at my inability to follow instructions or to do what he knew to be in my best interests. He never realized how much I enjoyed him shouting at me. Didn't realize what an effect his righteous indignation had upon the stubborn, bright-eyed, twenty-year-old girl in his class – not until she had seduced him and got herself pregnant with his child.

I looked out into the darkness. The dawn would reveal the view I'd fallen in love with; the landscape that I'd first glimpsed in one of the many property particulars that Cranham had insisted I leaf through when we first came to our arrangement. He would buy whatever property I wanted and provide a home for me to raise my fatherless son, and I would marry him in a chaste, courteous arrangement that permitted him to live as he wished.

'I fear that you no longer think you can trust me,' said Walt, the radio sizzling like an egg frying in hot fat. 'I ask you to reconsider. I didn't want you involved but now I am a man short and have enough plates to spin without having to worry about you clattering your way onto the stage. Stay where you are and

I shall send a gentleman to escort you the last leg of the journey.
You must be tired. And I know you will have questions. Put
the gun down and place your hands on the wheel and I shall
make sure you are treated like a maharani.'

I heard the faintest echo to his words, as if he was speaking
inside a small, empty room. I looked down at the gun on the
passenger seat and tried to use good judgement. Would handing
myself to Walt offer sanctuary or fresh dangers? He knew
about John and Felicity, that was clear. But was he the one
threatening their safety or the one in the best position to
save their lives?

'Cordelia, you can't do this on your own. There are people
involved who will not waste a moment's thought on ending
your life, or the lives of your friends. And while that might
actually suit my purpose, I have done my utmost to keep you
from danger, even if that may seem hard to believe. Please,
leave the gun where it is and keep both hands on the wheel.
I give you my word, no harm will . . .'

I heard him at the last possible moment – the faintest rustle
of a boot disturbing the long, damp grass. I saw him at my
window – yellowy eyes looming from the slot between jacket
and boilerman's cap. I grabbed for the gun but he moved
quicker than I did, dropping the radio and lunging forward.
He struck me with the butt of his gun, just below the jawline.
The world went dark: consciousness disappearing as if swirling
down a perfect hole in the centre of my vision.

The last thing I saw was Walt looking down at me and
checking my pulse.

He shook his head. 'Sorry, Hinny.'

And then there was nothing but the dark.

FELICITY

Transcript 0025, recorded December 1, 2016

I felt the exhaustion settling on me like snow. My clothes all felt too heavy and my legs suddenly didn't have the strength to hold me up any more. I had to steady myself against the wall, sploshing the hot coffee on my hand and cursing like the devil. John was on his knees facing the door, looking like he was about to start a hundred-yard dash. I think I may have started laughing. It all just seemed a bit farcical. I don't like new things. I'm not one who craves exciting experiences or a change from the old routine. I'm happy with my own four walls. I'm never more content than sitting on the edge of the bathtub waiting for it to fill up. I couldn't find my temper, though God and John know I've got one. I was just bone-weary. Tearful, I suppose, though it was more a case of my eyes leaking tears than giving in to that snotty sobbing you see on the telly.

'You hear that?'

'The arguing?' I asked. 'Aye, somebody's in a lather.'

'I couldn't work out who was saying what,' grunted John, pulling himself up and taking the coffee cup from my hand. He took a sip. Grimaced, and took another.

'The man with the gun seemed to have his dander up. I recognized the voice.'

'Was it the other who gave me a thump?'

'I don't think so,' I said, trying to untangle the different strands of recent memory. 'God only knows how many people are in the house.'

John leaned himself against the wall, his arm against mine. Pelletier had left a packet of cigarettes and a box of matches next to the flask; an unremarked courtesy that marked him out as less of a so-and-so than his mates. John took one from the packet and lit up. He pulled a face.

'American,' he said. 'Haven't had one of these since the war.'

'Our James got you that crate for your birthday,' I said. 'Him and Heron . . .'

I tailed off. The wounds were still too painful. Grief's a scab. You only know the wound is still raw when you start to play with the edges.

'They're still at it,' said John, cocking his ear. There were crashes and bangs and angry shouts drifting in from outside.

'I hope that Sera's OK,' I said, fretfully. 'She was proper lovely. Proper Florence Nightingale, that one. She and her brother are supposed to be telling their life stories to some important person. That's why they're here. I think they've been through a lot.'

'Guatemala?' asked John, testing the word. 'We watched that documentary, don't you remember.'

'On Guatemala? I've never watched a documentary on Guatemala.'

He looked at me like I was soft in the head. 'No, on Belize.'

'John Goose, we are not talking about blasted Belize!'

He sighed, irritated with me. Looked at the glowing tip of his cigarette as if he were trying to hypnotize himself into a better temper. 'Belize is next to Guatemala, Felicity. You said so yourself. And we watched that programme about Belize. On the BBC. Horrible pit of a place, jungle and swamps and a little group of British paratroopers guarding the border with Guatemala. Don't you remember?'

I waved a hand, sick of his prattle. 'I was probably reading my magazine.'

'It was about our soldiers. The Brits, like. The Guatemalans next door – they want Belize. And Belize is British territory so we had lads out there defending it. They looked proper miserable. Hot and bothered and complaining about being so far from home and not knowing what they were even doing there. They had the odd scuffle with the enemy but it weren't much more than lobbing bricks at them.'

I looked at him for a bit, wondering if he wanted me to add anything. 'And?'

'And nothing.' He shrugged. 'Well, maybe nothing. I just

mean, with Cordelia doing what she does and all the accents out there – I don't think they're going to open the door for us come the morning, do you?'

I didn't like the look on his face. I could see him working out our options and finding none. 'That thing in his pocket – it might alert somebody who'll come to help.'

'Aye,' he said. 'And it might not work, or it might tell the wrong person.'

'Cordelia,' I said, and there was some comfort to be found in her name. 'She'll know that we're not home. She'll have rung to see how we got on at the house and she'll have put two and two together.'

I felt his fingers against mine. Felt him give my hand a squeeze and I swear it was enough to make me feel as though we were seconds from the bloody end.

'Christ, back up,' said John, quickly, pushing me back against the wall. His hearing was better than mine and he heard the footsteps before me. A moment later the door was opening and Sera was thrown bodily into the room. One of the soldier-types had dragged her by the hair and then shoved her down, spitting out a swear word at her and then at me before slamming the door shut behind him. Sera lay where she fell, her dark hair covering her face, one arm over her head like she was expecting a beating.

'Jesus, Mary and Joseph,' I said, trying to stop myself from shaking. 'John, help her.'

'What am I supposed to bloody do?' he asked, looking as lost as me.

'For the love of God,' I muttered, and then I was down at her side, rubbing at her arm, stroking her hair back from her face like she was a nipper and I was her mam. She had a nasty bruise on one cheek and blood running from her nostril. There seemed to be a patch of hair missing from her scalp.

'Sera,' I said, trying to get her to sit up. 'John, grab that coffee . . .'

I took the flask and waved it under her nose, feeling hopeless. Her eyelids fluttered for a moment and when she started to open her mouth, her lips stayed half stuck together and she had to work her tongue into the dry places just to get some spit working around her mouth. She sipped at the coffee, sitting back against me, wincing as she raised her hands to her face and checked her bruises.

'Are you all right?' I asked, and it's never anything other than a stupid question.

'Something has gone wrong,' she whispered, looking up and seeing me and then glancing into the darkness where John stood. 'He is better? He is well?'

'I'm soldiering on, love,' said John. 'Grateful to you.'

'Who hurt you?' I asked, feeling my temper start to boil. 'Was it that nasty sod who dumped you here?'

She didn't speak at first. Got a grip of herself and then raised her hands to hold her cross. 'They have deceived me,' she said, and there was exhaustion in her voice. 'The people who tried to help me – they spoke of being on the side of the angels but there is a demon in their midst who will never permit the change that we are promised.'

I looked to John, worry writ in every line of my face, feeling so far out of my depth that I couldn't imagine ever nearing the shore. 'I don't understand,' I said, and it seemed to refer to so much more than the events of the evening so far.

'My brother, he knows now what has been done. I did not have his faith, you see. I had doubts and when I spoke them he quieted me and swore that our protectors could indeed be trusted. Now he sees the truth. That man . . .' She pointed at the wall as if expecting a monster to come through it.

'Go on, love,' said John, squatting down beside us and giving a hiss of pain as he remembered his open wound.

'A deal is being made,' she said. 'In there. Tonight. A deal that condemns my people, my country to a silent extermination. We came here to speak truth and to prevail upon the decent people to open their eyes to the suffering that they permit. Instead we are given more lies. I could take no more. Nor could my brother. This was done to me to silence his protests. But he will not yield. No matter what they threaten, he will not give them what they want.'

'What is it they want?' I asked, feeling her hands grabbing at mine and clutching them to herself like I was a priest giving the last rites.

She closed her eyes. 'They are waiting for a man. An important man. We were told we would be given the chance to address him – to explain what is happening and what we saw. Instead we are to be silenced. Lies will be told and if we do not cooperate then the killings will continue.'

It broke my heart to see the tears fall. I held her like we were sisters. John just squatted there, his face all grey and poorly-looking. He looked around as if he wanted to find the length of pipe but he gave up in the tic of a clock. What could he do? What could any of us do?

Then we heard it. A perfect pop, like somebody stepping on a brown bag.

And Sera, pushed up against my chest, began to sob.

CORDELIA

A sudden sharp sting at my wrist and then a great chill flood of pain spilling down from my crown. I woke up with a hiss and a groan, the taste of blood on my tongue and a spiteful tingling in my fingertips. Everything felt musty and thick, as if the air were full of grass seeds and feathers. I didn't open my eyes at first. I feared that if I let even a chink of light in then the lump of pain at the base of my skull would explode like a grenade.

'Her ladyship awakes.'

Walter Renwick. I felt the words on the bare skin at my neck. He was so close to me it took all of my willpower not to jerk away. Goosepimples rose on my skin where the warm air from his mouth touched my flesh. I realized how cold I was. How uncomfortable. I made fists with my hands, trying to make sense of myself. I felt cords bite into the skin at my wrists. Tried to shuffle my feet and felt the same rough material against my ankles. My bare ankles. My breath came out in a rush as I got the picture clear. I wasn't naked, not completely, but I'd been tied to a hard-backed chair, arms bound behind my back with my ankles tethered to the chair legs. My boots and socks had been removed. I started to shiver. Started to weep.

'Oh Hinny, I can't tell you how distressing this is to witness. Please, open your eyes.'

Gradually, painfully, I let my eyelids creak open. I was in a farm building. Tumbledown walls and rotten mounds of damp hay, chocolate-brown oak timbers holding up a roof full of holes. Walt was sitting on a picnic chair a couple of feet in front of me, a torch on his knee throwing a great cone of light into the space between us. I couldn't tell if it was the torchlight or the head injury but everything seemed to flicker; to shrink and grow, ripple and tear itself in two. The blackness beyond the glow of the torch seemed to shimmer like ink and it was impossible to properly discern Walt's features – the angle of the torch creating unnatural hollows and distortions. It was like talking to a pumpkin lantern.

'I thought we were friends,' I whispered, and it came out thick and blurry and the taste of blood on my tongue became more pronounced. I sniffed back snot and tears and blood. Hated myself for my weakness. Tried to find enough anger to show some fight.

He shook his head at me – an act of almost paternal exasperation. My thoughts became a maelstrom of conflicting impulses and emotions. I was scared almost witless, of course, but more than anything else I was confused. Why me? Why here? Why any of this? Memories started rising: scraps of recollection that floated on the still water of my consciousness like dead fish. Had the rumours really been true? Was Walt really working for the enemy? Was he the dissident, the Soviet sympathizer and national traitor that superiors and underlings alike had whispered about? The thought sickened me, though whether it was a betrayal of his country or simply disgust at my own naiveté, I was in too much pain to work out.

He ran a hand through his hair. The movement changed the angle of the light so I could make out what he was wearing. He looked smart. Fitted suit, tastefully patterned tie, white shirt. He wore a dark overcoat and had teased his hair into a neat side-parting. His skin still had that puffed-up, unhealthy look about it, but the scruffy little mess of my acquaintance had been replaced by somebody who looked every inch the professional.

'Cordelia,' he said, tiredness in his voice. 'A friend, you say?' He looked skyward, cocking his head as if listening to a voice. Sucked on the thought as if it were a boiled sweet. 'I don't think I have such a simplistic thing as a friend, my dear. I'm not sure I would have a use for such a person. But yes, there are those of whom I think warmly. And I do count you among that number.'

I shivered, using the motion to disguise my attempts to tug at the bonds. They were expertly tied. I wasn't getting out of here unless he released me.

'This is how you treat the people you like?'

He smiled, genuinely pleased with me. 'It is, yes! And I don't expect you to understand it or condone it and I certainly don't imagine that after the curtailment of this night's activities that you will be inviting me to any social engagements. But I do hope that somewhere in the distant future you realize how much it pains me to see you in this position, and that you perhaps feel a whiff of gratitude that I spared you the alternative.'

I opened my mouth wider, feeling the bruise on my jawbone bloom with pain. 'The alternative?'

'There are people who believe you are more trouble than you are worth,' he said, spreading his hands apologetically. 'They see no reason to spare you and have only indulged my mercy out of their dedication to the cause.'

He sounded strange; an eerie kind of apostolic zeal entering his voice. It sounded as though he was speaking for the benefit of a rapt congregation rather than to me.

'The whispers were right, then?' I asked, my voice croaky, throat dry. 'You're a Soviet?'

He reeled back as if slapped. Screwed up his face in utter confusion. 'A Soviet?'

'A communist,' I said, feeling lost. 'The other side.'

He put his head in his palm, taking a moment to gather himself. 'Oh Cordelia, have I really misjudged you so completely? A Soviet? A KGB infiltrator? That's the only motivation of which you can conceive? Good Lord, girl, how tremendously parochial you have become. Have I left it too long, I wonder? Perhaps the young firebrand of whom I thought so highly has already been transformed by the Whitehall machine. Have I really wasted time and resources on nostalgia?'

I couldn't face swallowing again with my throat in such pain, so I coughed the blood and spat into the darkness. I put all of my anger into the glare that I fixed upon him, even as my mind replayed his words looking for any indication as to his agenda.

'So who are you working for?' I asked. 'What's this all for? Who's the enemy, who are your friends? What is it you're here to do and why the hell am I involved?'

He rubbed at his face again, pursing his lips as if he were

tasting the questions. He screwed up his features again; a grimace of genuine pain. 'I'm not a well man, Cordelia,' he said, and his voice sounded a little more like his own. 'I won't still be here when you all reap the benefits of my manoeuvring. I've spent a lifetime working in the shadows, hiding secrets, forcing people to betray their better natures, preying on people's vulnerabilities, their weaknesses, their vices – I've placed people in danger in the pursuit of freedoms that do not truly exist and I have taken lives to defend a way of life that I do not condone.' He looked at me with those glassy eyes, his features sorrowful; lugubrious. 'I have done great and terrible things in service of the Crown, Cordelia. I have asked for nothing in return other than a sense that I was corrupting myself, and others, in service of a greater good.'

'You're the one who told me that patriotism is absurd,' I said, bitterly. 'When did you ever act like a nationalist? When did you ever hold up British ideals?'

He looked straight through me. I felt, for an instant, as if there were somebody behind me – somebody holding a blade or a gun, seeking approval to stop my impertinence.

'I don't mean patriotism, Cordelia,' he said, tiredly. 'I mean humanity. I mean the sanctity of life – the freedom of each individual to at least try and reach old age without becoming collateral damage in the war between ambitions and ideologies; nations and ways of life. I hold no ideology up as superior to another. Communist or capitalist – they are two scorpions in the same upturned glass. My duty, as I saw it, was to do something that might be considered "good" as opposed to "evil".'

'You sound like Ronald fucking Reagan,' I said, scorn twisting my lip. 'Moral superiority? A force for good in the world? Service to humanity? Jesus, Walt, were you always out of your mind or have you hit your head?'

I didn't see the blow coming. The back of my head exploded in a riot of clanging bells and fireworks as something hard struck me right on the top of my head. I saw stars. Oozed tears. I'd have thrown up were there anything in my stomach. I fell forward, slack, spit dribbling from my mouth, waiting for the great thudding agony to pass.

'Please,' I heard Walt say, tiredly. 'Please, a little compassion, yes? She will come to understand. I give you my word, she will understand.'

I tried to turn my head, groggy but desperate to see who was behind me. All I could make out was the sagging brick-work, a rusting metal feeder mounted on the nearest wall with a two-pronged pitchfork leaning at its side. The air smelled of damp and rot; of wet wood. Nobody had used this byre in a long time.

'I don't care what you're doing,' I muttered. 'Guatemala. Belize. I'm not important, Walt. And my friends, John and Felicity – they can keep their mouths shut. Whatever you're doing, I don't need to know. Everything you think about what we do, about the things we have to do in service of something greater than ourselves – I think the way you do. You've seen my file, you know my politics. I've worked for the company all these years because keeping busy and doing something exciting is the only way that I can stop myself going mad. Grief nearly killed me and catching a bad person revived me. I do this job because the alternative is misery and a noose. People matter more to me than a flag, Walt. I'd kick the queen in the ribs right now if it meant you let Felicity go.'

I became more animated as I talked, wriggling and writhing and desperately trying to loosen my ropes. I felt my skin tear against the rough surface. Felt tears leaking from my eyes and suffered a sudden flash of memory; years before, basic training, a hand on the back of my head and my face submerged in dirty water; my instructors simulating real-life torture and applauding me for holding out longer than any of the other recruits. I never yielded. Never gave up my secrets. But that had been years before when I was too damn stubborn to let anybody beat me. It wasn't real. I'd have told Walt anything he wanted to know if he just cut my bonds and told me to take my friends and go.

'It's not up to me to let them go, Cordelia,' he said, softly. 'I don't have them. The gentlemen at your house – the gentlemen who await my arrival – they have them. What they choose to do with them depends entirely upon the outcome of our little tête-à-tête.'

'You and me?' I gasped. 'Whatever you ask, whatever you want . . .'

He waved a hand as if briefly perturbed by a wasp. 'You and I? Good God, no. I've told you before, you are nothing but a nuisance here. You were not meant to be involved.'

'It's my house!' I shouted, unable to contain myself.

'A happy accident.' Walt smiled. 'A quiet place near an out-of-the-way airfield, far enough from London to be unobserved and still registered in the name of Cranham Hemlock. It's perfect. You said so yourself when I requested a safe place for my associates. Of course, I had long since identified it and begun preparations, but it did my ailing heart good to see that you were wise enough to concur.'

I gritted my teeth. My brain felt as if it was running out of my ears. 'Just fucking tell me what you want!'

Another blow from behind. This one crunched into my side, a perfect shot that snapped a rib clean in two and drove all the air from my body. My mind filled with red and purples, the pain so intense I couldn't conceive of a world where I could stand or walk or speak again. I let out a desperate little mewling sound, blood suddenly running from my mouth and nose. All I wanted to do was slide to the floor and lay there until the ground covered me up.

'Please, Luis,' said Walt without emotion. 'I did ask you to consider my fondness for the young lady. I appreciate your devotion to our purpose but I must ask that you refrain from causing her any more harm. If we are called upon to take more decisive action it would be a comfort to me to know it was an act of mercy. Clean, quick, efficient, painless. It saddens me to see her in such distress.'

A voice from behind me, strangely accented: Spanish but earthy; hard. 'No more talking. Do what you came here to do. He's arrived.'

Walt looked past me, eyes brightening. 'He has? Excellent. I suppose, then, that this is what we've been waiting for. I trust that I do not have to repeat your orders. We are all briefed, yes?'

'Si,' came the voice again. 'We will be listening.'

'And I shall give you much to listen to,' said Walt, with a

smile. 'I must bid you farewell, Cordelia. Your husband and I have much to discuss.'

He stood up, straightening his clothes. I could barely make him out for the tears in my eyes. As he came towards me I flinched, shuffling back in my chair and feeling the skewers of absolute pain push deep into my stomach. He put his hand on my cheek. Squatted down.

'There remains a softness in my thoughts, Hinny,' he said, one hand snaking behind my back and his hand fastening over my immobile hand. 'Please, remember the business we are engaged in. And do keep an open mind. I wish you the very best of luck.'

I felt him push the cold metal object into my palm. Felt the softest brush of his lips against my cheek.

'Luis, I believe our guests have irritated one another long enough. I will ask you to escort me. The others are to await the outcome of our discussions before decisive action is taken.'

He walked past me without another word. As I looked up, the shadows at the edges of the barn seemed to rearrange themselves. What had been darkness became men. Men in black clothing and balaclavas; men who had melded so perfectly with the crow-black air that it felt, through the tears and the pain, as if they were some other-worldly manifestation: darkness made flesh.

I counted six of them, trooping soundlessly past me. Saw the glint of light hitting the metal of the assault weapons slung over their shoulders.

In moments I was alone. Whatever presence I had felt behind me had disappeared with the others. I let myself sob for a spell, the pain in my side more intense than anything I had ever known. Only when I felt that I had wept myself numb, did I probe the surface of the metal object with my tingling finger and thumb.

Walt had left me the lighter. He had placed it in my hand and told me not to forget the business we were in. I didn't understand what he meant but I knew that, for whatever reason, he was giving me a chance to save myself. He was involved in something so very much bigger than me. I could burn through my bonds and slip away and never look back.

Saving my own skin never occurred to me. All I could think of was Felicity and what she would be feeling as wave after wave of danger engulfed her. I closed my eyes and willed her to be safe; to be strong – to be the woman I knew she was capable of being and not the timid little mouse who fretted in the shadows and let people walk all over her. I sent her a promise; a pledge that whatever it took, if she could be strong for a little longer, I would make things right. I would take the pain away. I would die to save her life.

I ignited the lighter. Felt my skin begin to blister, and the ropes begin to burn.

FELICITY

She finished the coffee. Drained it from the thermos like she was a working man tasting the first pint of the day. If it scorched her mouth she didn't show it. I wondered how long she'd been without a proper meal. Wondered what a proper meal even looked like to her. She didn't seem poorly-fed. In fact, there was a pleasing roundness to her features that suggested she ate well. But her world was unimaginable to me. Perhaps mine was to her. But we didn't seem particularly different as we sat by the wall, huddled up against each other, cold and sore and not knowing what was coming next.

John stood beneath the hole in the ceiling, looking up and occasionally running his hands over his bandaged side. The fabric was already stained an unhealthy pink and I could see how much pain he was in. Whatever strength he'd found over the past couple of hours was draining out of him in front of me. There was no way he was going to have the fight in him to climb into the roof space and wriggle through the dark and the filth towards something or someone who could help.

'It was a shot in the air,' said John, again. 'Somebody was making a fuss and one of the buggers with the guns fired a warning shot. I'd put money on it.'

Sera, her hand in mine, gave a weak little smile. Her eyes hadn't stopped pouring with tears since we heard the crack of the gunshot. All she could picture was her brother, laid out in the room at the end of the corridor, sightless eyes staring out at a distant, darkened land.

'I wish I knew why this was happening,' I muttered. 'I'm a grandma, you know. First bairn just out of nappies. Our eldest, he's living in Carlisle with a nice young lass. That's the way of it now, isn't it? Nobody marries any more, or that's how it seems. But they're a lovely little family. I've got their Christmas presents wrapped. We haven't got our tree up yet. Do you have Christmas trees in your country?'

I heard myself prattling on but couldn't seem to stop myself. I just whittered like we were old friends who hadn't caught up in an age. I don't even know how much of what I was saying she really understood, but she seemed to find the sound of my voice oddly soothing and told me to keep talking when I ran out of nonsense to say.

'We have Christmas trees in our church,' she said, quietly. 'There are mahogany trees near my home.'

'Mahogany?' asked John, surprised. 'Like the furniture?'

'I think the name comes from the tree,' said Sera, with that faint smile of hers. 'I too had planned a splendid Christmas. We had celebrated *La Quema del Diablo* – the burning of the devil, casting out the bad in preparation for the coming of Christ. We had begun the *Nacimiento* – the finest we had ever created.'

'The what?' I asked.

'The . . . I suppose you would call it a Christmas scene? Father told me the word. The . . . nativity?'

I nodded, catching up. 'You make them too, do you? We do this thing with candles and goose feathers and a red ribbon. We do something at Easter with hard-boiled eggs too. Steep them in onion skins and leaves and make pretty patterns on the shells. I don't really know why.'

'Tradition is important to us,' she said, and there was a little faraway smile on her face, even as the tears fell. 'The whole family joins in with the Nacimiento, dyeing the sawdust, collecting the perfect cloth, the right linens and flowers and stones. Each year we build a new one and we try to be the grandest in the village. Some of the folk religion – the old ways – they find their way into the nativity but if it were wrong to do so I feel sure Father would have told us so. It was he who said that while pride is sinful, so is sloth, and God wants us to do our very best. There is some competition between the families. It matters. My son, he had saved his own money to purchase this splendid cloth to adorn Christ's crib, and . . .' She stopped herself. Looked down at nothing and gripped my hand.

'You're a mam?'

'A mam? Oh, *si*, a mother. I do not know. Is there a word for a mother who has lost her child?'

My insides twisted up on themselves. It felt like there were roots wrapping around my throat. I didn't know what to say or even if I had the voice to do so. 'My lad was a grown-up when we lost him,' I croaked, my body so stiff it was like I'd died and nobody had told me. 'My friend – the lady who's house this is – she lost her baby when he was two. It nearly killed her. There's no feeling like grief. I'm so very sorry for your sadness.'

She nuzzled against me like she was a house-cat wanting a stroke and it suddenly didn't feel odd to hold her tight. 'He went back,' she said, quietly. 'As my brother and I fled, he went back to fight. Will I ever find a way to make sense of that, do you think? Eight years old and more courage than me.'

I couldn't offer anything of use. I just patted her arm. 'Bad things happened?'

She nodded. 'The same lies will be told, I am sure. I believed that I would be able to persuade the people in power that they should not listen to those lies. I came here to try and make changes. But I know now, even with God's grace, that I have been told more untruths. There is no "powerful man" who can change the mind of a president. There is no force for good working against the evil done by my government. There is no hope for my people. Nobody really cares.'

I didn't like seeing her so downhearted. What can you say to somebody whose unhappiness seems to reach all the way into their marrow? 'People can surprise you,' I said, hoping it didn't sound too pathetic. 'People do care about each other, I think. They just get caught up in their own silly stuff. I didn't know about some of the things that were done to people in France during the war. Then I met somebody who told me about them, and after that I cared a lot. I didn't know about Guatemala. Now I know about it, I hope that whoever's doing the bad things will stop doing them.'

'You are very kind,' she said, and she didn't sound like she was making fun.

'I just wish I could do something,' I said, meaning it.

'Your government,' she said, a little more animatedly. 'Tell your government the truth about what their allies do. Make them see that to look the other way is to collaborate.'

I looked up at John. He couldn't meet my eye. 'Me?' I asked. 'Who would I say that to? Why would anybody listen to me?'

'She doesn't vote,' grunted John. He'd lit another cigarette but seemed to be struggling to inhale.

'We yearn for democracy,' said Sera, turning to face me. 'That is all that we seek. The promises we were made, the purpose of the fight, it is all in the name of democracy – for the right to choose our rulers. That is the purpose of our struggle.'

I felt a bit picked on. I didn't vote because I felt it was none of my business. Cordelia always gave me a right ear-bashing for it and told me I was letting down all the women who'd fought for my rights, but I'd always get in a tizzy with her and say that I'd rather not bother than get it wrong.

'They're moving,' said John, suddenly. 'Listen, footsteps . . .'

We fell silent, straining our every sense. Sure enough, we heard the mumble of voices and the crack of floorboards as an untold number of figures passed by our door. They were moving towards the main body of the house. Cordelia only ever lived in a couple of the rooms when she called this place home. She built herself a big comfy nest out of drapes and rugs and clothes, all piled up in the centre of the empty living room and surrounded by pile after pile of books. She lived in there for months after Stefan died, too feckless to know how to turn the electricity back on or how to work the washing machine. She got thin and dirty and sank in on herself as if she were rotting. But we found each other and saved ourselves and did something half decent along the way. I kept trying to imagine her turning up and explaining things to everybody and John and me getting embarrassed at all the apologies and handshakes and back-slapping. I just couldn't make it feel like anything other than wishful thinking. I didn't want Cordelia walking in on whatever was happening in her home. I wanted her safe, wherever she was.

'American accent,' said John, moving away from the door. 'More than one.'

'They are American and Canadian,' said Sera. 'British too.

The big man who arrived in the expensive car – he sounded like the man who reads the news.'

'Your news?' I asked.

'BBC.' She smiled. 'Very . . . what is it Father used to say . . . very *well-spoken*. A large man. Well dressed but not particularly handsome. I do not wish to be unkind but he was quite fat.'

I shrugged, not expecting to recognize her description. 'And who was arguing?'

'The two American men were arguing with the soldiers. Something had gone wrong. They were being kept waiting. The man with the cigar was becoming very angry. My brother, when he found his strength, he began to demand to see the man we trust, demanded to speak to the man we were promised. Instead we were given this fat man and two more men in suits; eyes that saw everything but cared nothing. Then we knew, whatever is to happen this night, we will not secure change for our people. I would have been happier to die with my son than to be disappeared here in this unfamiliar place.'

'Disappeared?' asked John.

'That is the word that is used. Hundreds of men, women, children. Thousands. Tens of thousands. We do not know. The soldiers come, the agents come – people are taken and they do not return. Sometimes a farmer ploughing his field will unearth bones. They plough them back in, afraid of what their discovery will bring. It has been this way for twenty years.'

'And nobody's doing anything?' I asked. 'Why aren't we helping?'

'We?' she asked.

'Britain, I mean. Or the Americans. Why aren't we stopping them? What are we for if we don't do that?'

She shook her head as if she were a teacher explaining arithmetic to an uncomprehending child. 'The Americans finance our enemies,' she explained. 'Train them. Arm them. Give them images from their satellites. Your British, they permit Guatemalan soldiers, squads of assassins with no other responsibility than to hunt and kill – they permit them to enter Belize and hunt for those who have escaped the torture chambers and the guns.'

I shook my head. 'No, why would we do that?'

'Communists,' grunted John. 'Same as all that Cuba stuff twenty years ago. They don't want communists in their back yard, do they? The Americans either support the government or they have to be OK with the people rising up and governing themselves, and if they do that, they might just choose communism. So they have to pick a side.'

'And the side they have chosen is responsible for a silent genocide,' said Sera, a quiet malice adding barbed wire to her words. 'They talk about evil empires while funding the men who kill my people as if they were worth nothing at all. Our president, he is a religious zealot. He believes his actions to be ordained by God. I am a godly person. I believe in peace and humility and loving our Heavenly Father with acts of kindness and charity. Our president believes in a different god. He is born again, or so he claims. Communists are atheists, and atheists are the minions of Satan. And so he declares himself to be at war with the devil and all of his demons. Whatever he does in pursuit of crushing Satan is ordained by his god and the American evangelists who crow in his ear approve of whatever steps he takes to rid the world of the godless.'

I looked to John. 'Did you know about this?'

He shrugged. 'I just read the sports pages.'

'But you're here to tell our government the truth?' I asked, catching up.

'That was what I believed. Now, I believe I have placed myself directly in the hands of the very people who seek to kill and kill and kill again. A man I once knew, a good man who lost his life in a fight that was not his own – he told me of the man who was, in his words, "on the side of the angels". I sought him out and told him what I knew, risked my life, lost my family. And now I am here, in a stranger's home, waiting to see my brother's body before the bullet ends my suffering.'

John breathed out, a big greasy puff of cigarette smoke and bad air. 'Jesus,' he said, and reached out to put his hand on the wall for support.

'No,' I said, and it surprised me to hear it come out of my

mouth. I shook my head again. 'No, that's not what's happening. Not with the grand-bairn ready for Christmas. Not with what I've spent on shiny bloody wrapping paper. No bloody thank you.'

I hauled myself up. John started towards me but I gave him the look that scares him silent. I picked up the lantern and shone it into the hole in the ceiling. It was dark and dirty, all wires and cobwebs and grime.

'Right,' I said, and if I was scared in that moment I can't honestly say I remember it. It just felt like the only thing to do and there was nobody else who could do it.

I put my foot on the sink. Felt the pain in my joints and hoisted myself up. Then I reached up, standing on tiptoes, fingertips grabbing the rough wood. A moment later John was under me. Sera too. We must have looked like the worst bunch of silly beggars, but in fits and starts they shoved me high enough to get a grip on the wood and haul myself through sheer bloody mindedness into the pitch-dark space between the ceiling of one room, and the floor of the next.

I heard John's voice, muffled and far away. 'Your boots,' he hissed. 'Kick your boots off.'

I did what he said. My clumpy little shoes fell from my stockinged feet. They made no sound and I imagined John standing below to catch them. He said something else to me and I won't lie to you, over the years I've imagined that it was 'I love you' or something to that effect. It probably wasn't. It was probably something practical, or an instruction to keep the noise down. But I didn't say anything in return. I just wriggled forward, splinters in my belly, rough wood against my forearms; spiders and feathers and dirt in my hair, pushing forward blindly into a black, hungry mouth.

CORDELIA

The pain was excruciating. I could feel my skin blister and blacken as the flame chewed slowly through the bonds. I didn't know what I was tied up with but I started to smell something greasy and chemical over the sizzling bacon scent of cooked skin.

I felt the tears pour down my cheeks. Bit down on my tongue, spit frothing on my chin as I kept the scream inside. I pulled against my restraints, feeling the pain in my ribs bloom and grow. I tugged again and lurched to the side. One of the ropes had snapped and my right hand was suddenly free. I twisted in my seat, reaching behind me, the pain in my ribs so bad that I could barely breathe. I started picking at the blackened threads of the remaining rope, shuffling my feet as much as I could to try and work my legs a little freer. My fingers and toes began to tingle as the blood rushed back. I sobbed as my shaking hands disentangled the individual threads, my mind full of images from old books: the urchins in those dark satanic mills; their fingers all thread and blood, oakum and tar.

Suddenly I was free. The ropes fell from my left wrist and I toppled forward, clawing at the ropes around my ankles. I replayed all the sounds that had been beyond my comprehension during those terrible minutes of suffering. I'd heard an engine: a big powerful car. There had been quiet voices. A breeze had ruffled the sweat-soaked skin at the back of my neck.

Gradually I wriggled my feet free from the two expertly tied ropes. There was blood at my ankles and wrists where the cord had eaten through the skin. My thumb and index finger on my right hand were an ugly mess of black and pink: the skin scorched off in places. But the pain was nothing compared to the throb in my ribs. I took a step forward and the simple act of movement was enough to take my breath

away. Gingerly, biting my lower lip, I ran the fingers of my
left hand over my injuries. It was a clean break. If my attacker
had wanted to, they could have driven the split rib up into my
lungs and left me to drown in my own blood. Everything that
had been done had been intentional and professional. So
why had Walt helped me to escape? It was he who'd brought
me there; he who did little to stop the others from hurting
me. Why, at the time of whatever triumph he saw in his near
future, why would he jeopardize it to hand me the lighter and
give me a chance to make a difference.

'*Como te escapaste de puta puta!*'

I moved so fast I almost snapped my neck. A figure had
appeared in the doorway: black clothes, black hat, face paint
and the perfect sugar-white slits of staring eyes.

'*Te mataré donde estés, perra del diablo!*'

He was five or six paces away – the same distance I would
have to cross to reach the pitchfork by the wall. I threw myself
towards it, two manic paces and then a great ungainly leap,
crashing down into the mulch of straw beside the tumbledown
wall and seizing the wooden handle of the pitchfork with both
hands; all pain forgotten as the adrenaline flooded me for one
glorious instant of utter terror.

I heard him slip. Curse. Slither and tumble as he stepped
in my spilled blood and melted flesh.

I didn't think. Didn't aim. Just spun and thrust out with the
pitchfork, bracing the handle against the apex of floor and
wall.

It went into his chest like a table fork into a baked potato.
All the tines went through him and a hot spurt of blood spilled
down onto my upturned face; his eyes two perfect circles, his
mouth opening to vomit up a gout of thick crimson.

He staggered back, the fork sticking out of him like a flag-
pole. Then he clattered down onto his back, kicked out, and
was still. His last breath was an ugly, gurgling sound that I
can still hear if I pay attention to my worst memories. And
I just sat where I was for a moment, blinking a stranger's
blood out of my eyes, replaying the last moments. I'd killed
a man before; a terrible person who had been enjoying the act
of my slow murder far too much to be permitted to live. But

taking a life should always weigh heavily on a person's soul and I felt sick and cold as I realized that this person had died at my hand.

I crawled forward to where he lay. Tried to get a better look at him by the flickering light of the discarded torch, rolling this way and that on the uneven floor so as to cast air-raid lights upon the big, star-scattered sky. I used my good hand to check his pockets. He was wearing black combat trousers tucked into gleaming military-issue boots. American, as far as I could tell. He wore a black all-weather jacket and his belt contained a sheathed blade and half a dozen jacketed rifle bullets, not far off three inches long. I checked his pockets for ID but found nothing. I had to pull the fork from his guts to be able to open his coat, rummaging around in the cooling blood for anything he might be carrying. I found nothing. Only when I rolled down the face mask and pushed up the black hat did I get a real sense of my attacker. He was no more than thirty years old; handsome beneath the black face paint, with fine cheekbones and a pleasantly symmetrical mouth. He was well-built, too: muscled but lean, as if he were an athlete accustomed to living on meat and raw eggs. I almost didn't see the tattoo. The blood leaking from the holes in his chest obscured much of the definition of his torso, but as I was pulling his jacket back down I saw the symbol, inked amateurishly just above where his heart would be. It was a flaming torch held in a fist. I recognized it at once. This man was part of the Kaibiles, jungle warfare specialists and elite fighting unit. I'd read about them in the briefing report. They were the unit most feared by enemy combatants and recognized as one of the most dangerous and deadly in the world. They were trained through extreme force, hardship and suffering and were taught from day one to remove all sense of compassion and humanity. From somewhere, their motto rose into my consciousness.

If I advance, follow me. If I stop, urge me on. If I retreat, kill me.

I recalled reading something about their members being told to raise a puppy to adulthood and then being forced to kill and dismember it as a test of their loyalty to their unit. Their initiation into the full brotherhood involved drinking a cocktail of rum and gunpowder from a spent mortar shell.

And now they were here. They were taking orders from a disgraced member of British intelligence, and they had found their way to this desolate wilderness in a little fold of cold, rugged land.

I sat back, trying to control my breathing. I'm sure there are plenty of people who would know just what their duty was and how best to do it, but I'm not one of them. I needed to think it through. I could barely stand for the pain in my side and I feared that if I moved my head too sharply I was going to vomit up the little liquid left in my system. I needed to know more before I could formulate a plan of action. First I needed to know whether I was safe. Were there more men like this about to stumble into the little byre? I dragged myself upright and slouched towards the opening of the barn. I poked my head out as if expecting a bullet. Instead I saw the cold, black vastness of a bare field, muddy patches here and there and thick with tangled grass in others. I took a few steps forward across muddy ground, stones and slime on my bare feet, then turned to look back at the barn. I recognized it at once. The holes in the roof formed a shape I recognized and knew from the road. It was the furthest outbuilding on the boundary of my home. I'd been inside with Stefan when I first moved north, turning my nose up at the smell and vaguely entertaining notions of bricking up the holes and stabling a couple of horses. Grief ensured I never came back. Not until now. Now, agonized and aching and slick with spilled blood, I realized I'd been captive in my own damn barn. And that meant I was only two fields away from the house where Walt and the silent killers had disappeared to and where Felicity and John waited for whatever hell was coming.

I turned around too quickly and almost stumbled over the object at my feet. It was a sniper rifle, propped up on a tripod, thick scope mounted atop the dull black metal of the lethal piece of weaponry.

Grunting with the effort, I bobbed down. Lay flat on the ground, mud soaking through my tattered clothes, and pressed my eye to the scope. There was nothing but blackness. I inched my fingertip along the sight, sliding the little metal disc to one side and staring out through the grainy green of the night-vision scope. I could see the rear courtyard of my house. Could make out the big black car slowly pulling in between the outbuildings, parking between a big expensive-looking machine and a battered little Vauxhall. I felt all the fight leach out of me for a moment as I realized what I was seeing. Felicity, I thought. John.

I watched through the scope as a small figure climbed down from the big car. Recognized Walt just from the way he moved. As I watched, a tall man emerged from the back door. He greeted Walt with a handshake, pumping his hand warmly and opening his arms wide to direct him towards the house. Eight paces and he was gone.

I moved the rifle in tiny increments, left and right. It took time and intense concentration but they emerged from the grainy darkness like the outlines of ships appearing through the fog. Three of them. No, four. Five. Crouched down or laid down, squatting behind low walls or pushed up against the trunks of the trees that lined the back lane. They were dressed like the dead man. They were armed. They were waiting.

I crawled backwards, slithering towards the open door of the barn. Only when I was back within did I feel safe to stand. The pain was intense but I had no choice but to endure it. I stood over the dead man and closed my eyes, wishing there was another way. Then I stripped him. Took his boots and his knife, his scarf and hat. I rubbed the face paint from his cold, rubbery features and smeared it, bloodily, on my own. I pushed my feet into his stinking boots. Cringed at the touch of the cold sticky fabric of his jacket against my skin.

I picked up the pitchfork. Held it like a wizard's staff. Limped to the entrance and then moved towards the rifle without a sound. I snatched it up, feeling the pleasing heft of it against my hip as I slipped the strap over my shoulder.

And then I started out across the great empty nothingness; a crow-black figure moving towards the hazy rectangle of perfect darkness, eyes fixed on the horizon and the soft promise of light.

FELICITY

Transcript 0026, recorded December 1, 2016

The smell was worse than the darkness. It was worse than the cobwebs and the rotting wood and the mouthfuls of damp feather and fur. It felt like all the worst smells you can imagine were climbing into my mouth and nose; a big python of ugly stink pushing its way into my face even as I wriggled forward like a snake moving out of its skin.

I felt my clothes tear. Felt my shins rubbing raw on the nails and the crumbled roof joists. There was barely an inch between the top of my head and the boards of the floor above. I had no way of knowing which direction to take. I kept pushing out with my hand, pawing at the air, not sure whether I wanted to feel nothing or something. I wanted to turn back but there was no way to turn around and the thought of slithering back through the hole was worse than keeping going. It was a kind of madness, I think. All these years later I can't really believe I did it. I could never have done it before or after that moment, I know that. But desperation and temper can make you do strange things and I think it was having my mind so full of the grandson that really pushed me up and into that horrible little space. I'd known true grief in my life and I wasn't ready to inflict that kind of feeling on anybody I cared about, let alone my only son and his little lad. I had a duty, didn't I? A duty to at least try. And all I'd heard about Britain and America and those far-flung places we were turning our back on – it had all got under my skin. I was annoyed with myself. It was guilt, now I think on it, though it weren't guilt about what my country had done or not done. It was guilt at not asking more questions. Guilt at just plodding on with my little life when horrible things were happening to decent folk. Folk like me, maybe. Aye, that's it, right enough. I think it was what Sera said about her little village; her people out in the wilderness, left to their quiet little lives, celebrating their Christmas, raising their families. They weren't that different from me really, were they? And if my friends and family were being rounded up and slaughtered, I think I'd feel a bit sore at the people who paid for the guns and trained the killers. I might even expect them to do something about it. I couldn't do much other than find a way out. I had no plan other than getting as far away from that house as I could. Whatever came next was up to somebody else, but in that moment, half crushed between the ceiling and the floor, I had just enough courage to keep moving forward.

I touched something soft with my outstretched hand. Snatched it back and then probed again at the black air in front of my face. I could feel a length of metal piping, ice-cold to the touch. Beyond it was the damp roughness of bare brick. I kept patting at the air. Felt a slight warmth upon my palm and fingertips and reached out, putting my other hand in my mouth in case I made a sound. There was an emptiness – a space between the edge of the boards and whatever lay beyond. I wriggled forward, trying to get my bearings. I'd moved perhaps fifteen feet from the edge of the room where John and Sera waited. That must have taken me out across the hallway and over the room that backed on to Cordelia's study. I pushed myself forward again, hands above my head now, inching forward over the little biting teeth of the wood and the nail-heads. And at last I saw light. Beneath me, the distance impossible to judge, I could just make out a line of soft yellow light. I moved towards it, feeling like a creature underground: a little blind mole nosing its way through roots and bones.

Then I heard them. Heard the voices off to my left. The light changed. Shadows seemed to flicker and dance as if somebody had opened the grate on an open fire. I angled my head forward and saw another line of light. Then another, moving away, regular as railway sleepers. Somehow I'd found my way into the space above the study. I was directly on top of the high-ceilinged room where the men were assembled, and where a voice I didn't recognize was talking softly.

I stayed perfectly still, barely daring to breathe. I wriggled forward again. I needed to see. Needed to hear. I pulled myself forward with my fingertips and hauled myself up to the line of light, pressing my face to the gap.

It took a while for the blurry picture to make sense to me. Took a while before I could decide whether I wanted to put my ear or my eye to the gap. But a picture formed and I can describe it for you as clear as I can close my eyes and tell you what every inch of my own bedroom looks like.

A little man was standing by the chimney breast. There was no fire in the grate and the only light in the place came from a couple of those little lanterns that had been handed to John and me hours before. The little man had dyed hair slicked back over a scarred, mottled scalp and he was wearing an expensive-looking suit that didn't sit well on him. I can't say I know much about fashion but he looked like a little lad wearing grown-up clothes. He had an air about him, that much was clear. This was a moment he'd looked forward to. He was holding court and looked like he was enjoying it. He gave off an air of confidence. He was used to such rooms.

Half a dozen different men sat in a loose semi-circle in front of him. It was as if they were in a little theatre, watching a magician about to pull a rabbit from his sleeve. They were expensive-looking men, if that makes any sense to you. They were no strangers to rich food. They were the sort who'd order brandy after their pudding and then sit chewing on fat cigars, swirling their drink of choice in crystal glasses big enough to re-home a goldfish. The chairs didn't match. Four were high-backed and I recognized them from the dining room. The two men who bookended the chaps in the middle were reclining in bucket-style armchairs. It was all very neat. I shifted my weight as gently as I could and tried to peer into the far reaches of the room. I could just make out Cordelia's bookcases, still haphazardly piled with her old textbooks, hardbacks and photograph albums. I felt a pang of longing for her – a sudden wish for her to march in through the door and demand that every one of them get the hell out of her house and to apologize to me personally as they did so.

I could make out Pelletier, stood in the corner, lounging against the wall like he was at a cocktail party. The two men who'd roughed up John had taken up positions behind the men in the high-backed chairs. I couldn't see any guns. Couldn't see any need for them. Everybody seemed to be playing nicely together.

I looked closer at the big man in the furthest chair. He had one of those faces that make you think of uncooked pork; all waxy and plump. His hair was swept back from his forehead in a luxurious black quiff, the tufty grey at his temples the exact same shade as his three-piece suit, complete with pocket watch and a flower in his buttonhole. He was wearing thick spectacles, heavy enough to sink into the pudgy flesh either side of his nose. I'd met him four times. He didn't remember me from one occasion to the next. I was, after all, just a housewife from Brampton, and his wife's closest friend. He was Assistant Private Secretary to the Foreign and Commonwealth Office. It was Cranham Hemlock.

PART THREE

PART THREE

FELICITY

Transcript 0027, recorded December 1, 2016

I held my breath. Ignored the pain and the fear. Listened as the little man spoke.

'You know who we are,' he said, addressing the room. 'You've heard rumours of a division within the intelligence service – an international cooperative designed to undo the worst excesses of the increasingly politicized world of intelligence and counter-espionage. We were established only a few short years ago but already we recognize it as a different age. You all know as well as I do that decisions taken by politicians need to be popular with the electorate – and the electorate is made up of the average man and woman on the street. Unfortunately, the average man and woman on the street is a self-interested, venal and frequently merciless creature. As such, we end up with politicians who will do whatever is necessary to ensure they remain in office – even if that means doing things that, if they were done by the enemy, we would think of as evil.

'Well, now we reach a reckoning. Now we see how people react when the guns and the terror and the horror aren't at the far side of the world. Tonight we bring the fight to their doorsteps and give you, these men of influence and power, the chance to prove you are capable of doing more than that which serves your own purpose. You are being given the chance to see what monsters you unleash into the world with every secret handshake and each memorandum dashed off and signed in between your long lunches and fucking your mistresses. This has been a long time in the planning, gentlemen. But by God, you will see . . .'

I think he'd have kept talking for ever if the ceiling hadn't given way. I honestly think he'd have talked himself up into a full-on fit. But I was so intent on hearing every bloody word that I didn't even feel the floor creak or the ceiling joists give way. The floor simply split in two and I dropped into the room below in a great explosion of plaster, wood and dirt; a strangled scream cut off in my throat as I crunched into the projector and onto the floor; spun inside a great hurricane of pain and fear and sound.

The last thing I heard before the oblivion came was the sound of shouts and curses, wood on wood, fists upon bone, metal and leather and a riot of desperate pleas. And then it was all gunfire and darkness.

CORDELIA

A sickle moon overhead, gleaming white. Birdsong, brittle as cracked glass, pecked mercilessly at the threads of pain in my head, my ribs, behind my eyes. Everything felt muffled but hypersensitive, like a dead limb slowly returning to life. There was a numbness to everything and yet I fancied I could hear each individual blade of grass crunching beneath my boots. The rifle knocking against my hip sounded like a bass drum at the head of a parade.

I tried to centre myself. I needed to be in control. To be calm. To order my thoughts and listen to my training and identify each objective before executing the plan that would move me closer to my goal. I had to keep a sense of perspective. I had one responsibility, and that was to ensure the safety of my friends. I wasn't able to do anything else. It would be somebody else's duty to tidy up whatever mess Walt was making. Let him play out his game, manoeuvring his chess pieces around, sacrificing his pawns, manipulating bishops and rooks; his eyes set only on one decisive checkmate. I couldn't even fathom what it was he wanted, let alone whether I supported him in his mad ideology. All I knew was that he had brought a lethal presence into the heart of a community I used to call home. Somehow, one of the former leaders of MI6 had secured the services of an elite team of Kaibiles. Whether they were mercenaries or loyal to the ruling military didn't really matter. They were men who knew how to kill. Men who weaponized rape and horror. Men who had all sense of humanity juiced out of them during training and who revelled in their international reputation as the most merciless and barbaric of jungle warfare specialists.

I kept moving forward, trying to focus only on what I could hear and see and not to lose myself in the great tumult of thoughts assaulting me. Why had Walt given me the lighter? Why would a man who valued human life and who left the

Service over its moral decline suddenly make a pact with the
weapons of oppression? Why bring me into it? Why Cranham?
And why here and now?

I could have screamed with fury if not for my terror at
giving my position away. Every few moments I stopped to
look through the specialist sniper-scope; the world turning
green and hazy as I focused on the static figures scattered
around the rear of the house. There was a mad moment when
I considered pulling the trigger. I wasn't a terrible shot. I could
perhaps have taken down a couple of them before they started
firing on me in return. But it is no easy thing to take a life.
I've never been a killer. I've never had the cold blood needed
to stop a heart and never think upon it again. The lives I've
had a hand in ending still weigh heavily on me and there's
barely a night goes by I don't have nightmares about the things
I've done and seen and endured. More than anything, I feared
that any commotion might add to the jeopardy facing Felicity
and John. All I could do was get to the house. I think I enter-
tained some half-baked idea of grabbing whoever I saw first
and putting the rifle to their head – demanding to know where
my friends were being kept and then quietly escorting them
away to safety. After that I could contact the Service. I could
try and put the pieces together. I could call in the people better
equipped than I to deal with an armed death squad under the
command of a traitor.

I heard a sound away to my right. Glanced up and saw a
flurry of white-brown feathers: a ghostly outline swooping
down against the line of trees. Its hoot loud and shrill: an
announcement of breeding rights; of hunger and virility – a
warning to all.

I didn't even hear the man approach. One moment I was
alone and the next I was tumbling sideways; a leathery hand
across my mouth and a leg intertwined between mine, tugging
me down into the wet grass. It was as if the earth had suddenly
taken on human form. The shout of surprise and alarm caught
in my throat as a finger and thumb closed my nostrils. He was
much stronger than me and from what I could feel of his
outline he was absolutely solid with muscle. I tried to squirm
from his grasp, eyes wide and white as the moon overhead

and he released me for just long enough for me to turn my head and see his face: eyeball to eyeball with me. He had blood and dirt all down one side of his face and a great swelling around the orbit of his eye, but there was no mistaking the man from the train; the same man who I'd left to die on a country road.

He pushed my face down to the ground, his lips to my ear. He spoke so quietly that it felt more like a thought than the words of a stranger.

'If you make a sound, you're going to die.'

I felt the pain come in waves as he shifted his weight, my mangled ribs blazing with fire. I couldn't breathe for the hand at my mouth and my eyes were full of tears and dirt. His eyeball, an inch from my own, looked into me as if trying to read my very soul. He was waiting for me to promise him that I would obey. He wanted my vow that I would not scream.

I blinked. Managed to give the tiniest fraction of a nod. Slowly, moving his hand away in tiny increments, he let the air flood into my lungs. I wanted to suck in a great desperate lungful but I knew it would only make me burst into a fit of coughing so I forced myself to suck in small, gentle breaths, my eyes locked on his, watching through the mist of tears and pain as he raised his gloved hand to his face and put his finger to his lips.

There was a sound from nearby: a soft rustle, as if an incongruous gust of wind were moving through the under-growth. Something passed between the man and me, some insinuation of shared destiny, of entangled fate. I didn't even see him move. I closed my eyes for just an instant and it was enough time for him to spring soundlessly from the earth and to thud back down to the ground, a man in his arms, his hands behind his back; a great curve of bloody death carved into his belly and another opening an astonished mouth in his windpipe.

I lay on the ground without a sound. Listened to the sound of blood pouring onto the dark earth and the fluttering kicks of a life coming to an end. Then there was silence, and he was in front of me again, the smell of blood and sweat and cigarettes filling my nostrils. He lay down next to me, close as if we were lovers. Then he gave a little nod and reached past me to pick up the rifle. He placed it between us. He held a knife in his right hand and he wiped the blade on his trouser leg before sliding it back into the waist of his sodden, mud-spattered trousers.

I didn't know whether he was my death note or my saviour. I swear, I could have started sobbing there and then and felt no shame for it. Instead I just closed my eyes and lay as still as death. If I tried to move he could take me down in a moment. I felt him roll away from me. Heard the soft, damp little echoes of a body being searched. Then the ground shifted a little and he was back beside me, his lips again at my ear.

'I don't think you and I have got off to the best of starts,' he whispered, and his accent was no longer Scottish. He must have seen something in how I reacted to his words as the slyest of smiles creased his bloodied, pug-like features. 'Apologies for the deception, Mrs Hemlock. None of us are ever entirely what we appear to be, wouldn't you agree?'

I swallowed. Chose my words carefully as the cold seeped into my bones. 'I thought you were dead.'

'Thick skull, thankfully,' he whispered, and his lower lip tickled my cheek. 'The farmer must have thought I was Lazarus.'

Questions lined up in my mind. I felt as though I'd done nothing but fumble around in the dark, making a fool of myself and getting further away from whoever it was I used to be. Inside thirty-six hours I'd somehow become complicit in something far beyond my comprehension, and with potentially catastrophic consequences.

'What's he doing?' I asked, my voice cracking. 'Walt. I don't know what he's doing or what he wants from me.'

He smiled again, a little of the tension seeping out of his body. 'Nobody ever really knows what Walt's doing except for Walt. But you very nearly messed it up for everybody.'

'Me? I don't even know why I'm here!'

'You're not meant to be,' he said, chastising me with the gentle, avuncular tones of a benign housemaster. 'You were meant to deliver the information to six, then get off the train when I told you to. He was laying a trail, you see. He wanted you to be able to say you knew nothing of what was going to happen. He wanted you to have the credit not the shame.'

I ground my back teeth, tasting blood. 'The credit for what? The men at the barn – the ones who left with him. They're Kaibiles. You know what they do, what they are, what they stand for . . .?' I stopped myself, another wave of confusion twisting me in knots. 'If you're on Walt's side why did you just kill that man?'

He smiled at me again, a pleasant grin that suggested he was capable of looking quite handsome, albeit in a ruby player sort of a way. He seemed so different from the man on the train. What had Walt called him? How had he addressed him over the radio before he came for me?

'I'm Erskine,' he said, as if reading my thoughts. 'I answer to several names, just like you. But Erskine will do for now. Might I be permitted to call you Cordelia?'

I pulled a face that suggested he was mad. A moment ago I thought he was going to suffocate me to death and now he was worried about decorum. I recognized the type. He hadn't been lying when he told me he was part of the Deck of Clubs. He was every inch the upper-class gentleman: military in his deportment and frightfully polite; mindful of social niceties even as we lay on the ground beside a cooling corpse.

'Call me what you bloody like,' I said, and there was more than a trace of my own heritage in the way I hissed it at him.

'That's the Cordelia that Walt described to me,' he said, and moved a little further away from me, lifting the rifle and looking out through the scope. I didn't speak. Just waited until he was done. When he gave me his attention again I sensed that he was in real pain. He was trying not to let it show but his jaw kept flexing and one eye was flickering open and shut as if he was trying to keep the agony chained up inside him.

'I have friends in the house,' I said, and saying it out loud was nearly enough to tear me to pieces. I was holding myself together through sheer force of will. I took a leap of faith, desperate to cling on to the hope that Erskine was going to help me with the thing that mattered most. 'John Goose. He's the caretaker of the property. You know that I've used it before, yes? Assets in need of places to stay; the occasional meeting place for those in need of a quiet space to think, to recover, to talk. He's on the books, all above board. Plants the listening ears and picks them up again and gets a few quid in his pocket when he's done. He and his wife went there tonight at my request. They're caught up in whatever's happening.'

Erskine nodded, chewing his lower lip. 'I heard. Everything Walt said to you – everything you said in return, I heard it all.'

I screwed up my features as in pain. Felt the thought arriving through the fog. 'The lighter?'

'Bug and tracker. Quite proud of it. Quartermaster took my old Zippo and gave it a thoroughly modern makeover. Glad you had the presence of mind to take it. Walt's got the recordings you took from me, so that's a loose end tied up. Really, I hadn't expected you to be so virulently anti-orders. I really did think you would get on the next train back to London. Walt wasn't even that cross when I reported in. Said you were the sort who was always hard to read and that was why he never knew whether to bring you into the circle of Angels.'

The word chimed with something I'd read. *Angels?* Was there an operation? Something to do with Prickly Heat? I was too tired and groggy to be able to disentangle the great mess of words that floated as ripped-up pictures just outside my recollection.

'It will come to an end tonight,' said Erskine, a grimness to the set of his jaw. 'One way or another, Walt will make people do the right thing, or he'll bring the whole damn tower of cards tumbling down.'

I shook my head. 'Please,' I whispered. 'I just need to get my friends to safety.'

'We all have people that matter to us,' he said, a little steel in his tone. 'You're an intelligence analyst, Cordelia. You're a spy, like the rest of us. You serve queen and country and you're supposed to follow orders no matter what they are. When you disobeyed me on the train tonight, it got me wondering whether perhaps you do serve a grander purpose – whether you hold yourself to a different set of standards. Whether you understand the moral imperative of our position.'

His eyes had taken on a glassy look, the way that religious zealots can appear when they hear of God's everlasting love. A new fear gripped me. Erskine looked momentarily untethered from his sanity.

'Higher purpose?' I asked. 'You sound like Walt. This was what got him kicked out . . .'

'No,' he snapped. 'No, he chose a better path. A righteous path.'

'I don't under—'

The word was lost in a sudden burst of gunfire. Six shots, too quick to be from a single gun, and all emanating from the dark house just over the lip of the field.

'Shit,' snapped Erskine, rolling onto his belly and grabbing for the rifle. 'Cordelia, stay down, stay down . . .'

But I was already up and running.

Running towards the gunfight.

The only higher duty that mattered was saving Flick.

FELICITY

Transcript 0028, recorded December 1, 2016

can't be sure that what I'm telling you is going to be exactly right, I'm afraid. I've tried to be as honest as I can and if I've got myself carried away or missed something out or said it in the wrong order, just put it down to my age and the fact that I'm doing my best. This next bit – the last of it, I suppose – is mostly guesswork, if I'm honest with you. My head was all over the place, you see. I don't know how to describe it. You must have had a good old knock to the head once or twice in your life and maybe you've had bad ears when you were little – that feeling you get when your whole head feels as though it's been stuffed with damp rags and you can't hear or breathe properly. Well, imagine that and multiply it and throw in the fact that my head was ringing as if it was stuck in a coal scuttle and you might get a bit of an idea what I was experiencing and why all of the memories are a bit of a muddle.

I'll just tell you the scraps of it, shall I? I mean, I see you there with your mouth open, looking a bit of a silly sod, and I can tell you don't know whether I'm pulling your leg or senile or giving you the story that will make you rich and famous. I know that look. Being friends with Cordy, you get to see that look on people's faces more often than most. What's the word? Is it incredulity? Hark at me, eh? Incredulous – aye, that's how you look. So I'll just get on with it and you can decide whether you believe me or whether I'm half daft.

So you need to think of me all bloodied and bruised and covered in dust and paint and feathers, laid out on the floor of Cordelia's study. I clattered down like I'd fallen out of an aeroplane, I swear, and only managed to get my hands up in front of me at the very last moment. Even so, the impact felt like being run over by a truck. One moment I was up in the rafters trying not to make a sound and the next I was in so much pain I couldn't even find the breath to cry.

I can remember bits of what they were shouting at one another; all those men with their angry faces and their beetle-black eyes, faces all sweaty and pink; jumping out of their seats and spilling their drinks and diving backwards as if they were under attack.

'. . . good God, he's set us up! . . .'

'. . . how dare you!'

'. . . told you he couldn't be trusted . . .'

It was Pelletier who silenced them. Pulled a gun from his pocket and fired it into the roof – a look on his face that suggested this was all in a day's work. I half remember him looking down at me and giving a funny little smile. He looked almost pleased with me – impressed that I'd got as far as I had.

I can see the little man too. I know now that his name was Walt and that he was the reason that everything happened, but at the time I just thought of him as the one in charge. He wasn't smiling at me. He looked absolutely furious. He was the only one in the room who didn't react like the world was falling in when I fell through the roof. His world seemed to move at a different speed to everybody else's. He just stepped out of the way and leant back against the chimney breast, hands in his pockets and glaring down at me. He had the look of a kid who hasn't won any of the prizes at their own birthday party.

I lay there for a moment, head ringing, the sound of the gunshots seeming to reverberate off the walls. Then the two bruisers were hauling me to my feet. I felt a hand in my hair yanking my head back as I was pushed toward Walt. I felt blood running from my nose into my mouth. One eye was all blurry. He put his face so close to mine I could smell his hair oil and see the crumbs between his teeth. His glare was as startling as a bucket of scalding water. Then his features changed and a slow, sly smile split his face.

'Felicity,' he said, and gave a little flick of his hands in the direction of the men who held me. The man holding my hair let go and I sagged forward, Walt holding me up. 'Good Lord but you're every bit the surprise that Cordelia spoke of. What the blazes are you doing fumbling about up there?' He peered past me into the crater in the roof. 'You really did that? She will be most impressed.'

I was too banged up to really take any of it in. It felt like listening to a conversation but from far away or under water. He looked past me and gave a reassuring little smile to the men who'd flung themselves backwards when the ceiling gave in.

'Nothing to worry about, gentlemen. These old houses – the floorboards are held together with spit and wishful-thinking. Clearly the woodworm got tired of linking arms and holding the roof up. Would you care to re-take your seats? And please, Pelletier, do go and check on our other guests.'

I heard the door open. Heard muffled shouts and bangs and the scrape of chair-legs being dragged across the floor. Walt helped me to a chair, turning me around and propping me up to face the door. Pelletier and one of the big men came back with John and Sera. John could barely stand but when he saw the state of me, laid out in the chair and covered in blood, he did his damnedest to take a swing at the man holding him. He got a punch in the ribs for his trouble and went down to his knees. Pelletier held Sera by the arm, his manner as respectful as he could make it. She looked around urgently at all the eyes upon her. Looked at me and then past me, to where her brother cowered in the corner; blood seeping from a wound to his shoulder, one hand pressed bloodily to the hole and a gory, elderberry-coloured blood leaking through his fingers.

'Be calm, please, Sera,' said Walt, apologetically. 'Such things often look a great deal worse than they are.'

'This is her, is it?' asked a man with an American accent. He was a good-looking fellow, neatly pressed: an expensive black polo neck under a dark grey suit. He'd settled himself back in his chair and was looking around him as if this was all a pantomime. A heavily built chap stood a few paces behind him. He held a gun in his right hand and something told me he was a bodyguard of sorts for the American.

Groggily I took in the other faces, pausing when I came to Cranham. He'd put on even more weight since I'd last seen him and he looked downright silly standing there, wiping the

brick-dust off his suit with a big silk handkerchief and then
wiping his sweaty face with it, leaving smears on his cheeks
that looked like war paint. He was looking back at me, face
screwed up; a toddler with constipation. He was trying to work
out how he knew me. Trying to work out whether he was in
danger or among friends.

I heard a burst of that funny language again. The man who'd
first spoken it, hours before, was leaning by the back wall, his
manner as nonchalant as Walt's. He was a little man too and
his teeth, in that light, were enough to give you nightmares.
He was talking to Sera. Walt, at my side, spoke briefly in
something that sounded like Spanish. Sera looked from one
to the other and then to her own bloodied brother, and then
sank into the chair that Pelletier offered her. Another suited
man picked up the contraption that I'd knocked sideways as
I fell through the roof. I recognized it as a video projector: a
fancy little thing all sleek and shiny.

'This is a shambles, Walter,' said Cranham, shaking his
finger in Walt's direction. 'You gave us your word of honour,
man. This was a safe space, a protected space!'

Walt grinned in Cranham's direction, shaking his head as
if enjoying a private joke. 'I shall speak to the owner,' he said.
'See whether or not there are any more skeletons in the closets.'

Cranham blushed, his cheeks turning the colour of ripe
plums. 'An outrage,' he muttered. 'A bloody outrage!'

'Apologies for the rumpus, gentlemen,' said Pelletier,
smoothly. 'It's not a party without a cabaret, huh? Can we
freshen your glasses? I'm sure your hearts are pumping hard
so if you need a moment to catch your breaths, don't be in
the least bit embarrassed. You're among friends.'

I swallowed some of the blood and gagged on it. Blinked
the hot tears away. Slumped down in the chair and tried to
make myself as small as I could, to blend into the upholstery
and somehow disappear.

There were general mutterings from the assembled figures:
a few little laughs and jibes at one another's expense.
None of them wanted to admit to having had a fright. They
were like schoolboys teasing one another for jumping during
the scary part of a story. They got themselves smoothed over

and sat back down. I tried to make some connections between
them – to work out which of the men were together. There
were half a dozen figures standing in the shadows and each
seemed to provide some kind of security service for the figures
in the chairs.

'If you would be so kind.'

Walt pointed at the projector. One of the heavies clicked
off the lanterns and the other pointed the projector at the space
between the bookshelves. Grainy footage flickered on the wall.
I saw a row of crops, lit by an ice-bright moon. Saw soldiers
changing out of uniforms and into T-shirts and jeans, pulling
on armbands and little scraps of face mask patterned with a
symbol I could barely make out. They were laughing as they
got changed, pushing one another over, smoking their cigarettes
and holding their guns like lovers. Then the footage showed
them bouncing around in the back of a truck; eyes bright,
leaning forward on their rifles like they were golfers waiting
for their turn to take a shot. The footage lurched forward a
moment later. Suddenly I was watching a group of men, women
and children being led from their little dark houses and into
what passed for a main square. I saw chickens fluttering and
squawking away in the background. I saw a man trying to
wrestle with the soldier who held him and heard myself gasp
as two soldiers stepped forward and clubbed him in the side
of the head with their rifles. He went down and they struck
him again and again until he stopped moving. A little girl ran
in front of the camera, her eyes huge, mouth open in a silent
scream. The footage lurched again. I had to look away. I
couldn't stand it. From around me I heard the whispers of
disgust from the gathered men. I glanced up again. Men were
hurting women. Hurting them in the way that there's no getting
better from.

'Please, gentlemen. Please keep watching.'

They did as Walt said. So did I. Watched as the footage
sped up and leapt forward. Now the soldiers were standing at
the lip of a great hole in the ground. The soldiers were dragging the bedraggled, half-naked women towards the pit. One
carried a small girl by her ankle, dangling her upside down
as if she were something for the pot.

One by one, two by two, the men pushed them into the hole. The silence made it somehow even more terrible. I had to imagine the screams; imagine the sobs. Then they stood around, leaning on their rifles, smoking their cigarettes, exhausted by the exertions. Finally a figure stepped into shot. He didn't look like the others. His skin was pale and although there was no colour in the footage, his moustache looked blonde. This was a white man. A tall, slim-built, white man in combat clothes and beret. He stopped for a moment to survey the scene. The men in the room muttered little exclamations, as if the face was known to them. And then he moved on, and we watched as the soldiers on the screen started shovelling dirt and stone on the people in the deep, deep dark.

Then it stopped. The footage crackled to a halt and we all just sat there, not sure of the right response.

'Terrible, terrible,' muttered Cranham, as one of the men flicked the lanterns back on. He'd gone very pale. 'Atrocious.'

Walt stared at him, one eye twitching slightly. He looked to be in pain but was holding it in. 'An interesting choice of words, Mr Hemlock. Atrocious. Yes. An atrocity, you mean.'

'Well, of course,' muttered Cranham, mopping his face again. 'Will these paramilitaries stop at nothing?'

Walt shot Pelletier a look. He rolled his eyes and gave that enigmatic little smile again. At the back of the room the American muttered, 'Sweet Jesus'.

'You saw what we saw, Mr Hemlock,' said Walt, softly. 'You saw the soldiers changing out of their uniforms and into civilian clothes?'

Cranham blustered, clearly embarrassed. 'Oh, is that what I was looking at? Sorry, I don't think that's what I saw. They were uniforms, were they? So dashed hard to tell the difference, isn't it?'

If he was expecting a laugh he didn't get one. Nobody spoke at all for a moment. Then Sera sat forward in her chair. She looked up at Walt and gave him a little nod – a gesture of respect.

'I am very pleased to see you,' she said to him. 'I did despair. I thought I had been lied to. To see you here, even as my brother suffers – it gives me hope that you will keep your word.'

All eyes turned to Walt. 'Keep your word, Walt?' asked the American in the polo neck. 'What you been promising this little lady?'

Walt took a moment. He reached into his pocket and retrieved his cigarettes. He took his time about lighting it, igniting the flame on a golden Zippo lighter and glancing at the writing on the side of it.

'Big D's,' he said, to nobody in particular, reading the writing on the side of the lighter. 'You'll know that place, yes?'

A man in a sober black suit gave a little twitch of his lips. He had iron grey hair cut in a sensible military style and was sitting in his chair with his back ramrod straight. 'Belize City,' he said, quietly. 'Yes, I've read the reports.'

'The risks they've taken for us,' said Walt, looking at the tip of his cigarette. 'The lives sacrificed. The tortures they've endured. Please, Mr Hemlock, do have the decency to curb your xenophobia while in the presence of heroes.'

Cranham looked affronted. Turned to the military man as if expecting support. 'You hear this tripe, Gooden? Xenophobia's the thing we should be wary of, is it? Here? Every possible rule broken, security compromised – senior civil servants all but press-ganged into attendance – liberties taken with one's personal affiliations . . .'

Pelletier didn't let him finish. Just stepped forward and whispered in his ear. Whatever he said, all the blood seemed to drain from Cranham's face. He looked like a week-old loaf and it was all he could do not to wet himself in his fancy suit.

'Where's this all going, Walt?' asked a man with receding grey hair and a pair of spectacles so thick that they made his eyes look twice the size. His accent was English and very upper-class. He was the sort who could hear a joke and declare it 'very droll' rather than laughing at it.

'You see what we see, yes?' asked Walt, pointing at the wall where the film had been shown. 'They are Kaibiles. They are the elite military – the men adored and lauded by a litany of presidents. And they are changing into civilian clothes so that they can wipe out a village and blame it on the paramilitaries. That, in turn, gives President Reagan the excuse he needs to vastly increase government aid and training for the ruling military junta. And Great Britain, as America's lapdog, turns a blind eye for no other reason than because we wish to stay in the good graces of our strongest allies – those selfsame allies that very nearly ignored our every plea for assistance just a few short months ago as we found ourselves at war with Argentina.'

The man with the straight back reached into his pocket and produced a cigarette from a sleek silver case. He lit it with a match tucked in an invisible pocket, wafting the smoke as he spoke. 'It is an imperfect world, Walter,' he said, airily. 'We cannot only do business with people of whom we are fond. Guatemala, Honduras, El Salvador – they are integral in stopping the spread of communism. The paramilitaries, the agitators in Guatemala – perhaps they are not responsible for all of the horrors laid at their door, but they are hardcore socialists who could very well give the Soviets a toehold at the front gates of America. We have made pragmatic decisions, decent decisions, done our best to stop the—'

'You have let us die,' said Sera, simply, raising her head and letting everybody see her big brown eyes. 'We believe that more than a hundred thousand men, women and children have died in the last twenty years. Their deaths have all been at the hands of the military and those who support whichever puppet president the Americans are given to support. President Rios Montt – your Reagan speaks of him as a force for good; a true Christian man who will bring democracy to our country. He is a zealot. He believes he does God's work with every life he takes. He is backed by your evangelists. He is supported by your president. Your soldiers trained his elite fighters. Your taxpayers pay for the weapons he uses to wipe us out.'

'Reagan's going back to Congress in February to ask for millions more for his good friend, the President of Guatemala,' said Walt. 'He will show them the edited version of this recording. He will tell them of the dreadful communist guerrillas wiping out the native Mayan population.'

'He'll get it too,' said the American with the bad teeth.

'He's got the Christian right-wingers in his pocket and they adore Ríos Montt. He's doing God's work, after all.'

'And what do you want any of us to do about that?' asked the smooth man in the polo neck.

'You're going to stop it,' said Walt, simply. 'I have enough leverage against each of you to ensure that you spend your days either in jail or in the ground and that your legacies are utterly destroyed. Your names will become bywords for incompetence and deceit. I will see you painted as the very worst of traitors to your nations. If God has a ledger, your names are in it for transgressions that most would consider irredeemable. You, Cranham. You gave approval through your role in the Joint Intelligence Committee for the Angels operation to be rolled up and have its funding withdrawn. You approved the mission in Belize that led to the very best of my intelligence assets being obliterated. You, Gooden, you personally handed over to the Kaibiles a deep-cover operative of mine – a man who had risked everything to share with me the atrocities committed by government forces and to whom I promised a safe haven. I believed him to be safe in Belize – safe with a British army officer of impeccable breeding. Instead you informed your own paymasters. Informed Whitehall. Made a mess of everything and then gave him to the Kaibiles when they crossed the border and came looking. Shall I tell you how they killed him, Gooden? Or perhaps about the good Father, the missionary shot down over the jungle as he flew back from sharing vital intelligence about troop movements and the atrocities taking place in the jungle community that he had helped create, and where, worse luck, the government had recently discovered oil? I can play you the recording of the moments before his death, if you wish. He greets it with the fortitude one would expect.'

'No more,' said Gooden, standing up. 'I came because you said it was important. I came because I was intrigued. I will not be made a scapegoat for the things done by our enemies—'

Pelletier stepped forward and cuffed him around the head like a naughty schoolboy. At the back of the room, one of the security guards reached inside his jacket. One of the guards who'd hurt John raised his weapon and shook his head. There was silence for a moment. I realized I'd barely been breathing. I glanced at John who was staring up at me with glassy eyes.

'I'm tired,' said Walt, rubbing his forehead. 'Tired of the manipulation, the games, the lies, the secrets. I've been tired of it all for a very long time. There are plenty like me. We flock together, you see. Men and women whose conscience has survived immersion in the swamp of politics and espionage. We see beyond the back and forth of East versus West. We see humanity. We see the real lives affected by the power struggles we seek to influence. We tidy up the mess left by political decision-making. We have grown tired of watching politicians feed the slavering masses the meat that they crave. Things that happen far away do not trouble the conscience of the masses. You, Cranham – you can advise the Foreign Office from your position of pragmatism because it is not your door that the death squads are coming to. You do not have to wake up in the middle of the night to see a gun in your face, your family members being raped, butchered, buried alive in a well.'

'For God's sake,' muttered Cranham. 'You're every bit as insane as we feared! You ask why funding was cut and the Angels scheme mothballed? It's because it was a nonsense, Walt. It was a sop to the Lefties – something Carter thought up to ease his troubled conscience. It was a place to put nuisances like you, letting you feel like you were saving the little people while the real diplomatic corps got on with changing the world. Good God, is this your grand hurrah? You're going to slap our consciences and make us listen to two poor jungle-bunnies about how horrible it is to live as they live? Well, perhaps they shouldn't shelter guerrillas, how about that?'

'There are soldiers outside, right now,' said Walt, without emotion. 'They believe me to be one of the evangelists who props up their president. They believe they are on a mission of the highest national importance. It has been a lesson in tradecraft, manoeuvring them through airports, nations, their passports made up in the names of a whole rainbow of nations. And now they are here. A little rural community far from the goings-on of their national seat of power. This is a place where men and women and children sleep soundly and work hard.

They will wake tonight to the sound of gunfire. They will be shepherded from their beds. Those who talk back or protest will face violence. And when the dust settles and they have slipped away into the night, I will ask you all whether or not you believe that the difficult decisions you have made, whether the men you have so pragmatically supported, I will ask you whether you might not wish to change your minds.'

Each of the men in the room turned to look at one another. Faces creased in confusion. Mouths twisted, brows furrowed; the military man started to stand. Pelletier crossed to the window and twitched aside the curtain. He pulled a lighter from his pocket – the insignia on the side the same as Walt's. He ignited it once, a single flame in the absolute dark. There was an immediate ripple of gunfire, a sound like a tree-branch suddenly snapping in a dozen places at once. I heard the tinkle of falling glass from an upstairs window.

'You're insane,' said Cranham, his hand at his mouth. 'This is England, you halfwit! What kind of a man brings trained killers halfway around the world in the name of the greater good?'

Walt started laughing. It was an ugly sound, a strange snuffling that caused him to break into a bout of coughing. He turned away as it got worse but I saw the smear of blood on his chin before he wiped it away; caught the whiff of iron and corruption coming off him.

'You've got a man out there with an automatic, have you?' asked the American. 'Clever. Theatrical. But if you think I'm going to suddenly start actively working against US foreign policy because you've tricked a few diplomats into a gathering in this godforsaken place, you genuinely are as insane as we all feared.' He turned to the American with the bad teeth. 'How did you get yourself caught up with this fool, Bateman? God, this is what happens when you let the hippies cut their hair and put on a suit . . .'

Pelletier stepped forward again. Stopped, suddenly, hand raised. Something seemed wrong. He put a hand in the pocket of his coat. I looked at John. His eyes were closed.

The world seemed to slow down. Pelletier reached into his pocket and retrieved the bug that John had slipped there when he was still in charge of his thoughts. There was a little red dot blinking on the top. Pelletier looked at it as if he was holding something magical. He glanced at Walt, whose face seemed to freeze in a moment of absolute horror. Pelletier looked down at John, making sense of it. Closed his eyes as if trying to contain a rage that could overwhelm him completely.

'No,' said Sera, and threw herself down on him.

'Stop,' I whispered, though it was more to myself than to anybody else.

And then the shooting started in earnest. Machine gunfire followed by the perfect 'snap' of a rifle. A bullet whizzed through the top of the windows and thudded into the wall. The men at the back of the room grabbed for their guns while the enforcers and Pelletier shouted for them to stop, to stop, it wasn't what they thought . . .

The windows came through in a burst of gunfire, an explosion of glass and bullets and noise.

I looked up just as the figure came through the falling shards, bursting through the glass and the curtains and tumbling into the room in a storm of gunfire, hitting the ground hard and rolling like a barrel into the centre of the room.

The figure that stood was barely recognizable. It was all mud and blood, sweat and gore-caked skin. It blocked out the view of the men behind; the figures pointing their guns at one another, screaming, bellowing, ordering each other to drop their weapons, to hold, to hold . . .

The eyes locked on mine. Filled with tears. Filled with rage.

'Cordelia . . .?'

She moved quicker than anybody else. Crossed the space between herself and Walt before I could get a word out, pulling a knife from her belt and spinning to her left as he raised his gun, fury gripping his features, words of hate dying in his mouth as the bullet nicked her shoulder.

Then she was behind him and the knife was at his throat; her bloodied hands in his hair.

And suddenly there were two moons in the sky and the sound of helicopters and a loudspeaker and everybody was laying down their weapons and getting down on the floor.

Cordelia didn't move. Just held Walt with the blade against his throat, weighing up the cost of his life.

Then he smiled. Bit down. Started to shake; froth and blood on his tongue, tears and snot pouring from his eyes and nose; his body shaking as if he were being electrocuted.

Cordelia dropped him. Pelletier looked up from the floor and his face twisted with grief. Then he closed his eyes. Bit down. Started to shake and bleed. Started to die.

And then she was beside me, holding me tight, stinking like the devil and slick with so much blood I couldn't tell if she was a victim or a killer.

She cried first. When I started, she stopped and called me soft.

And for a while, I reckon, we were just two old friends, laughing and bleeding and hugging in the dark.

I won't call them good times, but I swear I can't think about it without a smile on my face.

CORDELIA

'd be dead if it wasn't for Erskine. Any one of those troopers could have cut me down as I ran through the field towards the house. Instead they dropped where they'd been standing; double-tapped through the top lip or the rear of the skull – brain stem separated and heart immobile before they hit the ground. I didn't take any of it in. Just ran, fighting the pain, gripped by the kind of madness that seizes you when somebody you love is in danger. I didn't think about any of it. Hurled myself through the window because it was the quickest way in. It wasn't until Walt was crunching through the cyanide tablet hidden in his back tooth that I actually allowed my brain to catch up with my actions. Then the shakes came and the tears and the shock and I swear if it wasn't for Flick I'd probably have drifted off into a darkness that didn't guarantee a return. Instead she kept me talking. Kept flicking away at my eyelids and squeezing the skin on my wrist and telling me over and over that I'd be OK and that she was going to read me the riot act once it was all over – that she'd been punched and kicked and John's stitches had ripped and she was bloody furious with me for not telling her that John was on the payroll or that he wrote poetry and who the hell did I think I was getting another woman's husband all in a lather with words and feelings that he wasn't equipped to handle.

It went on for a while. I drifted in and out. There was a lot of shouting. Nobody seemed to know quite who was in charge. I remember people pulling and poking at me and Flick telling them that if they touched me again she'd bite their arms off. Then it was bright lights and high ceilings and the awful tugging feeling of the little forceps moving through the meat beneath my skin and the 'plink' of the bullet hitting the metal kidney bowl. Then there was sleep.

It was evening again before anybody official came to see me. I was in a private room in a military hospital and how I'd got there or where 'there' was didn't really matter. I just know that the bed shifted for a moment and I woke up from wherever I'd been, and a man I knew to be Deputy Director of SIS was sitting there looking at me. He had a hat between his knees, silk-lined, and inside was a bag of pistachio nuts. He was shelling them as he watched me – taking the jackets off and then transferring the shelled nuts to a different section of the bag.

'Sir! Wh—' I began, struggling up and feeling pain grip me so hard it was as if I'd been taken by a shark.

'No names,' he said, a little jolliness in his voice. He raised his hand and put a finger to his lips, then gave me the kind of smile that you give a naughty child when they've accidentally done something helpful. 'A busy couple of days, I gather. How are the war wounds? I don't envy you the entry wound. Had one myself in '52. Still hurts on cold mornings.'

'My friends,' I said. 'They'd been hurt.'

'Don't worry yourself. The gentleman is being treated wonderfully well. I think he's struggling to believe that it's a specialist ward at Brampton Cottage Hospital, but he seems the sort who wouldn't call out a lie in case it was bad manners.'

I couldn't help grinning at the way he'd so perfectly skewered John Goose. 'Did he need more surgery?'

'A little,' he conceded. 'A couple of bleeds that he'd be better off not knowing about. Prognosis is good. Better than before, I'd say. Surgeon found a couple of other unpleasant little cysts while he was rooting about and snipped them off too. Rather marvellous, surgery, don't you find? Just a shame it makes the doctors so damn holier-than-thou.'

I didn't speak. Watched him shell the pistachios and wondered if he'd ever get round to telling me what he was here for.

'Your friend. The lady. Quite a tough soul underneath the cardigan and the vests, I'd say. Climbed through the roof, you know. I mean, fancy! Must have caused quite a stir when she clattered down. And thank goodness that the old bug picked up enough movement to start transmitting. Poor fellow listening in at GCHQ almost had a fit. Had to wake up two Cabinet members to get the green light. All very exciting, I shouldn't wonder.'

'She's OK?'

He made a face. 'I don't like these American expressions. She's flourishing, my dear, flourishing. Sitting up in bed like a veritable maharani. I think she's rather taken with the medicines she's been given. Not one for strong spirits, I gather.'

I tried to keep a straight face, picturing the scene. Failed, and was grateful to see my visitor join in.

'Bad business,' he said, eventually. 'A little embarrassing for all concerned. Our mutual friend was always a hard fellow to read, but it seems that the illness drove him quite round the bend.'

'The illness?'

'Multiple tumours, my dear. Quite potty. Faked a dozen internal communications documents and managed to get half a dozen gullible diplomats together at the home of a senior civil servant. Had this half-baked idea about blackmailing them into persuading their governments to sever ties with a foreign government until they ceased being beastly.'

I waited for a moment before replying, trying to work out which bits of what I was hearing were being laid out as a script and which might, just possibly, have the ring of truth.

'There were foreign soldiers,' I said.

He waves his hand. It wasn't something to concern myself about. 'He had lots of connections,' he said, airily. 'Always knew how to turn a fellow's head. An excellent analyst, in his time, though never a true team player. Very much his own man, which might have been quite an attractive quality back when the world was a simpler shape but no place for that in today's Service. If there were foreign soldiers on English soil, that would be cause for a diplomatic incident and after the Falklands, there's no appetite for that.'

'You have the transcript – the recordings, everything that was picked up at GCHQ . . .'

'Human error, I'm afraid,' he said, spreading his hands. 'Some issue with the recording. I wish I knew enough to explain it. Suffice to say, there'll be an enquiry. Heads will roll.'

I lay back against the pillows. I had so many questions but knew with absolute certainty that I wouldn't get anything close to an answer.

'Cranham,' I said. 'Is he . . .?'

'Hale and hearty,' smiled the DD. 'A little shaken. Dreadfully upset to hear that his darling wife was in a minor car accident on her return from a committee meeting near Lucerne. Broken collarbone, quite banged up. He seemed genuinely distraught.'

'He saw me,' I said. 'He must have seen.'

'People see what they want to, in my experience,' he said. 'Take your son and daughter. I see their similarity to their father. I do not see the uncanny resemblance to the gentleman with whom you were briefly engaged in a dalliance not long after you completed your basic training. I'm sure your husband sees also that which he wishes – as do his grateful family, so keen for children to further the Hemlock line. You've been such an asset to that family.'

I held his gaze. Watched him shell the pistachios. Thought, briefly, of the man called Heron and our all-too-brief romance in the winter of '71. Walt was right – Cranham had indeed been overjoyed at the idea of being a father, even if he found the children to have a little bit too much of a gypsy-look to ever truly pass muster.

'He wasn't wrong, was he?' I asked. 'Our mutual friend. The things we do, the alliances we forge, the people we persuade to risk their lives – none of it's in service of a greater good. It's in service of what's good for the ruling classes in our little pocket of the world.'

He looked at me as if I were a toddler playing dress-up. Shook his head. 'I rather think that the cinema will prove to be a backwards step for humanity in terms of the people's satisfaction with their lives and their place in the world. The Americans have it so simple with their cowboy films. There is a hero and a villain and the hero wins, albeit with a little tragedy, a little suffering, along the way. We are not in the business of removing the villains from the earth. It is the duty of governments to sustain the status quo; to maintain a way of life, and where possible, not make things any worse. For forty years it has been our job to stop the spread of communism. We have had some successes and some failures, but our way of life has continued and I take comfort knowing that, the people like you and I, have played a small part in that. People like our mutual friend – they sieve the world looking for morality, for justice, for this naturally-occurring mineral of decency. They are all constructs, my dear. They are as much a fiction as compassion and decency. You and I serve the real world.'

I closed my eyes, bone-weary and sore all the way through. 'He gave me the lighter,' I said, sleepily. 'Was he trying to save me or not?'

He finally popped a pistachio in his mouth. He grimaced and spat it discreetly into his palm. 'He seemed to want to ensure you weren't a victim to the fall-out of his actions. He wanted you to have plausible deniability. You weren't involved – you even tried to alert your senior officers through the correct channels. He sent one of his zealots to stop you making it north. We're all rather glad you did. The lighter had a tracker in it, I'm sure you've realized that. The man who came after you, the man from the train – he wasn't entirely as loyal to our mutual friend as his other disciples. He feared that the so-called Angels were entirely committed to the operation – they really would have unleashed all manner of horrors. He was there to ensure it didn't happen as our mutual friend intended.'

'He's with us?'

'*Us* is a very nebulous concept.' He smiled. 'Suffice to say, you should be glad he's a good shot, and a decent man.'

I watched him scoop up the shelled pistachios and tip them back into the paper bag. 'These are yours, by the way,' he said, chattily. 'I brought them as a little gift – a source of sustenance to aid your recovery. I fancied that they might make a severance payment, a goodbye gift. But seeing you as I do, seeing the way you understand entirely what I am telling you – perhaps they are not the correct gift.'

I must have looked as confused as I felt. 'I like grapes,' I said, sleepily.

'I'm sure you do.' He smiled again. 'There are fine grapes to be found in the markets of Tangiers. A marvellous place, Tangiers. I'm currently seeking a reliable soul to look after some business for the family firm. It occurs to me that you might benefit, when sufficiently rested, from some time in the sun. A year, perhaps two, looking after the office there. A busy office too. One could make a real difference in such a position. Good schools, should you wish it.'

I wasn't sure if I was being exiled or offered a job. I screwed up my face, feeling myself drift away. 'I didn't do anything for queen or country,' I said, my voice thick with sleep. 'It was for my friends, my family . . .'

He leaned over, moving without a sound. Looked down at me as my eyes closed.

'My dear, they are quite one and the same.'

EPILOGUE

Paolo Fergus looks up, face flushed, the final page held between forefinger and thumb. Dame Cordelia Hemlock is looking at him over the rim of her brandy glass, a little smile creating a dimple in her left cheek.

'Cut the mustard, does it?' she asks. 'I'm not a professional, but I gave it as much gusto as one can summon at my age. Better than Felicity's bumbling recordings, I hope. Did she ramble? Good God but that woman can ramble.'

Fergus doesn't say anything. Leans over and picks up the crystal tumbler from the tray and swallows the smokey amber liquid. Closes his eyes until he can get his thoughts in a row.

'I can't print this,' he says, his voice thin and reedy. 'They'll slap a section D on it as soon as I pitch it anywhere.'

'You can pick the bones out of it,' says Cordelia, shrugging. 'Make it work. Chop out the bits where we've doubled up and overlapped and make it sound like we're not a pair of daft old biddies in a muddle. There's paperwork at Kew that back up the situation out at Belize. You can't name names but you can tell people that we did what we did. They won't care, not really, but you can tell them all the same.'

He sucks his cheek, thinking hard. 'The pilot. The American vicar.'

'That's the spirit.' Cordelia nods. 'Works damn well on its own, that one. Good old-fashioned Texan preacher leads a group of indigenous Mayans out into the thickest part of the jungle and builds a village? Then the military come in and chuck them off so they can drill for oil? That's some righteous fury, right there. No wonder Walt got him on-side, gathering intelligence for the Angels. He even had a pilot's licence. Could get in and out of Belize with barely a blip. The Guatemalan authorities shot him down, you've worked that out, yes? He had a couple of Walt's assets on board with him, coming back from a drop. You won't be able to prove it but it was a CIA cable that alerted the Guatemalans to what the reverend was doing.'

'The Angels,' says Fergus, shaking his head. 'There really was a unit set up to do good?'

Cordelia grins at that, filling her glass from the decanter. She takes a sip and appreciates the flavour. 'After a fashion,' she says with a shrug. 'Walt was a nuisance but he was good at what he did. His intelligence network was the best around and the US needed him more than ever with all the uprisings happening on their doorstep. He was happy to share when President Carter was doing a half decent job of turning the US away from its deals with dictators. It was a different story when it became clear to him, to me, to bloody everybody, that a different type of politics was in the ascendency. He wasn't going to betray his network to a country that was funding the people who were responsible for genocide. Carter had pulled funding. Told the Guatemalans there'd be no more aid or arms until they cleaned up their act. Reagan made it clear that once he got in power, he'd turn America into heroes; a force for good battling the evil of communism. It was a vote-winner. And he did what he said he would. Made friends with a dictator who was later convicted of war crimes and told all his voters that he'd received a bum deal in the media and was actually one of the good guys, even as his own intelligence services were telling him that the death squads were killing people in their thousands. He got them everything they wanted. Even sent in the US Marines to help train the Kaibiles in the kind of counter-insurgency tactics they'd used in Vietnam. The one who got caught in the video – we never identified him but I know that the son of one of the US diplomats who were at the house in '82 was serving with the Marines at that time.'

'Can you give me a name?' asks Fergus.

'I think I've given you enough,' says Cordelia, and stretches out her shoulders in a manner that suggests she's tired and could do with some solitude.

'The house is a shell now,' says Fergus. 'I saw it on the drive in.'

'Still mine though,' says Cordelia. 'I get letters from the council insisting I do something with it. They don't seem to understand. It's got a life, that house. It deserves to die of old age, not the bulldozer.'

'It was the start of the high-flying for you, was it?' asks Fergus, chewing his pen. 'After what happened, you went up through the ranks like a rocket. Head of MI6 by the time you left. It surprises me you're willing to talk about all this.'

'You can't print much of it,' says Cordelia. 'But Flick's not long for this world and John's gone and I think it would give her a kick to see her painted as a bit of a hero somehow, even if it's only she and me that know it's her. You can do that from what we've given you, I know that much. I'll write the bloody thing myself if you don't.'

He scoops up the pages. Shuffles them. 'You haven't signed them,' he says. 'I've got a green biro, if you'd like.'

She gives a snort of laughter. 'I didn't write it,' she says, quietly. 'You ever say that I did and I'll grind you into the ground. I may be old but I still have friends.'

He starts to stand. Stops himself. 'The brother and sister. Sera and . . .'

She closes her eyes as if the memory pains her. 'They were flown home. Carried on the good fight. President Rios Montt was toppled a few months later and the new guy introduced something a bit more like democracy. It still carried on, though. The genocide, the disappearances, the death squads. Two hundred and forty thousand is the conservative estimate. She wrote to Felicity twice. We intercepted the letter so she never saw it. She was thanking her for what she'd done – the way she'd acted like a friend, like a sister, when they were together in that room and sharing their pain. Flick would have been embarrassed and Sera, well, she got all gushy and sentimental and started apologizing over and over for taking the book.'

'The book?'

'John's poems. She'd held onto it, gripped it like a talisman all through the night. Read every silly word in the blasted thing in the years that followed. Can you imagine? John Goose's ditties being read in the jungles of Guatemala? He was good, though. Nice ear for a rhyme.'

'You know where it was found?' asks Fergus, gently. 'What must have happened.'

'1986,' says Cordelia. 'Village in the west. Just one of many. A brave lady.'

'And her brother?'

'Never heard from after he got off the plane. He was the real hero of it all, if you ask me. Joined the Kaibiles, endured all the horrors of training to be one of them, just so he could feed information back to Walt's network. He was the one who filmed the carnage at the village. Kaapo, that was his name. Got himself out and his sister out and put all of his trust in a man who used a Belizean brothel as his base of operations. He joined up with another man. Alejandro something-or-other. Bit of a mix-up there. Foreign Office spivs got their wires crossed and had our poor boys hand him back to the very lads he'd just betrayed. Rather impressive work, other than the occasional hiccup. Got the pair of them all the way to a little village on Hadrian's Wall. Went home, and carried on. Last we heard a man fitting his description was claiming asylum in the US, though whether that's true or not I couldn't say.'

Fergus sits still for a moment. Looks around him at the cosy little room. Hears a thud from upstairs and looks to the ceiling.

'Don't worry, she won't come through,' says Cordelia with a smile. 'She'll be needing her bandages changing. Count down from ten in your head and before you hit three she'll be asking for a cup of tea, I promise you.'

Fergus enjoys the look of warmth and friendship that fills Baroness Hemlock's face as she talks about her friend. 'You've been through a lot together,' he says. 'It's a strange friendship – a spy and a housewife.'

Cordelia's face turns to stone. 'Nowt wrong with being a housewife, young man. Nowt wrong with being a mam or a home-maker. But she's a damn sight more than any one of those things. She's the bravest woman I know. Best of all of us.'

Fergus makes his apologies. Stands up. Hears the thin, gravelly voice of the lady from the recordings, shouting down the stairs and wondering whether the kettle's boiled yet.

'See,' mutters Cordelia, appearing at his side. She stands a little too close to him. Where the collar of her dress slides down her shoulder he can make out a puckering of the skin; a ragged circle of white lines.

'I don't know what I'll do with all of this,' says Fergus. 'It's not the story I set out to write.'

'Life's like that,' she says, without emotion. 'You think it's going one way and then it shoots off in another. You never really know where you are. All you can do is try your best to not make the world any worse for anybody else.'

'And do you believe you've achieved that?'

She pauses for a spell, considering the question. Her eyes, brilliantly blue, seem to darken with the effort of concentration. Eventually she gives a tight little smile, as if she's worked out the answer and doesn't feel the need to share it.

'I don't think I'm on the side of the angels,' she says, candidly. 'But I'd like to think I've had some of the devils running scared.'

Fergus makes a note of the line. Picks up his bag. One of the compartments is slightly open. Cordelia notices and reaches in without a word. She removes the little recording device. She opens it up and takes the tape. Crosses to the Rayburn and opens the cast-iron door, tossing the recording on the fire. She doesn't say a word to Paolo Fergus, who stands in the doorway looking embarrassed.

'She's enjoyed talking to you,' says Cordelia, as if nothing has passed between them. 'You've kept her memory sharp. For that, I'm grateful. Use what you can, ignore the rest. Don't make me look like a prima donna or a poor girl done good or I'll have your kneecaps. Are we clear?'

He nods. Feels an overwhelming urge to kiss her on the cheek and then run away. She has the look of somebody who doesn't like killing, but has done her fair share.

'She mentioned another incident,' he says, standing on the doorstep and watching the rain. 'How you met. Some body in a blue suit up at the cemetery. Could you maybe fill me in?'

'That one belongs to my grandson,' apologizes Cordelia. 'He'll tell that one when we're both dead and gone.'

'But you have more,' says Fergus, eagerly. 'Between you, you must have more stories to tell.'

Cordelia smiles. Looks at the ceiling and imagines her friend laying there, sulking, waiting for her cup of tea. Gives her attention back to Fergus and briefly enjoys feeling young again.

'There's always more.' She smiles.